Madam, May I

Also by Niobia Bryant

MISTRESS SERIES

Message from a Mistress

Mistress No More

Mistress, Inc.

The Pleasure Trap

Mistress for Hire

FRIENDS & SINS SERIES

Live and Learn

Show and Tell

Never Keeping Secrets

STRONG FAMILY SERIES

Heated

Hot Like Fire

Give Me Fever

The Hot Spot

Red Hot

Strong Heat

Make You Mine

Want, Need, Love

Reckless (with Cydney Rax and Grace Octavia)

Heat Wave (with Donna Hill and Zuri Day)

Published by Kensington Publishing Corp.

Madam, May I

NIOBIA BRYANT

KENSINGTON PUBLISHING CORP.
www.kensingtonbooks.com

DAFINA BOOKS are published by

Kensington Publishing Corp.
119 West 40th Street
New York, NY 10018

ISBN-13: 978-1-4967-1654-5
ISBN-10: 1-4967-1654-X
First Kensington Trade Paperback Printing: June 2019

ISBN-13: 978-1-4967-1655-2 (ebook)
ISBN-10: 1-4967-1655-8 (ebook)
First Kensington Electronic Edition: June 2019

10 9 8 7 6 5 4 3 2 1

Printed in the United States of America

Madam, May I

Prologue

1988

"Stay right here. Promise?"

The five-year-old girl looked up at her father with her brown eyes squinting against the sun. "Yes, Daddy," she said, taking a seat in one of the rocking chairs on the porch as she held her bright red Tickle Me Elmo doll in one arm and stroked the new heart-shaped locket her father had given her just that morning.

Her father patted her shoulder and gave her a smile that wasn't happy before walking into the house and closing the front door. She swung her feet back and forth as she looked over the edge of the railing at cars riding up and down the street, which was made up of rows of houses with nice front yards with flower beds. Kids rode their bikes or chased each other on the sidewalks. Their laughter and high-pitched squeals of fun were the only noises to break up the quiet.

It wasn't very different from where she used to live.

She hugged her Elmo close to her chest. It giggled. "That tickles!" the animated voice of the doll said as it vibrated.

"How could you!"

The little girl turned on the seat and looked to the open window at the sound of a woman's voice raised in anger. She winced at the crash of something made of glass. With eyes wide with fright and curiosity, she hopped down off the chair and walked over to the window to peer inside. Through the sheer curtains, she was just able to see her father holding the wrists of a woman struggling to hit him.

Who is she?

"Zena, stop," her father implored. "I'm sorry. I am so sorry."

Sorry for what?

"I can't let her go into the system, Zena. Her mother didn't have any other family. She's my child," he said.

"And I'm your *wife*, Daniel," she said, her words broken up by her ragged breathing. "You had no right screwing around and then making a baby with your whore."

Whore? His wife? Daddy has a wife? My mama was a whore?

The little girl winced at the memory of sitting on the front pew of the church next to her daddy as she locked her eyes on the sight of her mother in the casket. *Daddy said Mama is in heaven with God.*

She released a breath, and her shoulders slumped as she fought not to cry. *I miss her. He said if I talk to her she can hear me.*

"I miss you, Mama," she mouthed.

"Zena, I have to do what's right," her father said. "I *need* you to help me do what's right. Please, Zena. *Please.*"

The woman—Zena—stopped her fighting, and her body crumbled like her knees had given out beneath her as she began to cry and wail. Her father bent his body and wrapped his arms around her to hold her up from hitting the floor. He pressed a kiss to her face, and she found renewed strength to push both her hands against his chin, knocking his head backward. When he freed her to press his hands to his face, the woman quickly scrambled away from him on her hands and knees.

Why are they fighting?

The little girl's heart pounded and her arm tightened around her doll. Elmo giggled and vibrated against her chest. "That tickles!"

Both her father and the woman looked at the window.

With a gasp of surprise at being discovered, she dropped the doll and took several steps back before turning and reclaiming her spot on the chair. They had lowered their voices, because she only heard harsh whispers.

I'm so afraid without you, Mama.

The little girl turned her head as the front door opened.

Her father extended his arm and beckoned her with his hand. "Come on," he said, his voice deep and warm.

She pretended not to see the long, thin scratch in his neck as she walked over to the door and slid her hand in his. The drops of blood from the wound had already stained the collar of his shirt. With one last look at her Elmo lying on the porch beneath the window, she followed her father inside the house.

"Zena, this is my . . . my . . . daughter, Desdemona," her father said once they reached the living room where his wife awaited them.

The woman's hair was in disarray and her eyes were rimmed with red from crying as she kept them trained on her husband.

"Say hello to Mrs. Zena, Desi," her father said, releasing her hand to press his to her back to gently nudge her forward.

She quickly moved to stand behind her father instead, clutching at the crease of his pants with her small fists. "Hello," she finally said, wondering if it was loud enough for anyone to truly hear.

The woman nodded her head stiffly in greeting.

Her father stepped forward to draw his wife—this woman she did not know—into his embrace. "Thank you, Zena. Thank you so much," he said, burying his face against her neck.

Desdemona tilted her head back to look up at them. The woman's body was stiff in his arms, and the look in her eyes was cold and hostile as she peered over his shoulder at her. Desdemona felt a chill race across her shoulders, and more than ever she longed for the presence of her mother.

Chapter One

Thirty years later

Monday, June 11, 2018

The monotony of it all may very well bore me to death . . .

Desdemona Dean tapped her extra-fine-point pen against the pages of her journal as she looked out the floor-to-ceiling window of her apartment in the Tribeca section of New York. "Different day. Same shit," she said aloud as she picked up her cup of tea and looked out at the views—to the right the Manhattan skyline and with a shift of her eyes to the left the Hudson River.

Not that it wasn't beautiful, especially with the sun beaming in the sky and causing the water to gleam. What had started out as extraordinary when she first moved into the eighty-two-story high-rise building two years ago was now the norm. Because the building was part five-star hotel and part luxury residences, the amenities were amazing. She couldn't deny that. Housekeeping. Ordering meals from a world-class menu. Pool. Spa. Concierge. Valet parking. High luxury with low maintenance.

I ain't that *bored.*

She set the cup down on the saucer and looked around at the eleven-foot ceilings of her twenty-two-hundred-square-foot condominium with its cream décor, dark hardwood floors, and floor-to-ceiling windows. It was beautiful.

Still, she *was* bored.

Desdemona sighed, turning her attention back to her leather-bound journal. She sat at her slate dining room table with her bare feet tucked beneath her in one of the eight suede club chairs surrounding it. She struggled to find more to write for later reflections years down the line when she would finally read the journals she had been keeping for the last two decades of her life.

Written memories.

Her mother had always journaled; she could remember her sipping a glass of wine while curled up in her favorite chair writing away, sometimes smiling but often more reflective and sad. There were many things about her mother that Desdemona had forgotten, but others moments remained like an imprint on her life.

She pressed the pen inside the crease of the journal and closed it before finishing her breakfast of ricotta hotcakes with maple syrup and chicken-and-apple sausage. With one last look out at her views, Desdemona rose from the table and dropped the silk kimono she wore to the floor as she left the dining room, crossed the foyer, and turned the corner leading down the hall to the three bedrooms. Her master suite was in the rear. She walked down the short hall with large black-and-white prints in black frames on the left and two closets to her right—one of them a walk-in—and around the corner.

She paused in front of the large seven-foot mirror leaned

against the wall next to the hall entrance to the master bathroom. She stretched her arms high above her head as she took in her head full of blond-streaked chestnut hair that was wild and noticeable as it framed her heart-shaped face. With doe-shaped eyes surrounded by thick lashes and a pouty mouth above her small dimpled chin, Desdemona knew she resembled a less cartoonish version of a Bratz doll or one of the Disney fairies. She was pretty.

That wasn't ego, but what she'd been told since she was a kid.

Instead, she wished she had been told she was smart and capable—that she had had to learn on her own the hard way. Looks faded. Smarts lasted long after cuteness was gone.

Releasing a breath, she cupped her breasts and jiggled them as she turned her body this way and that to inspect her buttocks and hips. Although her breasts were a full and pert 38B, she imagined them fuller. "Should I double these to double Ds?" she asked herself, shifting her eyes to take in her empty bed and wondering if a man were lying there watching her what his opinion might be.

She frowned.

There was no man and no way she would allow herself to give a damn what he thought if there had been.

Moving away from the mirror, she entered the bathroom, barely noticing the white décor, Carrara marble, bright lighting, and glass shower door that gave the room a light and airy feeling that might have been missed because the spacious room lacked windows. She slipped a satin bonnet over her hair and paused to smell the fresh white daffodils in the large crystal vase between the double basins of the sink before taking a shower.

With a plush white towel with chrome monogrammed letters wrapped around her body, Desdemona walked back to her walk-in closet and emerged ten minutes later in a bright yellow floor-length halter dress that exposed the portrait tattoo of her mother on her right shoulder. The deep vee perfectly framed her breasts, and a low back emphasized her wide hips and buttocks. The matte jersey material flowed around her body with ease, and with nothing but a sheer thong as her undergarment she felt ready for the sweltering summer heat outdoors. Her heels clicked against the hardwood floors as she remembered her journal and retrieved it, quickly returning to her walk-in closet to unlock the safe and slide it inside atop the crisp stacks of cash and other journals stored there.

She lightly stroked the thing she cherished the most: it was not the money. Within those pages were her story. Her trials, tribulations, and triumphs. "To hell and back again," she said in a whisper before stepping back to close and then lock the safe.

Desdemona selected one of the dozen designer shades atop the island in the center of the closet that contained her lingerie. From the shelves, she took down a black Balenciaga tote and begun transferring her wallet and other personal items from the Louis Vuitton she carried the day before. She was just about to slide her two iPhones into the inside pocket when one vibrated in her hand.

Desdemona flipped it over and smiled. "I'm having a drama-free morning, Patrice," she said, zipping the tote and sliding it onto the crook of her elbow before cutting off the ceiling light and leaving the closet.

The other woman laughed. "Nothing major. The shipment of gowns from the designer from London—"

"Suzanne Neville," Desdemona said, almost offhand, as she entered her passcode on the iPad stationed by the front door and used the device to notify the valet she wanted her vehicle. With one last look around her condo, Desdemona slid on her dark round shades as she left her condominium and walked down the sleek and modern-style hallway to the elevators.

"Right," Patrice agreed. "The shipment arrived—"

"Good," Desdemona said, stepping on the lift and pressing the button for the private lobby just for the dwellers in the private residences of the building.

"Is there anywhere in particular you want me to display them?"

I could care the fuck less, Patrice.

Desdemona owned a small but very exclusive high-end boutique offering stylish and unique pieces from designers around the world. She catered to the wealthy and powerful who had no qualms about dropping five thousand dollars or better on a dress. And just like with everything else in her life, she was bored with that as well. "Wherever you choose is fine with me," Desdemona said, as the elevator smoothly descended from the sixtieth floor to the lobby with its abstract black-and-white décor.

It didn't particularly matter. The boutique was by appointment only, and only Desdemona met with her customers. It was Patrice's job to collect the shipments and stock the boutique—and that was hardly rocket science.

"But—"

Desdemona stepped outside the beautiful limestone building, and stood beneath the canopy. "Patrice, there are so many moments in life where everyone gets a chance to show and to prove what they are capable of. This is your moment, Patrice. Don't piss on it by being afraid to make a simple decision," Desdemona said, raking her crystal-encrusted fingernails through her golden curls just as her metallic black Maserati Levante GranLusso was driven up to the curb.

Desdemona was in her mid-thirties, and Patrice was ten years her senior. If the woman didn't learn to show initiative and claim her spotlight, she would forever be working for someone else.

"I got it," the other woman said.

"I know you do. Bye, Patrice," she said before ending the call as she walked over to the crossover and smiled at the young valet as she handed him a tip before sliding onto the red leather driver's seat. She set her phone and tote on the passenger seat as the valet gently nudged for it to glide forward before slowing down and closing softly.

Desdemona turned up the volume so that Meek Mill's "Shine" blasted through the premium sound system. She had an unspoken rule: nothing but hip-hop and trap music in her cars. During her fifteen-mile drive to the Riverdale section of the Bronx, Desdemona let the thump of the bass give her energy, the lyrics give her hope, and let herself be reminded of growing up in the nineties.

As she entered the affluent neighborhood, she turned down the sound of Cardi B's "Get Up 10," not wanting to disturb the peaceful vibe of the neighborhood with the pounding of her bass. She eased the Maserati down the tree-lined streets until she pulled up to a pair of wrought-iron security gates with intricate scrollwork. There were no neighboring homes for half a mile on either side or directly across the street. Mature trees and landscaped bushes around the entire property offered seclusion. She lowered the driver's-side window and leaned out a bit to enter the security code on the keypad. The gates slid open with ease, and she accelerated forward up the long, brick-paved drive to a more than ten-thousand-square-foot brick neo-Georgian home. To the left of the motor court was a three-car garage of the same design, and to the right there were outdoor parking spots for three more vehicles. Desdemona pulled her Maserati into one of those before climbing from the vehicle and crossing the paved brick to walk onto the colonnaded porch.

Using her keys, she unlocked the front door and entered the two-story entry hall, closing the door behind herself. Stairs leading to the next floor were to her right, but she crossed the polished hardwood floors to her left to pass the small entryway leading to a powder room across from an elevator, which she rode up past the second floor to the penthouse, housing a junior suite and office. She unlocked the door, loving the heavy sound of the deadbolts sliding out of place, before entering.

The summer light beamed through the windows on the rear wall displaying views of the hills of Riverdale as she removed her sunglasses and set them along with her keys and tote on the large wooden desk in the center of the room. It was clear save for a huge vase of white daffodils sitting on the edge. The sunshine hit them, releasing their sweet aroma into the air. She began to hum a melody as she buried her face in the petals before kicking off her heels.

"*Love* it," she said softly as she opened the top drawer of the desk and removed an iPad.

She resumed her humming while tapping on the tablet to turn on the seventy-inch television that hung on the wall over the fireplace. The views from the twenty security cameras inside and outside the furnished house were soon displayed. Entry gate. Front door. Rear patio doors. Backyard and pool. All living spaces inside the house, including the spacious chef's kitchen. The wine cellar, exercise room, media room, and bedroom suite in the basement. Each of the bedrooms on the second floor and finally the in-law suite on the first level with its own private side entrance.

Desdemona smiled at the sight of the naked man lying in the middle of the king-sized bed stroking his own erection. Denzin Anderson lacked for nothing. Good looks. Quick wit. Disarming smarts. Hard physique. Long dick.

She used the iPad to activate the intercom system in Denzin's suite before setting it on the desk. "Punctual as ever," she said, her voice sounding raspy and soft to her own ears.

He locked his deep-set black eyes directly on the camera in the corner. "Disappointment is not my MO," he said.

"No, it is *not*," she agreed with emphasis, sitting on the tapestry Parsons chair behind the desk before she removed a cash counting machine from the deep bottom drawer.

Denzin chuckled.

She walked over to the fireplace and hit a small latch hidden behind a carved leaf. The side panel popped open, revealing three shelves. Each was stacked with money. Her courtesans dropped her share of the cash money they collected from consorts into her office via the mail slot on the door. She hid the money in the fireplace. She removed all the bundles, carrying them in one arm back to her desk.

"Security alert. Front gate."

Desdemona's eyes shifted to the television. She recognized the face of the woman behind the wheel of the nondescript electric blue car: Jann Loomis, a beautiful twenty-something sous chef.

"Is that her?" Denzin asked.

"Right on time," Desdemona replied, using the tablet to unlock and open the gate because all visitor security codes required she do so.

"What's her name again?" he asked.

"It doesn't matter."

Desdemona turned off the intercom and removed the rubber bands around the ends of the first stack of cash and set it inside the hopper. The shuffle of the money through the bank-grade counter filled the air. "Remember it's about her, not you, Denzin," she said, her tone amused.

He chuckled again as he rose from the bed, his erection seeming to lead him across the spacious room and out the door. Via the cameras she watched him move with confidence out of the suite and into the entry hall through the door behind the staircase before reaching the front door.

Desdemona fed the counter another large stack and then reached in her tote for her personal iPad in a bright orange cover. After setting it on the desk, she walked over to the walk-in closet. It was empty save for the fifty bottles of her favorite 2001 Château Rieussec and a dozen wineglasses lining the shelves meant for shoes. She grabbed one of each.

"And they're off," she said, looking at the television screen as she uncorked the wine and poured herself a quarter glass.

The young woman—a slender beauty with waist-length blond hair—was as naked as Denzin and bent over his bed as he stroked her from behind.

Desdemona turned the intercom back on before reclaiming her seat with one foot tucked beneath her bottom. "Oh, sweet baby Jesus. It's even worse with the volume up," she said, tapping the stem of the glass with her fingernails.

There wasn't a moan of pleasure—feigned or real.

The sex was perfunctory.

Denzin looked up at the camera and shrugged with a bewildered expression.

Desdemona took a deep sip of wine and then refilled her glass to the rim this time.

The monotony of it all may very well bore me to death . . .

Desdemona sighed into her glass before massaging the bridge of her nose with her fingertips.

Procuring pussy has lost its shine.

She rose from the chair, sipping her beloved wine as she walked over to the windows overlooking the pool and landscaped backyard. For a few necessary moments, she allowed herself to forget that the woman in the room with Denzin—her in-house stud—trying to become one of her highly sought-after courtesans was the driest lay she had ever seen in her life.

She garnered a minimum of two thousand dollars an hour up to $100,000 for a weekend in Europe or Asia, and her patrons were not paying that price for the privilege of having sex with a beautiful woman. They wanted more—conversation, excitement, a sounding board, humor, intellect, and above all privacy—and she made sure to provide it.

Desdemona only hired smart women and men with clear goals that prevented them wanting to work in the biz for any longer than two to three years—also ensuring no hidden ambitions to claim her spot in the business. Each courtesan was thoroughly vetted—including a psych evaluation—before she even agreed to meet with them, and their skill in the bedroom was rated by a session with Denzin before they were hired. She sent each new courtesan through etiquette training to ensure they could properly move among the wealthy, famous, and powerful—particularly those accompanying them on events. They were required to stay in shape—including daily Kegels. Drug use was completely prohibited—no weed, coke, or pills of any kind.

She turned her attention to the screen and grimaced at Denzin scrolling through his phone as he continued to thrust inside her. "Oh, sweet baby Jesus. Oh, poor thing. Just clueless. Just...just...just wrong. So *wrong*," she moaned, pretending to clutch imaginary pearls.

Regardless of who, what, and when, sex was the common denominator, and good sex was key. And what she was watching was anything but good.

She is *beautiful.*

Desdemona could think of five of her patrons off the top of her head who went for the blond-haired, long-legged beauties. Big tits, blue eyes, and the pretense of blank brains. The Barbies of the world.

Beauty is never enough.

Her patron list was comprised of professional athletes, Hollywood celebrities, politicians, corporate bigwigs, and even some young royalty. New patrons were by referrals only and business was booming. The 2017 deluge of firings and suspensions of politicians and Hollywood's elite for sexual misconduct had sent those fearing a future fall from grace to the services she provided. And over the years she had become just as well known and sought after for the privacy she provided as she was for the exclusivity of her courtesans.

Prior to the house in Riverdale, she had leased a penthouse apartment in midtown Manhattan for those patrons wanting to avoid renting hotels to enjoy their time with a courtesan—or courtesans. Others wanted more of a home feeling during their downtime. The setup was good. Private entrance on a one-way side street for the elevator leading straight to the penthouse. The building had the right mix of all ages and races to make her patrons blend in.

The problems?

The busy midtown location and not enough seclusion.

The house in Riverdale solved them both.

It wasn't broke, but Desdemona fixed it before it could be. That was her job. One of many.

She walked back over to the desk. "Denzin, looks like you've been taking advantage of the exercise room downstairs," she said, taking the counted stack from the machine and loading another as she took note of the amount of fifty thousand before giving them her attention again.

The woman—Jann—looked startled.

Good. An emotion.

"I like to keep my abs right, boss," Denzin said, giving her a playful wink as he continued to stroke inside Jann with the passion of scratching an itch.

"It shows," Desdemona said, taking another sip of wine and letting it stroke her tongue before she gently swallowed. Still holding the glass, she sat back in the chair and took a deep breath that she released slowly and methodically.

"Jann, I guess you're wondering why the man having sex with you and I are chatting when he's about nine—maybe ten—inches in," she said, leaning forward to set the glass on the desk.

"Ten!" Denzin balked. "Try *eleven*."

"I concede," she said, her voice amused.

The woman looked about the room again.

Denzin patted her right butt cheek and pointed up to the small camera in the corner when she looked back at him over her shoulder.

And as Desdemona looked into her dull eyes she honestly didn't know which of them was more uninterested. That was slightly shocking. Denzin was well-endowed and skillful. Over the last few years, she'd seen him push many a woman over the edge of passion with ease.

Hell, usually it was like watching really good porn. Bury your vibrating rabbit between your thighs until you cum kind of good porn.

At a heated memory of climaxing with rough cries as she watched Denzin and a lover do the same, Desdemona cleared her throat. "Leave us alone, Denzin," she said, her voice firm.

He stepped back, freeing his hard inches from inside Jann before grabbing a pair of basketball shorts to pull on over his erection.

Viagra? she wondered with an arched brow and then a double shoulder shrug because she couldn't blame him if he needed a little blue boost occasionally. He was her dick on demand handling female consorts and testing new courtesans—sometimes without much notice.

"Get dressed, love," she said, turning her back to the screen to give Jann the same privacy she hadn't bothered to consider just a few moments ago.

She sipped the wine and smiled into her glass as a butterfly with an intricate black-and-white pattern fluttered its wings and landed on the window, pausing for just a moment before again taking flight. For a second, she was jealous of its ability to just fly away on a whim.

The smile she allowed herself was slight as she turned back

to the screen. "This isn't for you, Jann," she began, setting the glass on the desk and stroking the fragile leaves of a daffodil bloom. "My patrons trust me to deliver an experience, and while I think you are one of the most beautiful women ever . . . you are not cut out for *this*."

Jann's disappointment was clear even as she nodded in understanding and slid the strap of her crossbody over her head. For a moment Desdemona wondered if she should've gone downstairs and met with her face-to-face, but she decided it wasn't necessary.

"Selling your body means different things for different people. For some it's liberation—believe it or not—and for others it's disgusting and belittling. Then there is plenty in between. Guess what? Every feeling about it matters. There is no law that all women have to think, feel, be, or do the same thing," Desdemona said, her face pensive. "But what I just saw was a woman who couldn't hide the shame she felt."

The woman's expression revealed the truth of that observation.

"So, if I can give you some advice, love," Desdemona offered, picking up the counted stack and loading another onto the machine. Soon the rapid shuffling of bills filled the air. "If your situation is desperate enough to do something that disgusts you, then your final recourse may be using your beauty to marry very well or hustle twice as hard."

Long after Jann was gone, Denzin had reclaimed his bedroom and Desdemona had turned off both the video and intercom. She lay back on the bed with her eyes closed enjoying the feel of the sun's rays warming her face through the window. Spreading her arms and legs, she gave in to a moment of folly, flapping her arms and legs as if she could fly away like the butterfly on the window earlier.

In an instant she envisioned water quickly rising to swallow her, sinking beneath its depths and feeling drowned.

With a gasp, she sat up in bed and released a short breath as she ran her hands through her curls before tightly gripping the soft strands into her fists.

Cha-ching. Cha-ching. Cha-ching.

Her gaze went to her tote. It was the ringtone of the prepaid iPhone that she used strictly for her consorts. Each of her regulars was given a burner phone and assigned a number to keep proof of their communications to a minimum. She released her hair and rose from the bed to cross the room to retrieve the phone from her bag. Number one. "Congratulations on the win last night, Mr. NBA," she said, turning to lean against the edge of the desk.

The deep voice on the line chuckled. "Time to relax and get ready for game six, Mademoiselle," he said.

None of her consorts knew her real name or identity. She preferred it that way. Yet another attempted security measure. All called her by her preferred moniker of Mademoiselle.

"The usual?" she asked, looking across the room and out the window at the clear and pristine pool in the distance.

She knew him well. He had been one of her consorts for the past five years. Wins required a courtesan to pamper and adore him. Softly and sensually. Loss required one to berate him. Rough and harsh.

Desdemona knew both her consorts and her courtesans well. Rarely had she not been able to make a perfect fit of the courtesan's particular skill or personality to the consort's wants and desires. Wealthy men appreciated that talent.

"I wondered if such a big win was huge enough to bring out the big guns?" he asked.

Desdemona chuckled, but the humor did not fill her eyes. "Big guns mean big money," she teased, keeping it light.

"If we win the championship I might splurge to bring you out of retirement, Angel," he said, reverting to a name she hadn't used in years.

Once a whore, always a whore.

"Angel is dead, and Mademoiselle killed her. There's no reviving her, love," she said.

"I still have my memories."

"If I only I could get residual checks for them," she joked.

They shared a laugh.

After the details were set and the call ended, Desdemona knew she should reach out to the courtesan she already had in mind for her consort, but instead she made her way out of the penthouse and down to the first level via the elevator. She felt almost melancholy as she turned the corner to cross the far end of the foyer, the hall, and then the living room to step out onto the brick terrace.

She was thankful for the seclusion of the close-knit trees and shrubs around the perimeter of the large yard as she grabbed her bright yellow dress in her fists and pulled it over her head. Nude, she went racing across the hot blades of grass to dive into the pool. The water was warm from the summer heat as it enveloped her body. She welcomed it as she swam to the other end, wishing that when she emerged her past could be as easily cleaned as her body by the chlorinated water.

Chapter Two

Monday, June 18, 2018

Pussy has made me rich, and I plan to stay that way, because I will never ever rely on another person to sustain . . .

Desdemona stroked the trio of diamond line bracelets lying across her wrist. One was of tiny butterflies and the other was simple bands with exquisite diamonds. Did she need the trinkets? No, she had plenty. It was just nice to know that she could afford them if she chose.

There was a time when a pack of Ramen noodles was a struggle to buy.

"Will you be adding these to your collection, Ms. Smith?"

Desdemona. Say it. Say Desdemona. Ms. Dean. Say it.

How could he? He didn't know it.

Desdemona looked at the salesman, a tall, effeminate man with Nordic good looks and impeccable style. He had garnered many a commission from her. "No, not today, Clayton," she said, extending her wrist so that he could remove the jewelry.

Her eyes clung to the butterflies.

He saw that and lingered before placing it back in the jewelry case.

Diamonds are this girl's best friend.

She reached in her tote and withdrew a billfold to count out a hundred one-hundred-dollar bills.

"The butterflies?" he asked.

She nodded before stacking the cash and tapping the edges atop the glass jewelry case before handing the bills to him.

"Of course," he said as he rung up her purchase.

"I'll wear it out," she said, running her hand through her hair, now worn straight and parted down the middle.

Clayton set a small shopping bag holding the bracelet's bright red case and her receipt onto the top of the display case before clasping the piece around her wrist. "You look fabulous as ever," he said, turning the piece so that the clasp was not shown and it was close to her diamond Patek Philippe watch. His eyes took in the sheer fitted black tee she wore with nothing but a black strapless bra underneath it, paired with a form-fitting black satin skirt and red-bottom heels. "I love how I have never seen you in anything but dresses."

He's right. I only wear dresses. Winter, spring, summer, and fall. I wonder if he would still love it if he knew that I learned early in my "career" that dresses and skirts meant easy access and easy cleanup. Very uncomplicated clothing for a whore. And in time the dresses became more of a habit that stuck.

Desdemona gave him a soft smile before holding her arm up into the sunlight streaming through the glass doors of the private jewelry salon. The diamonds gleamed. The butterflies seemed to twinkle.

"Beautiful choice," he said.

"Yes, and thank you, Clayton," she said, picking up the shopping bag and her tote before leaving the midtown Manhattan jeweler.

The summer heat seemed to radiate from the concrete sidewalks, and the air was filled with the sounds of the congested New York traffic and the fast-paced bustle of pedestrians as she walked the half block to the large and modern eighteen-story building on the corner. She opened one of the glass doors leading into the lobby with its polished tile floors and beautiful design, walking across to one of the four elevators.

Her space was on the tenth floor. She loved hiding in plain sight among the many commercial and office spaces. The building contained everything from upscale doctors' offices to designer showrooms and artists' studios. Her thousand-square-foot boutique/showroom was in a corner unit at the end of the tenth floor. Nestled away from the elevator and prying eyes.

As Desdemona unlocked the double doors she briefly eyed the name "glitz" etched in lower-case letters in the frosting of the glass wall. She entered the loft-style space and turned on the overhead lighting as she took in the twenty shiny black mannequins displaying each of the high-end dresses she carried.

Desdemona set her tote and the shopping bag on one of the four leather club chairs situated around a round riser where a model could showcase a gown. Patrice's choice to display the black lace Suzanne Neville gown on the mannequin nearest the window wouldn't have been her pick, because the sunlight didn't bring out the detail work of the lace, but she fought the urge to move it. She didn't want to undermine Patrice's confidence, particularly since the business was mostly a front.

Her consorts couldn't care less about the dresses they purchased as part of their payments for the services of her paramours. For her, the boutique served a dual purpose—a front for her procurement business and a legitimate source of income allowing her to file taxes and still have a verifiable reason to be in contact with every consort on her list. The profit she made off the sale of the dresses was a bonus.

"Good morning, Mademoiselle."

She stroked her new bracelet as she turned and eyed Byron Levin entering the showroom and walking toward her, looking every bit the powerhouse Hollywood producer in his lightweight suit. He was in his mid-sixties, balding, Jewish, tall with a round belly that was indicative of good living, and wealthy beyond belief. "In town for the Tonys?" she asked, forcing a soft smile as she extended her hand and raised her cheek.

He shook the first and kissed the latter.

As required, he had left any staff downstairs. She only met with consorts and no one else.

"As a matter of fact, I am. Hoping to help get a play adapted to film," he explained.

She didn't bother to ask for any more details. "Care for something to drink? Or is it too early for vodka tonic?" she asked, remembering his favorite drink as she waved a hand in invitation to one of the club chairs.

He unbuttoned his blazer before folding his tall and wide frame into one of the chairs. "I don't like to turn down an offer from a beautiful woman," he said.

Desdemona was glad to turn her back to him as she walked over to the bar cart in the corner. She rolled her eyes. Byron had been a consort for years. He was big, loud, and boastful, covering up his arrogance with a charm that was as noticeable as a pile of shit on a hot summer day. She fixed his drink from the stocked bar cart in the corner.

"My visit here is twofold," he said when she handed him the drink and took the seat in the chair next to him.

He in turned handed her an envelope of heavy stock before taking a healthy swallow of his beverage.

Crossing her legs, she opened the envelope and pulled out

a raised print invitation to the official afterparty of the Tony Awards being held at the Plaza that very night. Something for nothing didn't exist in their world. She eyed him coolly and awaited an explanation.

"I have an associate who might want your offered... *services,*" he said.

This was nothing new.

Being added on as a consort of Mademoiselle was no easy feat. An accepted referral was a sign of clout. Her list was tight and manageable—just the way she preferred. To be accepted by her was a feather in the cap of the wealthy men and women who wanted something to brag about like new jets, concept cars, rare jewels, and deep-throated lovers desperate to prove that he was her number one.

"Byron," she began, holding the invitation between her index and middle fingers to extend to him.

"I know. I know," he said, finishing his drink. "Just meet him. I will only introduce you as my wife's favorite boutique owner and nothing else in case you decide not go any further with it."

Behind her contentment was an annoyance that she hid well. These days her thoughts were more inclined toward leaving it all behind, not adding to her roster of powerful people looking to buy sex, temporary affection, or ego coddling.

"I started to bring him with me this morning," he said, rising to move over to the dresses on display.

"Byron," she called over to him.

He glanced back over his broad shoulder, glass still in hand.

"That would have gotten you dismissed from my list," she said, her voice firm. She softened the truth with a smile.

He chuckled and nodded, turning his attention back to the frocks before him. "I know, and I don't want that," he admitted. "My little regular gal is dedicated as hell to get me over the finish line with a smile."

Plum—or at least that's the name she uses—draws some of my highest fees. And I even heard he tipped her well on top of that. For all that cash she better be dedicated.

"Let's surprise Dolly with this one right here," he said, pointing to a beautiful gold sequined gown that would look lovely on his wife—a former beauty queen who had dedicated the last thirty years of her life to his career, their family, and charities. "She already has a gown for the Tonys, but she can save it for some other shindig. Hell, she can use it as a fucking dust cloth for all the hell I care, long as I get *me* some Plum while I'm in town."

For a moment Desdemona allowed herself a vision of his bulky body drenched in sweat as he rutted away between Plum's thighs. She frowned.

"Would you like the dress delivered?" she asked as she rose to her feet.

"No, I'll take it. Good optics and all," Byron said with a wink.

"It's always about the optics, love," she said, her voice husky as she walked to the rear of the loft where they kept the inventory. "Mrs. Levin is a ten, right?"

"Like you don't know, Mademoiselle," he drawled.

"We only have that in a size six," she said, ignoring his sarcasm.

"That's fine; it'll give her a little motivation to fit in it."

Desdemona leaned back to give him a stern, chastising look. His back was to her, and he missed it. She eyed the wide expanse of his back and remembered well the roundness of his belly from too many vodka tonics and medium-rare steak dinners. *The nerve, you big-gut, wide-back son of a witless bitch.*

Desdemona pulled out a red lace gown with a wide skirt and thin sequin belt. "I do have this one in her size," she began, carrying it over her bent arm to then hang it on the garment bagging jack next to the large wooden desk serving as the checkout counter. "I think just selecting another gown that fits her beautiful figure is more appropriate than a low-key shot at her weight when it's insult enough that you just sang the praises of another woman's pussy. You know?"

He walked over to join her, setting the empty glass on the corner of the desk. He eyed her, and there in his eyes was his battle over whether to accept her opinion or not. Whether to be reprimanded by a madam—a black madam nearly half his age—or not.

Desdemona paused with the scanner to the barcode on the price tag for the nearly three-thousand-dollar dress. She couldn't care less whether he purchased the dress or some time with Plum—and he knew that. For every consort off her list were a dozen more waiting for entry to the promised land.

"I think Mrs. Levin will really like this one. Don't you?" Desdemona asked, looking at the dress and then back over at him. "Happy wife. Happy life."

Suddenly he chuckled and gave her the charming toothy smile. "Is it possible you're trying to help me be a better husband while helping me cheat?" he asked.

Desdemona scanned the tag before reaching into the top drawer of the desk for a pack of strong mints. She withdrew the can, opened it, and extended it to him in her palm. "It is my job to look out for you in any way I can," she said, going a softer route. "The same way I wouldn't want your staff to smell vodka on your breath, I wouldn't want you to pick an unnecessary fight with your wife."

He took a couple of mints and popped them in his mouth, giving her a nod of thanks.

Desdemona finished ringing up his purchase. "That will be three thousand, two hundred and sixty-one for the dress," she said, turning to slide one of her black garment bags with "glitz" in gold lettering up over the dress.

He handed her his credit card.

"And just the one session with Plum?" she asked, as she swiped his card and printed his receipt for his signature.

A session was two hours—and that was her minimum. Anyone looking for anything less wanted less than the experience she trained her paramours to give.

"Yes. I've been waiting for this all month," he said withdrawing a manila envelope from the inside pocket of his blazer.

"That brings your remaining cash balance to five thousand," she said.

He dropped the envelope onto the desk with a light *thud*.

Desdemona left it sitting there as she handed him the garment bag. "I suggest using the mansion rather than booking a hotel suite with your wife and a ton of colleagues in the city for the awards," she offered.

He nodded in agreement.

"I'll text you the details once I confirm with Plum," she said, coming around the desk. "And perhaps I will see you at the afterparty tonight."

"I hope so."

She walked him to the door, and he gave her one last tip of his head before leaving with a lighthearted whistle that filled the air. Locking the door, she retraced her steps back to the counter to check for online sales through their website. She recognized two of the names on the orders from her list. Leaving all the dress orders to be filled by Patrice, she quickly called the consorts from her prepaid iPhone and finalized their requests before opening the calendar and blocking out the times for the paramours.

Setting the phone down, she sighed and reached for the cash, pulling out a portable cash counter to double-check Byron was not short by even one penny.

In less than an hour, she had just profited three grand from the dresses and made ten grand from playing Geppetto to her marionettes. That was well over four hundred dollars a minute, and business was far from done for the day.

Maybe I've made enough to retire for good and leave it all behind.

And do what, though? This is all I know.

Desdemona closed her eyes and tapped the tips of her stiletto-shaped nails against her chin. It was in these quiet moments that the truth prevailed. It had all become so easy. There was no challenge. Nothing to overcome. Nothing to beat. Nothing to win.

Biting her bottom lip and tasting the crimson gloss she wore on her lips, Desdemona looked down at the invitation before reaching to have it in her grasp. If nothing else it was something to do and things to see outside of the norm.

Tapping the corner of the invitation against her palm, she walked over to the inventory hung on racks lining the walls and selected a size eight black strapless gown with a matching elaborate floor-length sheer cape with delicate 3-D silk flowers. "Just in case," she said aloud.

Hours later Desdemona stood in the midst of the elegantly dressed crowd at the ball sipping on a glass of pinot noir. The room's neo-classical styling was made all the more luxurious by the colored lighting, sumptuous tablecloths, and sweet-smelling floral arrangements. There were hundreds of guests in attendance celebrating the annual Tony awards lauding the very best of Broadway's musicals and stage plays. From the floral wall serving as the backdrop for photos to the DJ drawing the bodies onto the dance floor, it was a night meant for the pleasure of celebrities of music, film, and stage. Sumptuous couches intermingled with elaborately decorated tables gave the large grand ballroom some warmth. Wine and signature cocktails quenched thirst, and downstairs a buffet serving samples of delicacies like mini-sandwiches and caviar sated appetites. Winners of the coveted Tony socialized with their awards in hand.

"Welcome to the Tonys," she mumbled into her drink before taking a sip.

There was a time when Desdemona had been starstruck, but those days had long since passed. Knowing some of the inner cravings of the elite had dulled the shine. Nothing like knowing a world-class professional athlete liked being fingered in his rectum while he climaxed to dull the shine and let it resonate that celebrities were like everyone else.

Desdemona claimed a spot on the mezzanine and amused herself spotting current and past consorts. There were more than a few in attendance. A high-powered manager of a top-grossing pop star. An athlete or two. A politician who trusted her with his predilection for beautiful transsexuals. Some raised their drink to her in a silent toast. Others showed their discomfort with their spouses at their sides. She made a note to speak to them about that at a later time.

She squinted when she noticed Byron, his wife, and another man she recognized as A-List actor Dirk Blank looking in her direction. Desdemona easily moved in the opposite direction, the edges of her cape rising a bit as she took the stairs and mingled with the crowd.

Smiling and socializing with the spouses of her consorts. It was a level of phony she wasn't able to swallow.

Her heel slipped, and she fell forward with a squeal, her face landing squarely against a hard chest.

"I got you," a male voice whispered near her ear.

Desdemona looked up at the man keeping her from falling flat on her face. A streak of fuchsia lighting illuminated his face. He was handsome enough but smelled even better. Warm and spicy. It made her tingle. She gave him a smile she knew showed her embarrassment. "Sorry about that," she said, standing erect.

"You okay?" he asked, his hands still on her elbows.

"Embarrassed, but all in one piece," she said, stepping back from him.

"One beautiful piece."

The years had made her a good read. Desi eyed him and sized him up. His stance was that of a confident lover. The thickness of his fingers, lips, and nose was indicative of a large penis. She locked her eyes with his, and he held them for a good while before they shifted slightly. A tell.

Desdemona tilted her head to the side and shook her head. "We're not doing that," she said, her voice playful.

"Doing what?" he asked, bending to speak close to her ear as the DJ switched to a loud and thumping electro house song by Calvin Harris and Rihanna.

Desdemona leaned in toward him. "Flirting," she said.

He nodded as he looked around the room and then back at her. "Because..."

"I'm celibate and I don't plan to end that tonight with a one-night stand, and I'm not up for a relationship," she said, holding her hands up and shrugging her shoulders a bit.

He looked disbelieving.

She leaned in toward him again and rose up on the toes of her strappy heels. "I'm good, love. Enjoy," she said into his ear with a lighthearted giggle at her use of the soft-hearted rejection popularized by social media.

He smiled and shook his head as she walked away.

Desdemona was honest. Brutally so. It helped her consorts trust her. What she had told him was the truth. The irony was not lost on her. A celibate madam. It had been more than five years since she'd had a lover. A warm and hard body pressed down upon hers.

Sometimes I miss the intimacy.

She stopped and turned to look at him—the good smelling man—but he had disappeared in the crowd.

She took a sip of her wine and then another as she allowed

herself to regret letting the moment to be wild, reckless, and young pass.

To break up the fucking monotony.

Desdemona reached for her prepaid iPhone. It was a little after midnight. She was ready to call it a night and get reacquainted with her bed.

And my loyal, uncomplicated, trouble-free vibrator. Go, Rabbit. Go.

She texted Byron.

M.: It's a no for now.

"Another pinot noir, please," she told the bartender, handing him her empty wineglass.

Bzz . . . Bzzz . . . Bzzz . . .

As she accepted her wineglass with a thankful smile, Desdemona briefly glanced at her cell phone vibrating against the top of the bar. Byron. Would he accept her refusal or angle for another shot?

Either way, she had made up her mind.

Dirk Blank was a brilliant actor. Unfortunately, the respect garnered for his talent did not extend to his behavior once out of character on stage or film set. His career was troubled with arrests, multiple stays in rehab, and violent outbursts on set. His life and career were heavily chronicled on gossip blogs and celebrity-centered TV programs like *E! News* and *TMZ*. His talent was undeniable. Award wins. Rankings on Forbes's list of highest paid actors. A-list privileges.

One of Desdemona's many requirements was no drug use by paramours or consorts.

Dirk Blank seemed to be on the mend with his career on yet another upswing. She'd even read in the trades that Byron was wooing him back to the stage for his newest dramatic play. Still, she wasn't willing to take the chance of a relapse on her watch.

Ensuring the safety and protection of her employees was at the top of her long list of duties as a madam.

Bzzz . . . Bzzz . . . Bzzz . . .

She checked the incoming text.

45:???
M.: 1 bad apple can spoil the bunch

"Two white wines, please. Thanks."

Desdemona turned at the sound of the voice placing a drink order. She recognized it instantly. "Hello, stranger," she said, looking at the profile of Zora Lowell.

The woman faced her, and her smile faded a bit as she stiffened her back. Her eyes shifted about the room before settling back on Desdemona as she took two steps back, giving them distance.

Shame. Desdemona recognized it well.

"You did nothing wrong, Zora, and no one knows. So, relax," she said, giving her an encouraging smile. "It's good to see you."

The woman nodded and released a breath that seemed to vibrate into the air.

"I'm surprised to see you here," Desdemona said, accepting her glass of wine from the bartender and taking a sip.

"I'm an accountant at the firm that handled the counting of the votes for the awards," she said, her eyes brimming with pride. "I'm on track to become a junior partner."

Zora's wide-set eyes and innocence had made her a favorite for consorts seeking to be coddled and comforted. Her dalliances had never been about wild and adventurous sex, but sweet and tender lovemaking—not every consort's cup of tea, but for those who chose that, they paid well. After just two years she had earned enough to graduate from college debt-free and retired from service to establish herself in her accounting career.

"Not bad for a little black girl from Newark," Desdemona said, raising her glass to toast the poised and polished young woman standing before her.

Zora licked her lips and blinked her eyes as if to fight back some emotion tied to her upbringing even as she raised one of the wineglasses she held to touch it lightly to Desdemona's. "Are you still only taking fifty percent?" she asked, changing the subject and lightening the mood.

"The accountant in you is asking that, Zora," she said. "What would Kitty think?"

Kitty was the name she had used as a courtesan.

"Touché," Zora said.

Desdemona fell silent as a bald man of average height and cute looks stopped next to Zora and eased his hand on her lower back as he pressed a kiss to her temple. And in less than a few seconds, she took in their wedding rings, Zora's unease, and the proprietary look in his eyes.

He's picked up on Zora's vibe with women and is worried. He's not wrong. Some of her happiest consorts were women.

"I thought I lost you," he said.

Desdemona said no more and turned away from them.

"Who's that, babe?" he asked.

"I don't know her," Zora lied to him.

In truth, she doesn't. Hell, do I even know myself?

Desdemona left the party, ready to leave the celebrity and the fanfare behind. Once in the back of her Lyft Lux Black XL, she looked out the tinted window at the city still vibrant and alive with lights, noise, and movement, but her thoughts were on her disdain for the type of pretense and falsehood in which Zora and her husband dwelled. She'd had enough of that growing up . . .

"Now I lay me down to sleep. I pray the Lord my soul to keep.

If I should die before I wake, I pray to God my soul to take," six-year-old Desdemona said with her eyes pressed closed tight and her hands pressed together beneath her chin as she knelt by her bed. "God bless Daddy, Miss Zena, my teacher Miss Scott, new black Barbie doll, and the braids Miss Zena gave me today, and my momma up there with you in heaven."

"A-men," she said in unison with her father and stepmother, Zena, before lovingly stroking the heart-shaped locket she wore around her neck.

"Okay, up in bed," Zena said, folding back the covers of her twin-size bed in her princess-themed bedroom in shades of pink.

Desdemona did as she was bidden, smiling up at her father and Miss Zena as each bent to press a kiss to her forehead. She missed her mother and talked to her in heaven so much that people thought she had an invisible friend, but things had turned out to be nice at her father and Miss Zena's. Never enough to make her forget her mother, but enough to make her loss a little easier to take.

"Good night," she said, before turning on her side and hugging her sweet-smelling pillow close.

Miss Zena turned off the castle-shaped lamp on her nightstand.

They left the room together, leaving her room door slightly ajar, and Desdemona closed her eyes, falling asleep.

Desdemona blinked, pushing the sweet and tender memory aside as the car hit an infamous NYC pothole and jostled her body back and forth a bit on the back seat of the SUV. She was thankful when it pulled to a stop before her building. "Have a good night," she said to the burly driver before opening the back door.

"Same to you," he said.

Desdemona tucked her clutch under her arm as she crossed the sidewalk to the double doors of the building. She smiled and nodded at the doorman as he held the door for her. In the elevator she leaned back against the wall, lightly patting her clutch against her thigh.

I wish I didn't care. But I did. I do.

Once in her apartment, she didn't bother with many lights, preferring the beauty of the lit nightscape through her windows. She stepped out of her shoes, removed her artsy cape and let it drop to the floor, and pulled the pins from her knot now to let her hair free as she walked across the living room and leaned against the sill to look out at the reflection of the city against the Hudson River.

Crossing her arms over her chest, she lightly stroked her clavicle as her memories of her past reclaimed her attention. Loneliness was something she thought she had gotten used to. The death of her father just five years after her mother had been tough. The treatment of her by her stepmother after his death had made her mourning even worse.

Another death. More change . . .

Ten-year-old Desdemona stood in the doorway of Miss Zena's bedroom, hating the nervousness she felt about talking to this woman who had become a stranger to her again. Her eyes darted to her father's side of the bed, and she missed him like crazy. It had been just a month since he died, but everything was different.

She is different.

Desdemona eyed her stepmother sitting on the foot of the bed in her nightgown rubbing lotion on her arms. She stopped suddenly, and her face became tight with annoyance. Desdemona stiffened.

"What?" she snapped, looking straight ahead as if avoiding even laying eyes on her.

At that moment she wished she didn't have to bother her at all. But she did. She had no one else to rely on. "Could you do my hair?" she asked, her voice soft and hesitant.

She didn't bother to add that her fuzzy and unkempt braids were drawing too much attention from classmates.

Zena released an agitated breath before rising from the bed to retrieve the hair comb, brush, and hair grease from the adjoining bathroom. "Come on," she said with barely concealed irritation.

That's how it always was. The new normal. She would do what was required: cook, clean, wash clothes, and send her to school, but every second of it was laced with her annoyance. Her coldness. It was clear she did what she did out of obligation and not love.

She hates me.

Desdemona walked into the bedroom, her feet bare and her steps padded by the plush carpeting. She sat down on the edge of the bed, already knowing to hold her neck stiff because Miss Zena's rough movements would cause her head to jerk back and forth. It was why she waited to remind her about her hair for two weeks.

"If your little behind wasn't so grown you would tie your hair up like I said and make it last longer," Zena said.

"I will," she said softly, hating that pang of hurt she felt.

Miss Zena never hit her, but there were no hugs either. Not anymore.

Why do you hate me? *Desdemona mouthed, wanting to give voice to the words. To her feelings.*

But she didn't.

She knew the answer. Kinda.

The day of her father's funeral she overheard Zena telling someone how she was stuck raising the child her husband had with another woman when she wasn't able to ever have one of her own.

"Maybe, in a weird way, she is your chance to be a mother, Zena," the woman she had spoken to had said.

"Or she's a daily reminder shoved down my throat," Zena had replied. "His will leaves everything to her, and for me to get a stipend every week I have to agree to be her trustee. So, I don't have any choice but to raise her. Daniel fucked me over once again."

Well over twenty years and she remembered her stepmother's rejection of her so very clearly.

I don't have any choice but to raise her.

Being somewhere when you knew you weren't wanted was a bad feeling—particularly for a kid. It took adulthood for her to understand that her mother had been her father's mistress, and the façade Zena put on of the happy family faded with the death of her father.

It was one of the first lessons Desdemona learned about honesty and trust.

She turned from the window and looked around her apartment. The fine things in her life that she acquired on her own. She was thankful for it all. The highs and the lows. The lessons and the blessings. "Not bad, kiddo," she said, before turning to cast her gaze out at the view once more.

Chapter Three

One month later

"Yoweeeeeeeeeeeeeee!"

At the high-pitched squeal of pleasure, Desdemona and Denzin shared a look across the island in the kitchen of the Riverdale estate.

"Plum," they said in unison, both without a doubt who could make a grown man hit a falsetto note to rival an opera singer.

"Did you know the term 'pimping' is from the early eighteenth century?"

Desdemona tilted her head down to look at Denzin over the rim of her oversize tortoiseshell glasses. "It didn't mean then what it means now," she said. "And I'm *not* a pimp."

Denzin flipped the page of the book he was reading. "I agree you have no pimp-hand."

She dropped the pen she was using to check through the list of her courtesans' latest round of blood tests—everyone was drug and disease free. "If you would like me to backhand you, I can," she said.

He chuckled. "No thank you, Mademoiselle," he said.

"There's a level to this, and I'm not scaring or beating anyone and we all make good money together," she said, her tone offended.

"Yes, we do," he agreed, before falling silent.

Desdemona crossed her legs in the crimson red matte jersey floor-length skirt she wore with a matching cap-sleeved crop top. She settled back against the padded back of the high chair as she pushed her spectacles atop her curls. She eyed him. "How's your mom?" she asked.

Denzin's brows creased. "She passed away last month," he said, looking at her before shifting in his seat and looking away.

Desdemona eyed him curiously. "I'm sorry to hear that, Denzin. Why didn't you tell me?" she asked.

He shrugged a bit. "We're not friends," he simply said.

True.

She shifted her gaze away from his.

"You only know my mother was sick at all because you asked me why I wanted to get into the business," Denzin said. "Hell, I don't even know your real name."

She leveled her eyes with his. "None of that means I don't care about any of you and what you're going through," she said, reaching over to lightly grip his hand. "Are you okay?"

He nodded and turned his attention back to his book.

His mother had suffered from a rare disease, and he insisted on being her caregiver—physically and financially. He needed both the free time and fast money that work as a courtesan afforded him. It wasn't just his dedication to his mother and his beauty and physique that led Desdemona to hire him. She trusted him. There was no one she trusted more.

Desdemona used her pinky finger to flick her glasses back

down on her nose before turning her attention back to the file before her. Once she was done with it, she reached for the all-black cross-cut paper shredder at her feet to set it atop the island. She shredded everything.

The silence was broken up only by the steady *bzzz* of the motor of the shredder and the occasional flip of the pages of Denzin's book. *Fahrenheit 451*.

"Wasn't there a movie with Michael B. Jordan's fineness with the same name?" she asked, remembering watching the film on Netflix last year. "Is it good?" she asked, removing her glasses and folding them before placing them in the red alligator case.

Denzin glanced up at her. "Yeah, it's pretty dope," he said. "You can get it when I'm done."

She pushed aside the nervousness she immediately felt. "No thanks. I prefer TV to books," she said, removing three green envelopes and a stack of cash from her Louis Vuitton tote. "I get bored quick."

"Cool," he said from behind the book before turning another page.

Desdemona placed two thousand dollars in each envelope. Her task complete, she drummed her stiletto nails against the top of the island as she looked about the chef's kitchen. She sighed, crossed and uncrossed her legs, and shifted in her seat.

"You're bored."

She eyed him.

He folded the top corner of the page and closed his book.

"I am," she admitted, looking down at her diamond butterfly bracelet and stroking the wings of one that seemed to be in mid-flight.

"You've been feeling that for a while now," he said assuredly.

"I have."

"What's the end game, Mademoiselle?" Denzin asked.

"Who says there is one?" she countered.

He nodded.

"The same could be said for you... especially with the passing of your mother," she said.

His eyes flashed for a moment with pain that was haunting.

She knew the loss of a parent all too well.

"I'm not done yet. I'm not bored yet," he said. "*But* I have an end game."

She leaned forward, crossing her arms atop the cool stone. "Care to share?"

"Not yet."

Desdemona looked at her watch.

"And your exit plan?" he asked.

"Yet to be determined," she said, rising to stand in her black open-toe wedge heels with large bows at the ankles.

She didn't miss that over the edge of the book his eyes lingered on her breasts sans bra with her nipples affected by the chill of the air-conditioning. "There's a hair-thin line between employed and fired, Denzin," she said decisively, not wanting to encourage a level of comfort in which he looked to her as a sexual object.

His eyes went back to his book.

She had no interest in bedding Denzin and wanted him to return the favor in kind.

Cha-ching. Cha-ching. Cha-ching.

She picked up her iPhone. She frowned a bit as she answered the call. "Yes?" she asked, walking out of the kitchen via the French doors to the rear porch. The night did nothing to keep the summer heat from immediately pressing against her body.

"I didn't sign up for a threesome."

Desdemona frowned. "And I didn't arrange one," she said, her voice filled with steel. "Where are you?"

"I'm in one of the bathrooms. I lied and told them I had to shower first."

"Door locked?" she asked, as she paced the length of the porch.

"Definitely."

Desdemona had sent Neesa on a session with Reverend B. C. Hines, a married televangelist of a megachurch in Atlanta with forty thousand members in his congregation and reportedly $80 million in annual revenue. "You dressed?"

"Yes."

"Leave the hotel suite while I'm on the phone," she said, waving her hand as something lightly flew against her cheek.

"Actually, this is the only night I'm working and—"

"You need the payment," Desdemona finished, reentering the house.

"Yes."

"I'm on the way," she said, grabbing the envelopes, cash, and her other items to dump into her tote before she strode past the island and ended the call.

"Everything good?" Denzin asked, closing his book again and rising to his feet.

Desdemona nodded and gave him a reassuring smile. "Nothing I can't handle," she said over her shoulder as she left the kitchen.

She made her way to the elevator and rode up to the second floor. She had a full house. All three bedrooms were occupied. The father and pair of sons were celebrating their pharmaceutical company's recent $32 billion acquisition of its largest competitor.

She stopped at each door and dropped an emerald envelope in each plastic wall file holder attached to the wood with removable adhesive. Normally, the paramours collected the remaining fee beyond the profit on the dress purchase and the deposit before the session started and left the cash in white envelopes on the door for her to retrieve and divide. Green envelopes indicated everything in it was meant for them plus whatever tip their consorts gave them.

She skipped the elevator and quickly descended the rear steps to reach the hall leading from the mudroom to the back of the kitchen. She activated the automatic starter of her vehicle as she strode across the mudroom to the door leading into the three-car garage. Her Maserati crossover awaited her.

Behind the wheel, she dialed number twelve on her contact list. It rang once before Reverend Hines answered. "Which is the commandment about stealing?" she calmly asked.

He chortled.

"And before you start, there are no TV cameras and you are not in your pulpit, so save me the bible verses and hallelujahs," she inserted dryly.

His chuckles ceased. "Mademoiselle—"

"Who are your colleagues?" she asked.

"Two good servants of the Lord—"

She sighed heavily. "Rev, please play with your congregation and not me?" she asked.

"I'm the only one she had to service. They were just going to watch," he said, his Georgia accent heavy.

"And that would have cost you an additional grand. See how we circled back to stealing. You know this is all against the rules," she reminded him.

He fell silent.

"Who are they?" she asked again as she dipped in and out of traffic, intent on reaching Manhattan as quickly as possible without drawing the attention of highway patrolmen.

"They're two ministers from my church. I vouch for them."

"Their names, Rev."

"Walter Young and Luther Poll," he supplied.

"Thank you," she said even though she felt wary about whether he was telling the truth. "Get rid of them, please. I'll be at your suite in fifteen minutes."

Desdemona ended the call and accelerated forward, reaching the Ritz-Carlton in Manhattan on Central Park South in record time. She checked her car into valet parking and barely took in the grand design of the lobby as she made her way to the elevator. She gave a wealthy young couple and their toddler son a polite smile as they all stepped onto the lift.

On the way up to the fourth floor she reached inside her tote and felt for the retractable baton she carried with her everywhere. She hadn't used her "mood changer" since the days she was a prostitute, but she was sure, if need be, use of it would be akin to learning to ride a bike all over again.

"I had fun."

Desdemona looked down at the little boy, about five or six, with the biggest brown eyes that were currently filled with sleep. "You did?" she asked, her voice tender.

He nodded earnestly before leaning against his father's leg as if exhausted.

"Sightseeing all day," his mother explained, rubbing her son's back as her husband picked him up in his arms.

With his head nestled atop his father's shoulder, he gave Desdemona a sleepy smile. "Your hair looks like the sun," he said in the seconds just before his eyes closed and he fell asleep.

Cha-ching. Cha-ching. Cha-ching.

Desdemona joined in the stilted and polite laughter of the parents as she dug out her cell phone. She opened the incoming text from Neesa. There were photos of each of Reverend Hines's ministers. "And I didn't even have to ask for it," she mouthed with a shake of her head.

Loyalty begets loyalty.

The elevator slowed to a stop on the fourth floor, and she stepped off.

"She was beautiful, right?"

Desdemona spotted the two men waiting for a descending elevator and coolly headed in the opposite direction, not wanting to be seen walking to Reverend Hines's park view suite. She had to breathe through her anger at possibly being exposed as she kept her back to them and pressed her phone to her ear pretending to be on a call until the men finally stepped onto their elevator.

She immediately turned on her heels, her strides long and wide as she reached his suite. Quickly, she reached in her tote and pulled out her retractable baton to slide it into the pocket of her voluminous skirt. Two raps of her knuckles on the door before he opened it and she was inside, standing beside Rev who was wearing one of the hotel's plush white robes.

She pointed her thumb at the closed door to her right.

He nodded, shoving his hands into the pockets of the robe as he walked farther into the living room decorated in shades of gold.

Desdemona knocked on the door. "I'm here," she said.

Neesa stepped out of the full bathroom.

"Nice choice," she said with a nod of approval at her selection of a form-fitting Ralph Lauren wrap dress in a dark blue with neutral heels and subtle gold jewelry.

It was the perfect level of sophisticated sexy for the Ritz-Carlton. Desdemona hated for one of her paramours to look completely out of place, and nothing defined a proper place in a space more than clothing.

Neesa was Native American and black with straight hair she wore down the length of her back. Her height and dancer's build coupled with her natural grace and quiet intelligence made her a favorite. Only her pre-med studies at Columbia University kept Desdemona from elevating her to her top-tier paramours who traveled over the world at a moment's notice to service a consort.

Desdemona accepted the money she handed her and quickly counted off her share, pressing it into her hand with a smile. "Have a good night," she said, opening the door.

"Wait a Goddamn minute!" Reverend Hines shouted.

Neesa left without another word.

Desdemona closed the door and turned to face Reverend

Hines. "We have a problem," she said, eyeing the tall and wide man with the most beautiful dark brown complexion, short silver hair, and bright white toothy smile. He shoved his hands into the pockets of the robe. "You know that, right?"

His face became pensive as he claimed a seat on the brocade sofa adjacent to the windows offering the night view of Central Park across the street. "If you plan on keeping my money without my session, then we definitely do," he said with calm.

She claimed one of the armchairs across from him, setting her tote on the floor beside her feet. "What makes our business together work is mutual respect and mutual protection," she began. "Tonight, you pissed on both."

He held up his hands. "You want to be paid for ass that just left me high and dry?"

She nodded. "Yes, because you tried to get three dicks wet for the price of one, and you almost exposed me to people I don't know or trust. Lack of respect. Lack of protection. Two strikes."

He frowned. "Two strikes."

She slid her hand into her pocket and stroked her baton as she crossed her legs. "One more and you are off my list," she explained, before offering him a smile that didn't match the frost in her eyes. "*Or*. . . if you like, we can part ways now and promise to keep each other's secrets."

Knock-knock.

They both looked to the door to the suite.

"Housekeeping," a female voice said.

"I didn't order anything," he said, rising to his feet.

In his haste, the bottom corner of his robe opened, and she was offered a disturbing glimpse of his penis dangling between his thighs.

Uncircumcised? Fix it, Jesus, she thought, mimicking the voice of Phaedra Parks, former *Real Housewives of Atlanta* cast member.

"It's my wife," Reverend Hines whispered from the door.

Desdemona sighed as she grabbed her tote and rose to her feet. "Strike three, Rev," she said, before crossing the room with her hand extended.

He looked down at it and then back up at her, imploring with her eyes that she change her mind. She shook her head, refusing him.

With angry strides, he brushed past her and returned moments later to roughly press his prepaid flip phone against her palm. She gave him a withering look as she opened the door to the bathroom and stepped inside, closing it and leaning against the solid wood.

"Surprise!"

"Jennifer," the reverend said, pretending to be surprised.

He really is a good actor. I guess it's all the practice from his performances in the pulpit.

"And the Oscar goes to," she mouthed, as she checked her hair and makeup in the mirror over the sink.

I really am too rich for this shit.

She paused with her fingers raking through her large curls when she heard a slight thump against the wall and a loud moan.

"I'm the only one she had to service. They were just going to watch."

Her eyes widened, and she felt dread that he was going to screw his wife and force her to listen, fulfilling his kink to have sex in front of someone.

I've seen and done worse.

Desdemona sat down on the closed lid of the commode and withdrew her phone to scroll through Instagram.

Thump-thump-thump-thump.

She frowned, cutting her eyes from the feed of the online gossip site The Shade Room to the door. She thought of his wife, a short and rotund plain-looking woman who was active in his ministry and spoke with a soft, cartoonish voice.

Desdemona wondered if she lacked trust in her husband and that was the impetus for the surprise trip. *Smart woman.*

Thump-thump-thump-thump.

She was thankful when their rough cries filtered through the door as the thumping increased in speed.

Thump-thump-thump-thump-thump-thump-thump-thump.

"Finish strong, Rev," she mouthed with an eye roll as she stood, dropping her iPhone into her tote as she flipped open his burner phone and checked it. No calls or contact info except hers. "Good."

"I'm going to order us some dinner," Reverend Hines said. "Go shower. The bedroom suite is right through that door."

"Just order me a salad," she said.

Just get me the hell out of here.

The doorknob turned, and Desdemona reached for it to pull the door open wide. He stood in the doorway with his robe still open. She gave him a slow up and down look and shook her head before pushing past him to open the front door and leave him, his wife, and his uncircumcised penis behind for good.

His chuckles reached her just before he closed the door.

She stopped, turned, and pushed the door open as she pulled her baton from her pocket, snapping her wrist to extend it. His eyes widened in surprise just before she brought the baton up between his open legs against his hanging testicles.

She chuckled. "Laugh now, Rev," she said.

"Bartholomew, bring my suitcase," his wife called from the next room.

Desdemona lightly tapped his privates once more before turning and walking away as she continued to laugh, striking the baton against the floor to retract it and then she dropped it inside her tote.

The last laugh on me? Never.

* * *

Desdemona stepped inside the Barnes and Noble in Tribeca and looked around at an environment that was foreign to her. The abundance of books overwhelmed her. Stacked on shelves. Lining the shelves. Seemingly to the ceiling. Everywhere.

"Welcome to Barnes and Noble. Can I help you?"

She smiled at the thin, tall Latin man with spectacles and his store ID hanging from a black lanyard around his slender neck as she raked her fingers through her hair deeply enough to stroke her scalp to ease the anxiety she felt. "Uhm, yes, I was looking for the book *Fahrenheit 451*," she said, hating the nervousness she felt.

"That's right over here," he said.

She wrung her hands as she followed behind him.

After leaving the Ritz-Carlton she hadn't wanted to go back to her apartment for another night of checking in on the safety and cash drops by her courtesans. She thought of Denzin's interest in the book and wondered if it could help stave off the boredom claiming her lately.

Or would it make it worse?

"Thank you, Carlos," she said, reading his name tag as she took the hardcover book he handed to her and clutched it to her chest.

"Can I recommend some other fiction titles for you?" he asked.

"Trust me. One book is a big enough leap," she quipped.

He chuckled and held up his hands. "No pressure," he said. "We don't close until ten, so feel free to enjoy your book in our café. The stuffed pretzels are awesome."

Desdemona turned and looked toward the eatery that had the air around it swelling with the scents of sweets and coffee. Although her stomach rumbled in hunger, she decided to save her appetite for orecchiette pasta with a veal Bolognese sauce she planned to order a la carte from room service once she was in her condominium.

She eyed four women in their mid-thirties laughing and enjoying each other's company in between sips of caramel macchiato and pointing out sections from their individual copies of a book. "No thank you. I'm good," she finally said in response to him.

One of the women looked over and caught Desdemona's eyes on them. She instantly turned away, feeling like a loner caught peering at the popular girls in school.

I never really had a friend.

"If you're all set I can ring you up," Carlos said.

Again, Desdemona followed him, pushing aside the feelings of inadequacy from the past that surged forward. She purchased the book and left the store for the less than five-minute walk back to her building. She had valeted her car when she got in from the hotel and made the walk to avoid the hassle of street parking.

Tribeca bustled with activity, and there were plenty of those who lived in or were visiting the trendy section of New York. As she passed upscale bars with live bands and restaurants with their outdoor seating filled to capacity, the vibe was all about the convenience of city living. Beautiful views. Cobblestone streets. The industrial buildings that once reigned now converted to lofts that drew the creatives. Many celebrities and wealthy elite called Tribeca home.

Still, the summer heat had not diminished much at night. She was glad to stride up the street to the doorman holding the door open for her. "Have a good night," she said to him as she passed him to step into the sweetness of air conditioning in the lobby.

"Same to you, Ms. Smith."

She made her way across the marble floor to the elevator and pushed the button. The doors opened almost immediately. She was grateful.

Once in her condominium, she instantly kicked off her heels and wiggled her toes as she turned on the ceiling light in the living room and carried the cash she had in her tote to her safe. She reached inside it for her most recent leather-bound journal and removed the extra-fine point pen nestled in the bend between the pages.

Wednesday, July 25, 2018

Church is big business for those collecting all those tithes and offerings . . . and for those like me making sure the false prophets get just the type of pleasure they crave . . .

Reverend Hines and his particular type of pleasure were off her roster, but he was not the only man of the cloth her courtesans serviced.

With a breath, she closed the pen inside the journal and slid it back inside the safe before locking it. The silence of her large condo was especially mocking, and she walked around the entire space turning on every light available before turning on Chopin's "Nocturnes" to play throughout the house on her Sonos wireless speakers. The first chords of the composition were light and romantic as if the pianist barely stroked the keys. She lit candles throughout the house instead and turned down the same lights she now felt were glaring. The candles offered the warmth and comfort she needed.

She paused in running a bath to close her eyes and let the music calm her, opening her arms widc and letting her head tilt back until the edges of her hair lightly stroked her back.

Desdemona was first introduced to classical piano music by one of her johns, a wealthy white lawyer of seventy years or more, who wanted nothing more than to listen to classical music all night as they lay in bed naked with their limbs entwined. One time he even cried, and she held him close and let his tears wet her shoulder.

"What was his name?" she asked herself softly, crinkling her brows as she tried to recall him.

It had been more than a decade.

"It doesn't matter," she said, opening her eyes to reach for her bottle of Jo Malone London's Nectarine Blossom and Honey Bath Oil and pour it into the hot bath water. "The man I forgot. The music I did not."

At the sound of the doorbell, she opened the glass door to the lingerie closet and removed a black lace floor-length robe to pull on. She tied the thick satin belt at the waist and, giving in to the mellowing mood of the music and a whimsy she hadn't allowed herself to feel since childhood, Desdemona lifted up on her toes and with a series of clumsy pirouettes made her way to the front door with the aroma of fruit scented candles filling the air around her. She opened the door and turned on the lights in the foyer, living room, and dining room.

"I have your room service order," the waiter said, standing behind a tray covered with a tablecloth, small floral arrangements, a paper-covered glass of ice water, and a stainless-steel plate cover.

At the sight of her in the nearly see-through lace, he stuttered and struggled to swallow over a lump in his throat. She gave the young man credit for not letting his eyes dip down to take in her body.

Desdemona had lost her shyness about her nudity years ago. More men than the years the young man had been alive had been eager to witness her nakedness. *No need to put on airs now.*

"Thank you," she said, stepping back and pointing toward the slate dining room table. "Please set it up in there."

She moved to the sofa and retrieved cash for a tip and her purchased book before going back to the front door as he transferred everything from the tray to a seat at the head of the table. For his comfort and not her own, she clutched the book to her chest, blocking the sight of her nipples from him.

As he took the tip she offered, he seemed grateful for her sudden show of modesty.

She closed the door behind him and locked it before dimming the lights again to a subtle glow, giving the candles prominence once again. She walked over to the kitchen to wash her hands in the sink and to pour herself a large glass of Rieussec from a corked bottle on the counter. She took a healthy sip as she made her way to her dinner, setting the book and the glass on the table and claiming the padded seat of the club chair.

She pecked at her pasta and mostly drank her wine as she listened to the music and eyed the book, sitting there. Seeming to mock her. She reached for it and pulled it across the table. Closer. Her fingertips tapped against the hardness in beat with the piano notes resonating in the air around her.

"Olan Killinger," she said, suddenly remembering the man who had introduced her to Chopin.

In truth when she thought she had offered him comfort, it took her years to realize he had been the same for her in a way. It was one night a week where she had felt safe. A little less forlorn.

Two pitiful souls.

She took a sip of her wine and looked off across the dining room to the large realist painting above her unlit gas-burning fireplace. It was of her parents and her when she was just a year old. The painter had skillfully taken the small photo nestled inside her locket and created a massive painting on canvas in sepia tones. It was all the more beautiful by candlelight.

She raised her wineglass in a toast to them. She wore the locket as a charm on her bracelet. Regardless of their sins, their love had created her, and although she had been melancholy of late she never had any regrets about the life—the opportunities—she had carved out for herself. She never pondered whether they were proud of her or not. She'd taken the life she'd been given and made the best of it. Tried her best at every step to win at her own game of survival, to outthink, outlast, and outplay the law as she amassed wealth from a criminal enterprise.

Even though it was a deterrent to having friends . . . and love.

And so much more.

Over the rim of her wineglass, Desdemona eyed the book. As she set her wineglass next to her plate of unfinished food she opened the book, flipping through the first few pages to reach chapter one.

She used the tip of her fingernail to follow along with each line as she read the story.

Less than five minutes later she closed the book and gave it a little nudge to push it away from her.

Leaving her barely touched dinner for the building's housekeeping to clear away the next day, Desdemona refilled her glass and moved about the living area to place the lid on the glass holding each lit candle. Without oxygen, the flame soon burned out with the lid keeping the acrid smell of the burned wick from filling the air.

She paused to let her eyes adjust to the darkness before she made her way over to the other side of the condominium, moving down the hall to her marbled bathroom. The music continued to play. Soon the robe was in a pile on the floor by her tub and her hair was twisted into a disheveled topknot before she sank beneath the warm depths, massaging the beautifully scented oil in the water against her body and then resting her head against the edge of the tub and closing her eyes.

The book had been a challenge to herself, and she had failed. Frustration got the best of her. There were far too many of the words lost to her. Those whose meaning escaped her. She couldn't pronounce or spell. Some of it might as well be foreign.

Desdemona raised her leg above the water, high in the air, pointing her foot to the high ceiling. With a sigh and the music as her backdrop, she decided she had done far too much in her life to let her lack of education be her biggest shame.

Chapter Four

Thursday, August 16, 2018

They have no idea just how good they have it . . .

Her life was a constant juggling of anywhere from five to ten balls in the air at one time. Her brain and instincts were always in overdrive. Tell this. Keep that. Do this. Don't do that. Every move and decision were critical. If this happens that may follow. Maintaining a "Chinese wall" between her consorts and paramours. Protecting everyone. Ensuring no one person would lead to her downfall. Covering all bases. Chess over checkers.

Freedom over incarceration for promoting prostitution.

Think. Think. Think.

Constantly.

Even something as simple as having the house cleaned took strategy. Inviting strangers into a house used as a brothel was an invitation for trouble if not handled properly. So once a week she had a cleaning company come in to keep the house immaculate. She rotated between four companies, not wanting anyone to have consistent access to the house. She made sure to have it thought of as a vacation rental and every Thursday she made sure to personally sweep the house for anything incriminating.

I've seen some shit.

Standing on the doorstep of her rental house in Riverdale, Desdemona felt tension nipping at her neck. The tightness across her shoulders was undeniable. Anxiety. It was mild and didn't induce panic, but it was there. She closed her eyes and did the 4-7-8 breathing method talking herself through the steps in her head.

Exhale.

Inhale for four seconds.

Hold breath for seven seconds.

Exhale for eight seconds.

"Relax, Desi. Relax," she mouthed, wiggling her shoulders before she smoothed her palms down the skirt of the black tennis dress she wore with all-black Yeezys.

Inside the house, she removed the Gucci leather backpack she wore and reached in the side pocket for a pair of gloves to pull on. The house was empty. Denzin had been flown to Greece by a long-time consort for their annual week-long tryst. His fluidity in the sex department made him a favorite of gals and guys.

She was headed toward the elevator with a garbage bag in her gloved hand when she paused at the thought of lounging nude aboard a mega-yacht as the sun toasted her skin to a deeper shade of brown. Not that something of that caliber was beyond her reach. It would barely dent her savings—in the bank, in her safes, and in safety deposit boxes in several banks—to charter a superyacht for a week-long cruise in the Mediterranean.

Should I?

She shook her head, denying herself as she continued into the house, wishing she had enough room on her plate to trust one more person. To throw one more ball in the air to juggle by hiring a full-time maid.

I wish.

Desdemona took the stairs to the second level and entered the first bedroom to the right. It was decorated in neutral shades with pops of dark blue for color. None of the bedrooms had heavy comforters over the covers. The high thread-count sheets and lightweight blankets were easier to clean and keep in abundance in the linen closets. The bed was still unmade from its use just last night.

She opened the drawers of the nightstands flanking the bed. One was filled with condoms and lube. The other held sex toys of every nature. She locked them both before checking under the pillows and covers for any left-behind condoms. She found two. With a snarl of her upper lip she carried them to dump into the garbage bag.

Most consorts made sure to dispose of their own condoms. Most. Not all.

"What a session," she mumbled, finding a Viagra pill nestled in the high fibers of the throw rug by the bed.

At the end of her search of all three bedrooms and adjoining bathrooms, she had tossed another used condom, several empty foil wrappers, an anal plug, and a torn sheet. "And a partridge in a pear tree," she sang dryly, mocking the oddball list as she carefully removed the gloves and dropped them into the trash as well before tying the bag.

Ding-dong.

"Perfect timing," she said, hoisting the bag as she made her way out of the room and down the hall to the stairs, jogging down the steps. She dumped the garbage bag inside the automated garbage can and retrieved her book bag before finally making her way across the foyer to open the front door.

"*Buenos días, Señora Smith,*" the middle-aged Latina woman said as she entered, pulling a rolling utility cart filled with her cleaning supplies behind her. Her five staff members followed behind, all dressed in polo shirts with her business logo on the pocket and black uniform pants.

"Good morning," Desdemona said, smiling at each one as they immediately set off to different areas of the house to begin cleaning.

She paused in the entry and let the sun framing the doorway coat her body as she closed her eyes. The heat felt good. Almost as good as it would aboard a yacht in Greece. Or a beach in Turks and Caicos. Or lounging on the balcony of a villa on the Amalfi Coast of Italy. Or riding through the town of Versailles in France on a bike.

Something lightly brushed against her nose, and she opened her eyes just as a colorful butterfly fluttered away. She wiped at her nose as she stepped back inside the coolness of the house. The sounds of vacuum cleaners and Dustbusters hummed in the air as she made her way to the in-law suite, Denzin's private quarters.

Desdemona tried to turn the knob. It was unlocked. "Good thing I checked," she said, opening the door to turn the lock.

She paused and looked around; her eyes landed on the built-in shelves flanking the television that were filled with books. She looked away from them with shame and stepped back out of the room to close the door and try the knob again to ensure it was locked. His space was off-limits—even to her.

Upstairs on the penthouse floor, she unlocked the door and immediately poured herself a glass of wine to wait out the hour it would take for the team to clean nearly all of the eleven-thousand-square-foot house. She turned on the surveillance but got bored watching the crew clean.

Swiveling in the chair, she turned her back to the television and looked out at the sweeping view of the hills as she mindlessly played with her diamond butterfly bracelet.

The all-too-familiar tension around her neck and shoulders returned. "Shit," she swore, hating to feel imbalanced and out of sorts.

Hating that it was steadily becoming her new normal.

Cha-ching. Cha-ching. Cha-ching.

With another sip of her wine first, she opened her book bag and removed her prepaid iPhone. Number nine. Setting her wineglass down, she swiped the phone with her thumb to answer the call.

"*Bonjour, étranger*," she greeted him in French, one of the few phrases she knew in the language.

"We need to meet. We have a problem."

Desdemona stiffened at the serious tone of his voice. Normally he would respond to her playful greeting of "Hello, stranger" with a chuckle or a quip.

Problem? What kind of problem? Jail time type of problem?

"Problems are my specialty," she said, thinking of the tall and bald light-skinned Haitian in his early fifties with hazel eyes. "I'm sure you remember that I have plenty of resources on this end."

"This matter will need *both* of us, Mademoiselle," he insisted, his French accent heavy. "We shouldn't discuss it by phone. I am sending a car for you."

Her curiosity was piqued, but she didn't like to be ordered about. It was one of the reasons she had stopped servicing consorts herself. The days of even being told just how a man liked to be made to ejaculate were over. Fast strokes. Doggy style. Blow job. Rim shots.

No more. Control was always hers. Whenever. Whatever.

"No," she asserted. "And are you in America? Hell, are you in New York?"

"Yes. The car can be there in ten minutes."

Desdemona released a short laugh that was mocking. "Where?" she asked.

His pause was noticeable, before his all-too-familiar chuckle followed. "Okay, tell me where you are and I'll send the car there."

"I'm handling some business," she said, turning to eye the surveillance screens on the television. "But I can meet you in two hours."

"Okay. You picked the time so I'll send the car."

She tapped her fingernails across the top of the desk.

"This can't be a pissing contest; only one of us has a dick, Mademoiselle," he mused.

"I will be more than happy to personally deliver two beautiful dresses to you," Desdemona said.

Time is money.

Again, he chuckled. "Fine. You win. Two hours—"

"Outside my showroom," she interrupted him smoothly before ending the call and claiming the win.

"We're here, Mademoiselle," the driver said.

Desdemona handed the garment bags to the driver before accepting his hand as she exited the back of the black Cadillac Escalade with her tote. She adjusted the large black shades and scarf she wore around her head and covering the bottom half of her face.

She had changed into a black one-shoulder dress with an asymmetrical hem that exposed one lush brown thigh.

"Have a good day, Mademoiselle," the driver said, closing the door of the SUV and laying the garment bags over the arm she offered.

"Thank you," she said, moving the short distance across the tarmac of the private airfield to the black jet.

Her steps were briefly cushioned by the black welcome mat before she carefully climbed the steps in her six-inch heels to board the luxurious plane.

"Welcome aboard, Mademoiselle."

She smiled at Antoine Pierre rising from his seat to hand

her a flute of champagne as she neared him. She draped the garment bags over one of the leather seats and placed her tote on the seat. "Where's your crew?" she asked, taking the flute and enjoying a sip.

"Privacy is key with you," he said, unbuttoning his suit jacket and claiming a seat. "They're not onboard."

She nodded as she moved to the seat across from where he now sat.

"Are you Muslim now?" he asked, his tone bemused as he eyed her scarf.

"This is not a hijab and you know that," she said, removing it and her shades with her free hand to set both on her lap before leaning back against the seat and crossing her legs. Slowly.

His eyes dropped to take in the innocent move, clinging to the sight of her exposed thighs. He swore under his breath and smiled. "*Entre tes cuisses je trouve le paradis,*" he said, his voice deep.

"Translation, please?" Desdemona asked as she uncrossed and then crossed her legs again, knowing she was teasing him . . . and herself. Five years of celibacy and being in the presence of the first john who ever made her climax was titillating. Not that it was emotional and sensual. Or that he was the most voracious lover. He just was the first man to ever care if the sex was as good for her as it was for him.

He also was the last john she serviced.

Antoine set his drink in the holder in the wood-grain panel running alongside his seat beneath the windows of the plane. "Between your thighs I find paradise," he said. "*Nommez votre prix.*"

That one she knew well. She shook her head, denying his request of naming her price.

Antoine was wealthy and once politically powerful in Haiti, now running his multimillion-dollar tech business out of Paris. Although single, he had been attached to a beautiful Swedish model for the last five years. Desdemona was well aware their relationship had ended a few months ago. The foreign press followed his activities with precision.

"What's the problem we need to fix?" she asked, taking another sip of very good champagne. "Have I finally been discovered?"

He shook his bald head. "No."

Inwardly she felt relief. She was well aware that it may not be her own criminal activity that brought the law upon her, but that of one of her consorts who didn't cover their trail well or traded her in to save themselves.

"I'm in need of your services," he admitted, moving to sit on the edge of the seat with his knees spread as he pressed his elbows down upon them and locked his fingers in the air between them.

Desdemona eyed him over the rim of her glass, noticing his erection pressed against the seam of his tailored pants. She cleared her throat. "Things have changed since we last spoke, Antoine," she said.

"I know."

She looked pensive, curious about the discussions being had about her. A lot of the consorts were friendly with each other, particularly since new consorts were by referral only.

"There are more than a few men unhappy with your decision," Antoine admitted, clasping his hands as if forcing himself not to reach across the short divide to touch her.

Desdemona took another sip.

"Knowing that you haven't been with any of them anymore makes me want you even more, Mademoiselle," he admitted. "*Nommez votre prix.*"

"There is no price. Not anymore," she said. "I can set you up with one of my consorts, perhaps someone more to your taste."

Their eyes met.

His ex was foreign, tall, slender, and naturally blond. Everything Desdemona was not.

"In fact, I have a set of twins that would be perfect. Lyla and Lola would be twice the fun for you," she said.

He did reach to press a warm hand to her knee. "It would take both of them and more to match you," he said with such determination. The Johansen twins were concierge level courtesans ready to fly around the country at a whim to service her elite consorts. The blond, blue-eyed twin beauties of Swedish background were aspiring actors, frequently out of work, but loved acting and improving their craft. They had just arrived back from an excursion to Vegas with a high-roller gambler, but Paris would give them renewed energy.

"True," Desdemona admitted, allowing his hand to remain. "But I have taught all my courtesans very well. I've even shown them videos of me doing what I do, how I do it, and why you all used to pay me very well."

"*Nommez votre prix*."

"No."

Antoine sat back in his chair in frustration, wiping his hand across his mouth.

"Trust me, the twins are what you need," she said, reaching into her bag for her phone. He was a man used to having his way. What her consorts failed to acknowledge was that they all were.

"Fly with me to Paris," he said. "I can just lie inside you all weekend and all will be right with the world."

Paris.

She was tempted. It would be so easy to say yes and get away from the normalcy of her routine. Something different. Spontaneous.

"I am the center of protection for my consorts and courtesans," she explained. "I need to be here in case something happens. That's my job."

"*Nommez votre prix,*" he repeated. "Anything."

She set her flute inside the cupholder and rose, coming over to stand beside where he sat. She reached for his chin and tilted his head back. "The next man I lie with will be because I choose to, not because he pays me," she said to him softly, stroking his chin with her thumb.

Calmly he reached around her body and pressed his face against her belly. "Then choose to," he requested.

The fleshy bud of her core throbbed to life as she looked down the length of the aircraft and her eyes landed on the king-size bed just beyond the open door. It would be so easy to lead him there and ride them both to a climax. So damn easy.

She shook her head, denying them both. "We have done business in the past, and to offer my body to you for free now would be bad business. Right?" she asked. "Right."

He said nothing.

Desdemona moved out of his grasp. "I brought three dresses for you to choose from," she said, walking over to the first seat, where she had laid the garment bags, to pick them up.

"I don't need *dresses*," he said.

She eyed him as she unzipped the bag, "I didn't *need* to come here today," she volleyed back. "I could have just as well denied you over the phone as I did on this plane, Antoine."

"I've never married, but I didn't want to cheat," he said as he reached for his flute. "So I left you alone."

Desdemona removed the three dresses.

"And now that I am free again, you have left me alone," he finished, before taking a very deep sip.

"Not just you," she reminded him, coming over with the gowns held by hangers in her hands. "All of you."

Over the rim of his flute, he eyed the elaborate garments she held before him before reaching inside his suit jacket to withdraw a thin billfold, from which he removed a black

American Express card and set it on the table beside him. "I'll buy all three *if* you model the middle one for me," he said.

Desdemona matched his gaze with her own as she picked up the card and held it between two fingers as she eased her dress down over her body until it fell to her feet. Naked, she continued to look at him even as his eyes left hers to travel up and down the length of her frame. At ease, she withdrew her iPhone from her bag and attached the card reader, tapping her foot as she rung his purchase.

"Name your damn price, Mademoiselle," he ordered, his eyes intense as they finally shifted up to lock with hers again.

"That will be eighty-one-hundred dollars with tax. For the *dresses*. Don't worry, I'll cover delivery," she said, before swiping the card through the reader.

She reached for the dress of his choosing: a sheer black lace halter dress with a low back and the mystery of the nudity beneath it hidden by the folds of the A-line skirt that fell to the tops of her heels. With a twirl, the dress rose up high around her waist. "You like?" she asked, coming to a stop.

"To hell with this," he said, quickly undoing the button and belt of his pants to free his erection where he sat.

"Antoine," she chided, like a teacher scolding a misbehaving child, as she picked up her flute and took a sip.

He bit his bottom lip as he stroked the length of his penis with a tight grip.

She removed the dress and hung it back on its hanger before calmly placing all three dresses back inside the garment bag. He began to grunt in the back of his throat at his rising pleasure, and she closed her eyes as her clit swelled to life, wanting to be pleased as well. She bent to pick up her own dress.

"Shit," he hissed from behind her, his urgency clear.

Desdemona released a breath, recognizing the pleasure in the depth of his hazel eyes as he stroked himself.

She desired a climax, but not him. She did not want *him*. He was just a man—a john—attached to a decent penis. She could achieve the same climax back at home with her two fingers or one of her toys.

She stepped over to him and pressed the side of his face against her flat belly. She felt his body tremble at her nearness as she looked down at him working himself so feverishly that his hips seemed to uncontrollably jerk forward. And when he roughly cried out as his cum shot from him like a cannon, some landing on her cheek and nipple, she stroked his head, comforting him. His moans and cries subsided as he became flaccid.

I owed him that nut.

She stepped away from him and stepped into her Lycra dress before dropping his card onto the table and picking up her tote. "Never contact me again, Antoine," she said, using the back of her hand to swipe his ejaculation from her cheek.

He looked up at her, his breathing still ragged, before his eyes squinted in understanding.

That one moment between them had cost him access to her courtesans.

He nodded. "It was worth it," he said.

With her clit throbbing and starved, jealous of his climax, she slid on her shades and scarf and turned to leave him on the plane. She didn't bother to retrieve his burner phone and just blocked his number on her end.

I could be in Paris.

Not that she'd never been before. She had. She had just never gone on her own. Just to go or for vacation. It had always been for work. Sex. Servicing. She'd seen no more than the Charles de Gaulle Airport and various luxury hotel suites. Never the landmarks she'd heard about or seen in TV shows and films. The Eiffel Tower she'd glimpsed from a window, and that was no more effective than a postcard. The Louvre or the Champs-Élysées? The Latin Quarter and Versailles? Never.

Just fly in. Screw. Fly back out.

"You're tensing up, Ms. Smith. Is everything okay?"

No.

Desdemona released a breath and forced her body to relax as she lay atop the padded massage table of the spa located in her building. "Everything's fine," she said, her face resting inside the padded headrest.

"Good," the woman said.

Desdemona couldn't remember her name.

She closed her eyes and tried to enjoy the feel of her skilled fingers working the muscles of her back with deep glides. In truth, it was the area below her navel that needed the massaging with a little toy that vibrated. After watching Antoine climax she'd felt like a cigarette—or fifty deep and hard strokes. Over and over and over—

Desdemona sat up on the table, her heart and clit pounding in unison, and reached around for the white sheet to cover her breasts. "That's enough," she said.

Her erotic thoughts plus the woman's hands gently kneading her body made things really awkward, really quick.

"But you have more time available," she said.

Desdemona looked at her name tag with a stiff smile. *Roberta. That's right.* "I'm fine, Roberta. You were wonderful. I just remembered an appointment," she lied, accepting the robe the woman handed her.

"Yes, ma'am."

She covered her face with her hand when she was left alone, but visions of Antoine's ejaculation plagued her. Teased and taunted her.

The times have really changed.

Cruising through Greece. Jetting to Paris. Men content with pleasing themselves.

It was so far removed from her days streetwalking. She lightly touched the spot on her cheek where his seed had been as she remembered seeing and doing far more for much less. Twenty for a hand job. Fifty for a blow job. The roughness. The fear. The long nights waiting on corners and in dark spaces for a car to pull up. The hits and punches from men just as angry as they were horny. And then those bums who paid up front then robbed her for the same money once they were done with her.

She closed her eyes, hating that she could almost recall the moldy scent of cheap motel rooms. And back then, that half hour in those dingy damn rooms with their scratchy sheets and lumpy beds had been a respite from the street.

She had had no wealthy consorts, just johns. Tricks.

Sometimes, she honestly forgot.

Desdemona doubted any of her courtesans had the gumption to survive the shit she'd seen and done. And she made sure they didn't have to. No violence. No pressure. No obligations. No degradation.

She tried her best to be to them what others hadn't been to her. Kind. Empathetic. Protective.

"Shake it off," she said, rising to her feet and closing the robe. "Look at you now, kiddo. Look at you now, Desdemona."

Notching up her chin, she refused to wallow. Refused to dwell on the middle between streetwalking and being a madam with a roster of wealthy and powerful consorts. She had taken the hard knocks, learned the tough lessons, and made sure that any consort looking to buy pleasure between a woman's thighs paid the high price and provided nothing but luxury surroundings to do so.

Dark corners. Park benches. Dingy motels. The back seat of cars. Anywhere and everywhere. Never again. Not for her or anyone who worked for her.

Upstairs in her condominium, Desdemona took a hot

bath and was just pulling on a short, sublime ivory and silver silk kimono with wide lace sleeves from Agent Provocateur when her doorbell rang.

Still in a Parisian state of mind, she had ordered delivery from a nearby French restaurant. She grabbed cash from her wallet to tip the porter who brought all deliveries from the concierge desk to residents.

She closed her robe tighter before opening the door, smiling at the uniformed middle-aged man. "I have a food delivery for you, Ms. Smith," he said, his tone polite as he averted his eyes.

They swapped the plastic bag of containers for the cash tip. "Thank you," she said, closing the door with her foot as she carried the food to the dining room table.

The smell of the cuisine already filled the air before she even opened the bag. Atop the containers was a folded card. She opened it and frowned in confusion. She assumed it was a handwritten detail of everything she ordered. A nice touch, but a waste for her. The French looked like gibberish and some of the English translation beneath it was lost to her as well.

"*Parlez-vous français*?" she said with a comical imitation of a French accent.

She had discovered the restaurant via Yelp. Great reviews. Beautiful photos of delicious and artistic looking food. She gave it a go, but when she ordered online she just picked things at random and prayed for something edible.

She had decided on an oyster dish for an appetizer, lobster and scallops stuffed in cabbage for her entrée, and a strawberry tart for dessert.

That was life among the wealthy and famous. She faked it until she made it. Picked up and learned what she could, and the rest she just played it by ear. Now she moved about them with ease and even gave them a reason to pause when she cast them a disapproving eye. It worked, but...

Desdemona paused in plating her food, having long since given up eating from plastic or aluminum containers, and reached for the card.

"Hoo-hootres gra-granite ox... aglue?" she read aloud, hesitant and unsure.

Not a good feeling at all. Foreign or not. The root issue was her inability to read well.

She set the card down and retrieved a long-handled fork from the drawer before she poured a large glass of her favorite wine. The food was delicious. Well-seasoned and buttery. So much so that she didn't allow herself to eat too much, thinking of her waistline. But even as she enjoyed the meal, her eyes kept going to the card, and she was reminded of her inability to comprehend it.

She retrieved her phones from where they were charging and went into her contact list, dialing number three. It rang once and went straight to voice mail. "Call me, Mr. President," she said, before hanging up and setting the phone on the counter.

She tapped her fingertips against the counter as she eyed the portrait of her parents. Both had been college educated, her mother a nurse and her father a pediatrician.

"Do better. Be better, Desi."

How many times had he said those words to her when she was a child?

Cha-ching. Cha-ching. Cha-ching.

She looked down at the screen and answered the call, placing it on speakerphone. "Ready for the new school term, Mr. President?" she asked, turning to lean her buttocks against the counter.

"Ready as ever," he said.

"Good," she said, with a genuine smile. "And how are you?"

The line stayed quiet for a little bit. He knew what her question entailed, and perhaps the pause was him dealing with a sudden pang of pain and regret.

"I miss her," he finally answered, his agony palpable even via a phone line.

"I know because it equals your love, Francis," she said, turning and bending over the counter next to the phone.

"If it wasn't for my children I would..."

His words faded, not giving voice to darker thoughts.

She clearly remembered the short and slender man in his early seventies with a head full of white hair that was once a sandy brown and blue eyes filled with intelligence but also some other emotion she couldn't name at the time. But it became obvious as he spoke of his beloved wife of more than forty years slipping into a coma after a burst aneurysm that the emotion was grief. Pure. Unbound. Brimming.

For nearly an hour he had sat with her in her boutique, fresh off being vetted after a recommendation from one of her consorts who was a governor and fellow classmate. She listened. She empathized. She tried her best to console him.

Desdemona understood grief all too well.

She'd accepted Francis McAdams as a consort. She'd been surprised to learn that the president of a private college earned seven figures, and he was at the top of the highest earners when totaling his million-dollar base pay, another million in bonuses, his retirement plan, and living for free in a large home owned by the university. He could more than afford her rate, she made sure of that. Before entering the education sector he was a brilliant attorney with a stellar law career.

After meeting with him and seeing his devotion to his wife, she wisely chose a courtesan with a trashier look and less education. Red was someone he would never connect with on a deeper level. That was important, because he was only looking for a physical release. No connection. No communication. Just sex. Once a week for the last year.

"How is Kimber?" she asked.

"The same."

"I'm *so* sorry, Francis," she said, the truth of her regret present in her tone.

"I know."

She regretted calling him, seeming to help nudge him toward his sadness over the loss of his wife. "I . . . uhm . . . I was just . . ."

"It's been a year and you've never called me. It's always the other way around," he said, amusement now present. "It must be important."

Desdemona picked up the phone and unplugged it from the charger before she walked backward into the kitchen to eye her parents in the portrait again. "I, uhm, I could use your help," she said, hating the way her fear and shame caused her heart to pound. "I . . . I—"

"Yes?"

She looked up to the high ceilings. "I need a tutor to help me study for my GED," she said, the words rushing together and almost colliding.

Her shoulders deflated, and she exhaled through her open mouth.

If he was surprised by her revelation, he covered it well. "A tutor is not a problem, but *our* business—"

"Is *our* business," she said, intervening.

"Good," he stressed. "Actually, I think Loren Palmer would be great. Let me get me back to you tomorrow?" he asked.

"Yes. Thank you," she said, amazed at the lightness and relief she felt even as her fear for the new, the unknown, the challenge butted against everything she thought she defined herself to be.

They ended their call.

She set the phone down on the table and opened the container holding her dessert. With a small gasp of surprise, she lightly touched the wings of the 3-D chocolate butterfly on top. The pastry chef had to have a steady and delicate hand to make something so fragile and decadent. "More butterflies," she said.

With a curious look, she picked up her phone and pressed the home button. "Siri, what is the symbolism of butterflies?" she asked the virtual assistant.

"Here is what I found on the web for 'what is the symbolism of butterflies?' "

Desdemona opened the website and highlighted the text before choosing the speak button, activating the text-to-speech option on her phone.

"The butterfly is primarily associated with change and transformation."

Desdemona looked down at her bracelet, to which she had been so inexplicably drawn, and felt like she was ready for whatever was to come.

Chapter Five

Monday, August 27, 2018

My biggest regret? Dropping out of school. Thank God my streets smarts and common sense got me this far. Time to see what a bitch could do with some education . . .

"Why am I nervous?" Desdemona asked her reflection as she smoothed her hands over the black T-shirt dress she wore with fluffy fox fur slides.

A millionaire worrying about earning a GED.

"Am I crazy?" she whispered.

Knock-knock.

She looked down the length of the hall to the front door in the foyer, with a light clap of her hands as if to pump herself up. The light slapping of her slides against the wood floors echoed as she made her way to the door to open it.

"Ms. Smith? I'm Loren Palmer."

Her eyes widened in surprise at the tall man in his mid-twenties standing before her. "You're Loren?" she asked, pointing a newly polished nude nail at him as she looked him up and down to take in his wild mane of hair pulled up into a ponytail with his edges trimmed and his beard neat. His V-neck T-shirt was fitted on his slender frame with the basketball shorts he wore with vintage Jordans and colorful knee-high socks. His arms were covered with black-and-white tattoos and with it all his black-rimmed vintage Cazal-style glasses seemed out of place.

He nodded. "Yes," he answered with his raspy voice, hooking his thumbs around the wide straps of the book bag he wore on his back.

"I thought you were a girl," she said.

He shrugged, reminding her of the emoji. "It's with an 'o,' not an 'au,' " he explained.

She continued to eye him. His hair was jet black, soft and shiny, and matched his brown complexion well. Behind the glasses, his eyes were slanted and intense in a deep shade of brown.

"Listen, I was told someone wanted a tutor?" he said.

"Uhm, yeah . . . uhm, me," she said, tapping her hand against her chest as she finally stepped up. "I want to be tutored."

"You have to be willing to learn," he said. "Are you?"

She nodded. "I am."

Loren walked inside, looking around at the condominium. "Dope place," he said, tilting his glasses down on his nose with his index finger as he looked over the rim.

That amused her, and she smiled as she closed the front door. "Are those prescription or for show?" she asked, coming over to lead him to the dining room table.

"Prescription," he said, easing them back in place over his eyes.

Atop the dining room table were school supplies. Notebooks, pens, and highlighters. Even tape, thumbtacks, and index cards. "I thought the view was so nice we could work right here," she said. "I hope I have everything we need."

He chuckled. It was deep. "More than enough," he said, removing his backpack.

Desdemona noticed him eye the chair by which she stood and then looked back up at her. She realized he was waiting for her to be seated first. She pulled the padded club chair back and took a seat before waving her hand at the chair before him to do the same.

"Is it a problem that I'm not a woman?" he asked, unzipping his book bag and removing a large and thick workbook.

"No, it just surprised me," she admitted.

"Do you want to do the tutoring in a more public place?" he asked, as he looked inside his book bag and removed a case of pencils.

Desdemona rose and walked across the dining room and living room to the hall leading to her bedroom. She removed her baton and her wallet from her bag, heading back to the dining room table to set both on the table with an arched brow. "No," she said definitively as he eyed it.

He visibly swallowed over a lump in his throat.

She reclaimed her seat and set her chin in her hand as she placed her elbow atop the table.

"Okay, so I am a teaching assistant while I am studying for my PhD in creative writing," he said, tapping the eraser end of a pencil atop the workbook. "I have been a tutor since undergrad, and my hourly rate is twenty-five dollars. I'm only available when I'm not in class or teaching."

Desdemona reached out and clutched his hand to stop the drumming.

"Nervous habit," he explained, easing his hand from under hers.

"Why are you nervous?" she asked, watching him pull his iPhone from his back pocket.

"No reason," he said. "I always have a lot of energy."

Desdemona remained quiet.

"The areas of study you will be tested on are mathematics, reading, writing, science, and social studies," he said, looking at her through his glasses. "To gauge which areas we need to focus on and just how much time you will need before you try for your GED, I have an assessment test for you to take."

She nodded.

He rose and set a booklet in front of her with a sharpened pencil. "What's the last grade you completed, Ms. Smith?" he asked.

"I heard you selling ass at night. Can I get a freebie?"

Desdemona closed her eyes at the memory of being teased at school when word spread that she was tricking. The day she walked into English class and felt the stares and giggles of her classmates before she took her seat and finally saw the cause for their amusement on the chalkboard. "Desdemona's price list. Blow job $10," she had read as her heart pounded hard and fast, and her stomach was tight with embarrassment. There were most tricks listed. More humiliation.

The laughter had burst and filled the room. Slurs and insults had been hurled at her.

Desdemona had jumped to her feet and run from their laughter—their lack of understanding that she did what she had to do to survive. She had pushed past her teacher entering the classroom and raced down the hall at full speed with her tears racing down her cheeks even faster.

She never returned to school again.

Desdemona closed her eyes against a wave of pain that hate still breathed inside of her. "Uhm, I dropped out in the tenth grade," she said, forcing a smile and opening her eyes.

Push through, Desi. Push through.

"Okay, so, here's the test," Loren said, setting a workbook, a sharpened pencil, and a notepad in front of her. "You have two hours to complete all sections. Do not open the test until I say to begin."

She eyed him as he walked to the opposite end of the table and took a seat. "So, this test will cost me fifty dollars?" she asked.

He looked around the grand apartment and then back at her with a twinkle in his eyes. "Is there an economic hardship?" he mused, biting away a smile.

Dimples. Two of them. Deep.

He was a cute kid.

"I'll figure it out," she said, picking up the pencil.

He tapped on his iPhone. "Begin," he said.

Desdemona nodded and traced her fingertips across the top of the table before releasing a breath and tearing the tab on the booklet. She looked across the large space to the painting over the fireplace. She could almost envision pride in the depths of their eyes.

Several times during the test she looked up to think and noticed Loren looking pensive himself as he sketched away on a drawing pad. The quiet was often interrupted by the turning of a page or the swift back-and-forth motion of his large eraser. The time flew by far too quickly.

Beep. Beep. Beep.

"Pencil down," Loren said.

She looked up at him just as he did the same. "I think I may make you rich trying to pass the test," she admitted, her voice soft but still filled with her awkwardness.

She hadn't felt so out of sorts in years. More like Desdemona and less like Mademoiselle.

I don't like it.

Loren came down to take the test. "I'll score it this evening and call you with the results and my teaching plan for you," he said, before setting a card before her. "This is the website for the GED, and I want you to sign up for an account. It will let you enroll for your testing *when* you're ready."

Nodding, she slid the card under her baton before she rose to her feet and walked down the length of the table.

"How are you feeling?"

She stopped and looked back at him, her surprise clear. "What?" she asked.

Loren picked up his book bag and began sliding his supplies back inside of it. "I'm sorry. I saw a sadness in your eyes and I was just checking on you," he said. "It would have bothered me all day—maybe even longer—if I didn't at least check on you when I saw your sadness. So how are you?"

Desdemona looked away from him, finding his stare unnerving. "Sad," she admitted, surprising herself.

"Why?" he asked, coming down the table to pick up his sketchbook.

She held his hand, stopping him from closing it. "Is that me?" she asked in wonder, taking the sketchbook out of his hand.

"I hope you don't mind."

The sketch was so realistic, picking up every nuance of her face. Her frustration at this moment was clear. As was her sadness.

"You can keep it if you want," Loren offered, taking it back from her and tearing the page free to hand over to her. "My girl would act up if she knew I was tutoring you anyway."

Desdemona stroked the edges of the page with her thumbs as she held it. "Why wouldn't she trust you?" she asked. "Have you given her reason not to?"

Loren zipped his backpack and hitched the straps up his arms with an incredulous face. "Me? Definitely not," he said with a laugh.

Desdemona shifted her attention to something she was familiar with: sizing people up. For the majority of his life, he had given more attention to his education than women. So much so that he was unaware of his looks and his appeal.

"Listen to what she asks of you and give it to her if you're able. Her jealousy will fade, and if not, she has more issues then you're required to handle," she said, setting the sketch on the table before retrieving her wallet and pulling out the cash she owed him from her wallet.

"Sounds like good advice," he said as he walked across the room to the foyer.

Desdemona followed him. "Thank you for helping me right a wrong in my life," she said, handing him the fifty dollars plus a tip.

"And is that why you're sad?" he asked, with those eyes on her again.

She gave him a half smile, looked down at her feet and back up at him. "I regret dropping out of school," she admitted.

He gave her a warm and toothy smile. "No worries. It's never too late to right a wrong," he said, before turning to walk out of the condo.

Desdemona caught the front door before it swung closed and peeked her head out to watch him walk down the hall as he whistled without a care in the world.

"I can't do this!"

Desdemona flung her pencil across the room and covered her face with her hands.

When the room remained silent, she split her fingers and looked at Loren calmly standing before the whiteboard on an easel that he'd brought to help tutor her. He looked unbothered as he stared at her through his spectacles with his hair in cornrows going back, emphasizing his high cheekbones and slender face.

She felt silly.

"I'm sorry," she said, raking her fingernails through her mass of blond-streaked curls. "But I feel more stupid than I did before."

He nodded as he put the cap back on the dry-erase marker, leaving behind the algebra on the board to come and stand beside where she sat on the sofa. "I won't lie to you; we have a lot of work to do if you want to be ready by January," he said. "You were weak in all subject areas—especially reading at a seventh-grade level. We could slow it down and you take the test later."

"No," she said, shaking her head as she refused him.

He fell silent.

It had been two weeks since she'd taken the assessment test. Two weeks and four tutoring sessions. "This is humbling as hell, Loren," she said.

He nodded in understanding. "What's your plan?" he asked suddenly, crossing his arms over his chest in the orange Polo shirt he wore with fatigue cargo shorts.

She looked past him to the sun just beginning to set in her views. "I want to go to college," she said, filling the silence.

"Cool."

She looked to him. "Because I'm older?" she asked.

"Nah, because you are already living well and you still want what some people take for granted," Loren said. "What do you do?"

Sell sex.

"I own a clothing boutique," she said, giving him her half-truth.

"Dope."

"But I want my education," she added, her voice determined.

He removed his glasses and locked his eyes with hers. "And that's the dopest thing ever, Ms. Smith."

Desdemona. My name is Desdemona.

"How's your girl?" she asked, rising from the sofa to walk over to the kitchen. She pulled two bottles of Pellegrino bottled water out, closing the fridge door with her hip.

"I took your advice," he said.

"And?" she asked as she handed him the drink.

"Things are better."

"Good for you, kid," she said, reclaiming her seat, pulling on her glasses with her free hand, and dragging the mathematics workbook back onto her lap.

"Close your book," he said, before taking a deep guzzle of the sparkling water and setting it on the low-slung modern glass-topped coffee table of hand-forged iron, with bronze finished end caps.

"Why?" she asked, even as she did as he said.

"You're too wound up. You're thinking too much," Loren said, coming to stand before her and extend both of his large hands. "Come on. On your feet. Time to unwind."

Desdemona eyed his hands and then cut her eyes up to his face. "Are you serious?" she balked.

"No, not at all. Not hardly ever," he said. "And you? Way too much."

"I'm too serious?" she asked, pressing her fingertips to her chest.

"Laugh more and you'll live more," he said, clasping his hands together before he did a two-step.

"Trust me, I laugh," she said. "Just not with you."

"Let's change that," he said, extending his hands once more.

Desdemona stared at him, ever aware of the way her heart pounded in surprise. With Loren Palmer, the monotony had been broken. "How are you able to be so happy all the time?" she asked.

"I am forever thankful for the lessons and the blessings," he said with a carefree shrug. "The lessons are in the lows and the blessings in the highs. Both are necessary. Both serve a purpose."

"Find the good in everything?" she asked.

He nodded.

"You're young and idealistic," she said.

"Good word usage," Loren said.

Desdemona tilted her head to the side and eyed him. "Really?" she asked, unable to stop her chuckle.

"What?" he asked. "That's my job."

"I knew the word 'idealistic' before I met you," she countered.

He bit his bottom lip, causing the soft flesh to dimple, as he looked away from her for a few moments and then returned his attention to her.

"Yes?" she asked.

"The person who talks to me and the person who struggles to grapple with reading and algebra are not the same," Loren said. "I would never guess by looking at you and talking to you that..."

"That I'm ignorant?" she asked, her voice soft as she eyed him.

"No," he asserted firmly. "You're not ignorant. Just unschooled."

Desdemona gave him a soft smile. "I am an observer. A mimic in a way. I have learned over the years to do and say the right things, but I'm tired of the façade. The pretense. I want to truly be everything I appear to be."

Loren walked over to the board and reclaimed the marker before turning to look over at her, his eyes reflective. "So how do you feel?" he asked.

"Hopeful," she said, feeling joy that spread a smile across her face and a warmth across her chest as she looked away from his approving eyes and down at her studies.

Desdemona covered her mouth with the back of her hand as she yawned while answering some sample social studies questions Loren had given her to complete.

"We need a change of view."

She looked over to Loren standing before her windows with his hands in the pockets of his slim distressed jeans, which he wore with a vintage basketball jersey.

"People pay a high price for that view," she said, reaching for her glass of wine to sip before setting it back on the coffee table.

"Does this place have a gym?" he asked, turning to face her.

"Yes."

"I think ten minutes of cardio will shake things up."

She arched a brow. "You're free to go. The gym is on the third floor. You can use one of my guest passes. But I'm docking your gym time from your pay. I'm not paying you to work out, little boy."

"Not my gym time. Yours."

Desdemona looked disapproving. "Make it make sense, Loren," she said.

"You're getting bored and yawning. I thought a little run on the treadmill would wake you up so we can stay focused on getting you ready for your GED test," he explained, crossing the room.

"I'm focused," she said.

He quickly reached out and snatched her workbook from her lap. "What did you just read about?" he asked.

I don't know.

"Exactly," he said at her continued silence.

She gave him a begrudging smile before she rubbed the bridge of her nose. "I have a treadmill in one of my extra bedrooms," she said. "No need for the gym."

Loren's eyes shifted down the length of the hall to the other half of the apartment before resting back on her where she sat on the sofa. "You're going to trust me in another part of this huge place besides the living area and the guest bathroom?" he asked, his voice amused and falsely shocked.

"I'm not worried about you, young man," she said, giving him a full smile as her eyes twinkled with mischief.

Loren held out his hands. "Finally," he said. "I did notice you finally stopped carrying that little stick."

As Desdemona rose to her feet, she quickly dipped her hand inside the top of the dress and withdrew her retractable baton from beneath her left breast. "It's always around even if you don't see it... and it's not that little," she said, flicking her wrist to extend it to its full length with a snap.

Loren's eyes widened comically behind his glasses. "So, I have *every* right to be slightly offended because I would never do anything to make a woman feel unsafe. Definitely down for the #MeToo movement," he said, making a power fist.

Desdemona scratched her brow and closed her eyes as she laughed a little.

"But I have lots of women in my life that I care about—girlfriend, family, and friends—and I'm okay with y'all feeling protected. Some of my brethren are knuckleheads," he continued. "But *I'm* not."

She retracted the baton and tossed it onto the sofa. "Don't worry, kid," she said, walking past him to the hall. "I don't even need it to beat you."

"That's insulting," he said dryly from behind her.

She glanced back at him over her shoulder. "My apologies, Loren," she said, teasing him by sounding as if she hardly meant it.

"Let's see who can run the longest," he said.

Desdemona fully turned to face him, leaning against the hallway wall. "A challenge. Interesting. What's to win?"

"If you beat me I will give you two free hours of tutoring," he offered, crossing his arms over his chest.

"And on the slim chance you beat me?"

"You pay me double for two extra sessions," he offered.

Desdemona squinted at him. "Either way I get two extra sessions," she said.

"Exactly. It's a win-win for you because it's my job to

push you as hard as I can to reach your goal," he said. "It's my job to help you be the best you can be. You deserve it."

"Why do I deserve it?"

He frowned in disbelief. "Why *don't* you?"

"Find the good in everything, huh?" she asked.

"I see the good in you."

And that one little statement of assurance struck a chord within her. It touched on every insecurity, every bit of loneliness, every single bit of fear she felt being alone in the world. It was touching to just have her goodness seen and acknowledged. "Thank you, Loren," she said.

He clasped his hands together and rubbed them. "You ready to do this?"

"Honestly? No."

He chuckled.

"Let's meet in the middle and I'll just pay for two more sessions, regular rate. Deal?" she asked, extending her hand.

He took it and shook it firmly. "Deal. Now let's get back to work."

Desdemona led him back into the living area, surprised that the kindness of this stranger motivated her even more to reach her goals.

Desdemona couldn't sleep.

She lay in the middle of her bed with her arms open wide and her naked body sandwiched between bright white fifteen-hundred-thread-count Egyptian cotton sheets that felt like cool hands on every spot of her body. Her six pillows were soft and full—and the only things joining her in bed these last five years. Those and her vibrator.

Am I crazy to be celibate?

Sex was hers; to be had and sold.

Why am I lying here horny?

They were plenty of consorts who were skilled and willing to have her and to please her.

But that's not what I want. They're not what I want.

She rolled over to her side, knocking one of the six plush pillows on her bed onto the floor as she opened the bedside nightstand and grabbed a distraction from the rise in her nature. As she rummaged, her hand hit her sex toy and it vibrated to life.

Bzzzzzzzzzzzzzzzzzzzzzzzzz.

She picked it up, her hand shaking from the movement. She paused, looking at it as she pressed her thighs together. With a sigh, she turned it off and dropped it back in the drawer to remove the book she had stashed there weeks ago. Setting it on the bed, she pulled her body up to a sitting position and grabbed her reading glasses before opening the book.

On the very first page of chapter one her brows furrowed in frustration. "The . . . hearth and the . . ."

She didn't know the word. "Sa—sa—sa," she said, struggling. "Shit."

Sound it out.

Advice from Loren.

Desdemona pressed her finger beneath the first letter of the word. "Sa-la-man-der," she said. "Sal-a-mand-er. Salamander."

Am I right?

She picked up her iPhone from the nightstand and searched for "how to pronounce salamander." A YouTube video came up first in the search.

"Salamander," the robotic voice said.

Desdemona smiled. "I was right."

"Every word in a story is important. Every single word. Nothing should be overlooked or skipped or misunderstood to make sure you comprehend—or understand—the story."

More Loren in her head.

More and more her young tutor and his teaching were

there with her throughout the day, and she was realizing more and more that a lot of what she was learning was already there in her life.

Even how you pour your wine at a certain angle to control the pour is geometry.

She chuckled. She had ten years on him easily, and he had taught her so much already. And not just about math and reading. Even about looking at a life differently.

Snuggling down in the bed, she pushed through with her reading and kept her phone close in case she had to look up the sound or meaning of a word. The more she read, the more she became lost in the story, admitting that she liked the way the writer described things and the story that unfolded.

Seeing the movie first helped her, but she enjoyed the details lost in the translation from book to film.

Slowly she pushed through, having to reread sentences or look up words for clarity until she came to the end of the first of three sections of the book. She folded the corner to keep her place in the novel and checked the time on her phone. It was well after midnight. She had been reading for hours.

Desdemona felt emotional and pressed her hands to her bare lips. Had it been easy? Had she stumbled? Did she get lost in the words she didn't know or understand? No, yes, and yes. But she did it.

"I did it," she whispered, lost somewhere in between happiness and desire to learn even more.

"Maybe I really can do this," she told herself, starting to believe in herself.

Funny thing, she was playing catch-up to Loren.

I promise one day you will pass the test and go on to college and do whatever you dream about and wonder why you ever had any fear about it all.

Who could she tell about her victory when she told no one of her defeat?

Desdemona looked at her phone. It was her prepaid—her business phone. Flinging back the covers, she rose from the bed and retrieved her personal iPhone from the Balenciaga bag she had worn earlier that day to run errands. She rarely used it and often forgot about it. Sitting on the padded leather bench at the foot of her bed, she folded her feet beneath her bottom and scrolled through her contacts. There weren't many. The majority of the people she interacted with were not friends and definitely not family. Of that she had none.

She paused, and her finger hovered over Loren's listing in her phone. "It's so late," she said.

Desdemona set the phone down on the bench.

"But I feel like he would be proud."

She picked it back up.

"But I don't want his girl mad at him."

Back down again.

"Hell, I'm hunting up congratulations and nothing else."

She picked the phone up again and settled on sending a text.

DESI: I just finished reading the first part of—

She paused to crawl onto the bed and grab the book to double-check her spelling of the title.

DESI: —Fahrenheit 451.

She finished the text with a few celebration-type emojis before sending it and dropped the phone back inside her bag, which was hanging on the door handle. She turned off the lights and climbed back beneath the covers, snuggling her head among the pillows. She felt giddy like a kid and couldn't help smiling, even as she closed her eyes and tried to bring on sleep.

When that failed, she thought of her little vibrating buddy

in the drawer. It would send her right to sleep right after she was done with it.

Why not?

Turning over in the bed, she opened the drawer again and reached for the vibrator.

Her minuet text tone filled the air.

Desdemona dropped the vibrator and sat up in bed as she eyed the illumination inside her purse. Cloaked by the darkness, she flung back the covers and got up from the bed again to move toward the light until her phone was in her hand.

Loren.

She pressed one foot atop the other as she leaned against the door and opened the text.

THE_TUTOR: SO PROUD OF YOU!!! THAT'S A CLASSIC.
DESI: Thank you! I'm proud of myself. Why are u up?
THE_TUTOR: GRADING TEST PAPERS.
DESI: Ur girl there?
THE_TUTOR: NAH.

Desi sent him a sad face emoji.

THE_TUTOR: WE'RE GOOD. SHE'S OUT OF TOWN.
DESI: Good. Don't mess it up.

He sent the shrugging emoji.

She sent the praying hands.

THE_TUTOR: IS THE BOOK GOOD?
DESI: Yes. Better than the movie.
THE_TUTOR: . . .

She awaited his next text, tapping her thumbnail against the screen.

THE_TUTOR: . . .

Maybe he went back to sleep.

THE_TUTOR: I JUST ORDERED A COPY. WE CAN TALK ABOUT THE BOOK AS WE READ IT. NOT A PART OF TUTORING. JUST FOR FUN. COOL?

Desi smiled and nodded as she texted him back:

Cool.

There were no more texts, and she dropped the phone back in the bag and climbed in her bed once again that night. As she snuggled beneath the covers and finally felt herself drifting to sleep, she was happy in knowing that for the first time in a long time she had a friend.

Chapter Six

Friday, October 19, 2018

Another year older. Time to do this next one differently from the last one . . .

"What's with the crown?" Loren asked as soon as she opened the front door.

Desdemona tapped her pencil against the metallic leaf and organza headpiece adorned with rhinestones and pearls. "It's not a crown," she said, stepping back to admit him into her condo.

Loren turned his mouth downward and nodded as he removed his ever-present book bag. "Is there a reason for whatever it is?"

She smiled and gave a one-shoulder shrug. "It's my birthday, Lo," she said hesitantly, using the nickname she had given him over the weeks.

"Happy birthday, Ms. Smith," he said, his face filled with pleasure.

"Thank you."

"Happy birthday to you. Happy biiiiiirthday," he sang, off-key, boisterous, and not caring one bit about it.

Desdemona smiled and covered her mouth with her hands as her eyes filled with the same mirth she felt. She applauded when he finished with one last long note and bowed.

"Wait, you're spending your birthday being tutored?" Loren asked, his face bewildered.

"I don't normally celebrate it," she admitted.

And no one knows it, she added to herself.

"Time to do this one different from the last," he said, reaching to clasp her hands. "Birthdays should be celebrated."

Desdemona felt uneasy. "It's no big deal," she said, trying to pull her hands from his grasp.

He held on tighter, his eyes locked on hers. "No tutoring tonight. No studying. Just celebrate your life. Being here. Being alive. Being healthy. Damn sure wealthy," he said, looking around at the condominium. "And for getting wise."

She eyed him. This young man was filled with such warmth and kindness that he had the power to change a mood with his dimpled smile. "Are you sure?" she asked, her hesitance clear.

"Life is for the living. I'm sure."

Desdemona took a breath, thinking back to the last time she had celebrated her birthday. "When I was a little girl, before my father passed away, he took me to an amusement park. Just the two of us," she said. "One of the best days of my life. Definitely the best birthday to date."

Loren's eyes were soft as he leveled them on her. "Now go have another one," he said as he reached for the front door. "It's one thing for other people to overlook you, but when you don't claim happiness for yourself that's worse."

He left with a wave.

Desdemona caught the door before it closed and stepped

out into the hallway. "You're pretty damn wise for a twenty-something," she said.

Loren paused and turned. "I've been told I have an old soul," he said, before turning to continue down the length of the wide hall to the elevator at the end of the floor.

Desdemona admitted that she hated to see him go.

His eternal good mood was infectious.

Back inside her condo she put away her study materials and walked over to the window to look out at her view just as the sun was beginning to set. "Thirty-five years old," she said. "I deserve to be celebrated."

For so long her life had been tied to everything but her happiness. She stroked her diamond butterfly bracelet. "Transformation and change," she said as she looked down at the butterflies in midflight.

As she looked out at the water in the distance, her instincts made her run through every single thing that could wrong if she took her eye off the ball for just one second.

What if...

What if...

What if...

Her eyes focused on her reflection in the window, and she reached up to stroke her ornate tiara. "Life is for the living," she said, before turning and picking up her iPhone from the coffee table.

She called Denzin.

"Boss. How can I help you?" he asked when he answered.

She hesitated. Trust was not easy to give. Relying on someone else could become a liability.

"Denzin, I need you to be available for me tonight and tomorrow," she said, rushing the words and speeding past the fear. "Nothing major. Just if I call you to go somewhere. To check on someone. I need you to be ready at the drop of a hat. Possibly jump on a plane to get somewhere. Can you do that for me?"

"Is everything okay?" he asked.

"Yes," she said, smiling at his show of concern. "I need to handle something. Can you do this for me?"

"No questions asked?"

"None at all."

"Done."

"Thank you," she said, ending the call as she walked over to her laptop, which was sitting on the corner of the kitchen counter.

Loren was right, and now that she agreed with him that she should celebrate, she wanted to extend the day. There was only one way to do that. "Let's use these time zones," she said, thinking of the west coast.

Beach vibes and shopping in Cali? Or gambling and partying in Vegas?

Let's leave it up to fate.

Desdemona's fingers flew across the keyboard as she pulled up available first-class flights out to Vegas and Cali.

"Vegas it is," she said, eyeing the info for a first-class flight to the state leaving from LaGuardia in an hour.

She booked it and a suite at the Bellagio on the strip.

Knock-knock.

Desdemona looked over her shoulder at the front door before turning and walking toward it to open it. Her eyes filled with surprise to find Loren standing there with an open black to-go box holding a cupcake with a lit candle stuck in it. "I thought you were gone," she said, the flame from the candle flickering in the depths of her eyes.

"Every birthday girl should make a wish," he said, his eyes serious as they searched hers.

Desdemona closed her eyes and leaned forward a bit to make her wish before releasing a smooth stream of air to get rid of the flame. She felt transported to that birthday she had shared with her father, hating that the wish she had made that day never came to fruition.

God, please let my daddy live forever.

"Happy birthday again," Loren said, his voice deep and warm.

She opened her eyes and looked up at him. "Thank you," she said, her whisper so soft but the movement of her lips clear as the acrid smoke from the candle rose in a swirling stream in the air between them.

Their eyes locked. For a brief—very brief—moment they held.

Loren cleared his throat. "I better get going. Gonna surprise my girl," he said.

It felt like he was placing her presence in the midst of whatever that very brief moment was as if to remind himself of her.

"Be safe," Desdemona said, accepting the cupcake as she stepped back from him. "Good night, Lo."

"Night," he said just before she closed the door.

Desdemona held the to-go box behind her back as she leaned forward to look out the peephole. Surprise caused her heart to double pump. Loren still stood there, looking downward, seeming to be lost in thought. Just when she reached for the doorknob, he walked away with one last quick look back at her door before he disappeared from her line of view.

Checking her diamond watch, she strode across the space to slide the container in the glass-fronted fridge. She needed to get to the airport and decided on a whim not to bother packing. She called for a Lux Black before going to her safe to retrieve several bundles of cash to drop in her Louis Vuitton tote.

The October weather in NYC was chilly at night but not in Las Vegas, so she chose a lightweight blazer to pull over the long-sleeved black sweater she wore with a distressed short denim skirt and thigh-high leather boots.

It wasn't until she was in the back of her Lyft that she

allowed herself to think of just why Loren had paused at her door. She shook her head at the thought of a crush, determined to count it as nothing but a quiet moment she had happened to see. Loren adored his girlfriend and had never been anything but polite and friendly to her.

Desdemona refused to let her ego ruin their friendship or get in the way of him continuing as her tutor.

Vegas was beautiful and warm and everything she needed. She went straight from the airport to shop at Crystal's before heading to her suite. As soon as she was inside the luxurious suite, she tossed her numerous glossy shopping bags and new designer carry-on luggage onto the king-size bed and took a shower in the spa-like bathroom.

With her damp body wrapped in one of the plush hotel robes, she raked her fingers through her hair as she walked out into the suite. The décor was sleek, modern, and colorful. With the curtains already open, the sight of the strip was her background. It would be made all the more majestic once night fell. She unpacked the clothing in her bags, hanging them in the closet. The lingerie, those things that would be pressed intimately against her body, she left wrapped in tissue paper in the shopping bag.

She'd removed the bottle of Gran Patrón Platinum tequila she'd purchased from her tote and poured herself a shot, sipping from the glass as she moved about the spacious suite. Her steps paused at the adjoining door, noticing it for the first time.

Her robe had fallen open, but she clutched it closed as she turned the knob and jerked on it to ensure the door was locked. She gasped when it flew opened and hit the wall. She gasped again at the man standing in the next suite with nothing but a towel loosely wrapped around his waist.

His face changed from surprise to pleasure at the sight of her, his eyes taking her all in from head to toe and showing his approval.

Desdemona gave him a quick appraisal as well and found the man, with his Idris Elba–like looks, to be attractive. Tall, strong, with broad shoulders and a good build. Dark skin. Bright eyes. Square jaw. Grown-man sexy. Definitely in his early forties.

With a mischievous smile and a flirty wave, she closed the door and locked it. She listened to see if he did the same from his side. He did not.

Was he alone in the suite? Was there a wife, girlfriend, side piece, or lover?

She glanced back at the door, curious about whether he had dropped the towel or not. With a little smile, and ready to get her birthday night in Vegas started, Desdemona lotioned her body with toiletries she had purchased before doing her makeup with a dramatic smoky eye and a glossy lip. Her hair she wore long and straight. She had no time for calling in a glam squad.

She loved the look and feel of her strapless cocktail dress with an internal bustier that gave her figure even more of an hourglass shape. The short length showed off her legs. The jacquard print covered with floral applique and crystals made her feel beautiful.

She locked her cash in the safe, changed the password, and grabbed the do not disturb tag before heading toward the door. She stepped into the hall, pausing when she spotted the man from the next-door suite leaning against the wall by his own door. She had to admit he looked just as good in all black—blazer, shirt, and slacks.

Damn good.

"Hello," she said, closing the door and slipping the tag on the door.

"Hello, neighbor," he said.

Desdemona almost gasped. His voice was deep, and he had a British accent.

"Are you Idris *Elba*?" she asked in a whisper as if it were top secret.

He chuckled. "Definitely not," he said, pushing off the wall.

Desdemona felt silly. "Right. I mean, you two aren't identical. I just...uhm...the accent threw me...for a second," she said, shaking her head a little as she tucked her blond tresses behind her ear.

"Brent Yarborough," he said, extending his hand. "And you look stunning by the way."

She opened her mouth to give him her alias but stopped herself. He was not a consort. This was her birthday. She didn't want to be anyone but herself. "Desdemona Dean," she said, sliding her hand into his. "And thank you."

"Can I tell you a secret?" he asked.

Desdemona eyed him. "If you want," she said.

"I've been waiting out here for you," he admitted.

"Why?" she asked, opening her clutch with her finger and preparing to withdraw her baton if need be.

"I wanted to meet you but I didn't want to intrude if you were with someone," he explained. "This way I could play it off."

She smiled. "I wondered if you were with someone as well, Mr. Yarborough," she admitted.

"I'm not."

"Neither am I," she replied.

A hotel room door opened, and a crowd of twenty-something women exited it. They fell silent as the women passed by them on the way to the elevator at the end of the hall. When the hall was quiet once more, they shared a smile.

"I'm in town to celebrate a friend's engagement," he said,

coming over to stand beside her. "But tonight, I would rather have dinner with you, Desdemona Dean."

Life is for the living.

"Today is my birthday, and I would rather have dinner with you than eat alone," she said, offering him her arm.

Brent chuckled as he slid his arm through hers and reached in the inner pocket of his blazer for his phone with his free hand. "Max. I'm skipping out on dinner tonight. I'll catch up with you tomorrow," he said, giving her a wink.

His friend laughed. Desdemona could hear his friend's voice echoing through his phone.

"How pretty is she?" Max asked.

Desdemona looked up at Brent, knowing he was unaware of her eavesdropping.

"A Lamborghini," Brent said.

Well, that's definitely better than a Hyundai. I guess.

"I don't blame you then," his friend said. "Breakfast in the morning? Or you're hoping to sleep in?"

Brent looked down at her.

Desdemona gave him a curious eye before slowly arching a brow.

He looked surprised, and then his eyes widened a bit in understanding.

She lifted up on her toes so that her mouth was near the phone. "Hey, Max. This is the Lamborghini, and Brent will be right on time for breakfast because he *won't* be sleeping in with me," she said, before reaching with a finger to end the call.

It immediately vibrated.

She walked away from him down the hall with her sultriest walk, glancing back at him over her shoulder, enjoying the flirtation. "Vroom vroom," she said, imitating the sound of a Lamborghini's engines being revved.

He slid the phone back in his pocket and followed behind her.

Desdemona paused, wondering what Loren's reaction would have been. He would have enjoyed seeing the lighter side of her and made some kind of joke to make her laugh as well.

Maybe that's because one was a grown man and the other a boy.

Still, as she stepped onto the elevator and turned to watch Brent join her, she thought of how enthusiastically he had championed her celebrating her birthday, and she wished *he* were there.

Desdemona had fun.

More than she's had in a long time.

The dined at Picasso's in the Bellagio. Played high stakes poker at several casinos on the Strip and slots in Old Vegas. Danced like crazy at 1 OAK. Made it rain on strippers at Club Lacy's.

As soon as they stepped on the elevators at the Bellagio and the doors slid closed, Desdemona pressed her body close to his, gripping the lapels of his suit to jerk his tall frame down toward her. Her eyes searched his before she licked at his bottom lip and made a little grunt of pleasure in the back of her throat.

Brent gripped her hips as he captured her mouth with his own.

Desdemona broke the kiss, sliding her hands up to the back of his head to take control and kiss him. First a soft peck and then as she smiled against his mouth, she deepened it with her tongue. He moaned in pleasure.

She did the same at the feel of his growing hardness pressing against her stomach. The elevator slid to a smooth stop and the doors soon slid opened. "Your suite or mine?" she asked against his lips before kissing them again.

He raised his head to look down at her, his eyes showing surprise and then filling with desire. "Your choice," he said.

Desdemona turned from him, taking his hand to lead him into the hallway and down to the door of his suite. She chose to use his because as soon as they were finished making love she planned to leave him sleeping while she went to her own bed.

As soon as the door closed, he picked her up in his arms with ease and carried her to the sofa. He turned and sat down with Desdemona straddling his lap with the skirt of her dress up around her waist.

This five-year dry streak is finally over.

She sighed when he pressed kisses across her clavicle as he reached behind her to unzip her dress.

"You're sexy as hell," he whispered in her ear before sucking her lobe.

"Am I?" she asked, as the top of the dress fell and revealed her breasts to him from the glare of the Vegas lights streaming through the open curtains.

Immediately he ducked his head and captured a nipple in his mouth.

Her moan was satisfaction, hunger, pleasure, and need all in one.

"Yes," she sighed, stroking his head as she tilted her own back.

For the first time in a long time, she felt normal. Every piece of her body felt alive. Their chemistry was not explosive, but he was skilled and she was horny.

As he switched his attention to her other breast, he dipped one hand down between her buttocks to stroke her core with his middle finger.

A fuck you before he fucks me?

She gasped at the feel of that finger slipping inside her.

I am so clever.

He soundly smacked her buttock, causing it to jiggle, before he released it to press his hands down between them to slide another finger inside her while massaging her throbbing clit with his thumb.

She bit her bottom lip and winced in pleasure as she slowly circled her hips and tightly gripped the shoulders of his blazer.

"Kiss me," he whispered up to her.

Shifting her hands up to his face, she tilted his chin up before lowering her head to suck his mouth before she traced it lightly with the tip of her tongue.

"I'm so hard," he said into that space between their lips.

"Good," she replied, kissing him again. Slowly. Deeply.

It was nice. Really nice. Her body was warmed with desire for him. But she wanted more.

More of a rush. More excitement. More action.

"Suck your fingers," she ordered, rising from his lap to stand between his open legs.

He did, easing them into his mouth as he cut his eyes up to her.

"Want more?" she asked.

He nodded eagerly as he sucked away.

Slowly she turned, giving him a flirty look over her shoulder as she wiggled her buttocks before bending to grip her ankles. She knew that the move framed her buttocks like a heart shape and exposed her core like a moist pit in the center of a peach.

He grabbed her hips as he buried his face between her cheeks, turning his head slightly to kiss each one before dragging his tongue right up the middle.

She twerked a little.

He chuckled.

Suddenly the room was flooded with light, and a high-pitched squeal filled the air like a siren.

Desdemona closed her eyes and released a sigh as the feel of Brent's mouth disappeared, and he jumped to his feet with a lot of "baby, baby, baby" that would put James Brown to shame.

"You with a Vegas prostitute!" the woman said moments before loud slaps echoed in the air.

Not a prostitute but you're close, lady.

Desdemona rose and turned with calmness as she watched Brent valiantly trying to block the open-handed blows the woman was throwing at him with the speed of Ali. She walked over to the bar, naked and in her heels, to pour herself a drink. She chose a shot of bourbon.

"No, she is not strutting around here naked."

Desdemona glanced at them over the rim of her glass as she sipped the brown liquor. The woman was thick and tall with bright red hair and pale skin. "I really should get dressed," she agreed, finishing the drink and walking over to the sofa to pick up her frock.

"Who *are* you?" the woman shrieked, trying her best to walk past Brent, who blocked her like a defensive lineman.

"Who are you?" Desdemona asked in return as she eased her dress up over her body and reached behind her to zip it up.

"His wife," she stressed, poking her chest with her finger.

"Could you leave *please*?" Brent asked, his voice tight with anger.

"Yes, just as well, as you could have told me you were married," she said, picking up her clutch and tucking it under her arm. "My apologies, Mrs. Yarborough."

"Get the hell out!" he roared, pointing toward the door.

"No," she told him before shifting her focus to his wife standing behind him with her hands on her hips and her chest still heaving with her hurt and anger. "Do you have any questions for me before I leave? That's the only way you'll get the truth tonight, and you deserve it."

"Bloody hell, are you crazy?" Brent asked, his accent thick.

Desdemona gave the wife one last look of question before nodding and turning to walk to the door.

"Baby, please let me explain. I was drunk—"

Desdemona shook her head at his pitifulness as she turned the doorknob.

"How long have you known my husband?" his wife called over to her.

Desdemona paused, hearing her hurt and need for clarity on the true standing of her marriage.

"Amanda, please," he pleaded. "Let her go."

She turned and faced them. "I just met him tonight. We happened to have adjoining rooms. We've never had sex. He doesn't have my number. I don't live in Vegas and he has no clue where I do live. He agreed to spend my birthday with me—"

Amanda grunted as she pushed against his chest with both hands. "You celebrating birthdays?" she snapped.

"We had dinner downstairs at Picasso's, gambled, went to 1 OAK and then a strip club," Desdemona told her.

"But all night you were sneaking and calling me," she said, her tears falling in earnest.

"She's lying," he lied, trying and failing to wrap his arms around his wife to comfort her.

"He paid. Check his credit card statement when it's available," she said, walking back over to the bar to pour another shot. "And of course, you saw how we were going to end the night for yourself."

The woman's body crumbled to the floor as she covered her hands with her face and cried with loud wails.

"Amanda, I will never see your husband again, and I'm sorry I ever met him," Desdemona said, moving toward them as she swirled the drink in the glass she still held.

She watched as he dropped to his knees to pull his wife's body close to his chest and whisper comforting lies to her. At this moment, in the midst of flames that might very well destroy their marriage, she was clear on why she never wished to wed.

Her chest ached with a pain that she knew was nowhere near what this betrayed wife felt.

She tapped his shoulder, and he whirled to look up at her with anger in his brown eyes. Desdemona raised her hand swiftly and gave him a wicked backhand that echoed in the air, caused his head to swing to the right and made her hand sting.

"That's for treating me like a whore," she said, her eyes like steel as she met his hostile stare.

He jumped to his feet.

"No, Brent," his wife yelled, falling forward on her knees to wrap her arms around his legs and pull at his arms.

Desdemona turned and walked to the door when he helped his wife to her feet. "Maybe it's a one-time slip and y'all can work your way through it, but the best way to do that is with the truth, and I just wanted to make sure you make the best decision possible for yourself, Mrs. Yarborough," she said, opening the door and leaving without another look back at them.

In her suite, she undressed and showered, hating that she felt she had to be cleansed of Brent's touch and his kisses. Of another bad decision. Bundled in the plush white robe offered by the hotel with her wet hair wrapped in a towel, Desdemona retrieved her iPhones from her clutch and made her way over to the chaise lounge sitting before the windows. She eyed the majesty of the Bellagio fountains. The movement of the water and the light display were simply beautiful. "Happy birthday to me," she sang softly with a half smile as she raked her fingers through her wild mane of loose waves.

What a night.

She allowed herself just one brief moment to wonder what had become of the Yarboroughs after she left their suite before pushing thoughts of them away. She was a footnote in their life as far as she as concerned. Nothing more.

Picking up her prepaid iPhone, she checked in with her businesses. All of her courtesans were booked for the weekend except for Denzin, but she would compensate him for serving as her backup while she was out of town. No calls throughout the night alerting her to trouble. All was well.

Unlike her business phone, Desdemona had her personal phone on Do Not Disturb mode, silencing any calls or texts. She had just one notification. Just before midnight, Loren had texted her. She unlocked the phone and opened it.

THE_TUTOR: ONE LAST HAPPY BIRTHDAY BEFORE MIDNIGHT AND YOUR SPECIAL DAY ENDS.

She chuckled at the animated gif of exploding balloons revealing a dancing dog wearing a party hat and holding a birthday cake.

He really is a sweet kid.

DESI: In Vegas. It was memorable. Thank you for pushing me to celebrate.

She set the phone down on the chaise and lifted her legs atop it as she settled back and looked out the window at the strip.

Her minuet text tone played.

THE_TUTOR: I WISH I WAS THERE TO SKYDIVE. DID U?

Desdemona smirked. "Humph. Skydived into some bullshit," she muttered as she typed with her thumbs.

DESI: Definitely not!

THE_TUTOR: DON'T YOU WANT TO KNOW HOW IT FEELS TO FLY?

THE_TUTOR: LIVE LIFE WITH NO REGRETS. FLY!

Desdemona tapped the edge of the phone against her chin and looked up at the night sky.

"No regrets," Desdemona said the next morning on the airplane, attached to the harness of a tall and lean skydiving instructor.

She was moments from a tandem jump, at the edge of the open doorway of the plane thousands of feet above the ground with nothing but blues skies in her view. Her heart pounded wildly. Her knees quivered a bit, and she felt anxious beyond belief. Her adrenaline was in overdrive. She felt trapped somewhere between terror and euphoria.

She did as instructed, and within moments they were leaning forward and jumping from the plane. "No regrets!" she yelled, forcing her eyes open to take it all in as they free fell through the air.

Chapter Seven

Monday, November 19, 2018

Holidays are the worst. Now is the time for family, and I have none . . .

The heels of Desdemona's shoes clicked against the polished tiled floor as she made her way to her showroom. She pointedly ignored the tasteful Christmas décor in the halls as she unlocked the glass door and entered. She paused in the doorway at the sight of a huge Christmas tree near the large wooden desk serving as the checkout counter. "Patrice," she said, with a twist of her lips in annoyance.

She turned on the lights of the showroom and unplugged the lights on the tree with a rough jerk before flinging the cord away. Thanksgiving was in a few days, bringing on constant conversations about turkeys, traveling, and quality family time. Desdemona couldn't care less about all three.

Turkey was dry.

Traveling during the holidays was hell.

Family was nonexistent.

Top all of that off with a considerable slowdown in her business as everyone wanted to be the perfect family man or woman during the holidays. "Fa-la-la-la-la-la-la-bullshit," she sang.

Still, this year she was taking advantage of the break and was booked to spend the week between Christmas and New Year's Eve in Dubai. She shifted the sleeve of her silver fox fur coat, diamond bracelets, and watch to stroke her newest tattoo. "No regrets," she read the words inscribed on her inner wrist beneath a black-and-white butterfly in flight.

Her trip to Vegas and the skydive had created a desire for more in her.

And upon her return from Dubai, she was scheduled to take her GED.

Possibly the biggest leap of all.

She removed the fox coat and slid her hands into the pockets of the pencil skirt of her tailored black suit as she walked over to weave her way among the dress-covered mannequins. Each was posed in a different position, and they were more than a foot taller than her in height because of the black boxes upon which they were placed. It felt almost like being lost in a beautiful bedazzled forest.

Click.

She turned at the sound of the lock.

Patrice, her showroom manager, entered. "I thought I turned off the lights," she said to herself.

Desdemona remained quiet, cloaked by the dresses.

Patrice was a middle-aged woman with short hair with silver flecks and a tall figure that was thick and shapely. A full-figured goddess with a good sense of style. Desdemona liked the crimson off-the-shoulder sweater she wore with a wide leather belt and wide-legged wool crepe pants.

When she bent to plug in the Christmas tree, Desdemona stepped forward. "Good job on the display models," she said.

Patrice jumped back, startled, and clutched at her chest with her eyes wide.

"Are you going to join Elizabeth?" she asked, referencing reruns of the 1970s sitcom *Sanford and Son* where Fred would fake a heart attack and say, "Elizabeth, I'm coming to join you, honey!"

Patrice chuckled. "You scared me, Ms. Smith," she said, placing her hands on her hips.

"A holdover from Halloween," she said dryly. "Boo!"

Patrice released a nervous laugh that was more of a high-pitched shrill that increased in pitch as her mouth became wider, for a pretty horrific looking facial expression.

"Ooooo-kay," Desdemona said, rubbing her hands together as she walked past her employee, giving her a chance to regain her composure. "So, I actually came to—"

Cha-ching. Cha-ching. Cha-ching.

She eyed her black alligator Hermès bag. "Excuse me a sec, Patrice," she said, walking over to where she had set it in one of the club chairs in the center of the showroom.

"Number one," she mouthed, surprised by his call.

Desdemona gave Patrice a quick eye as she moved to the door and stepped into the hall.

Cha-ching. Cha-ching. Cha—

"Hello, Champ," she said, holding the iPhone with one hand and pressing the other to her back as she paced a bit.

He chuckled. "Maybe this season," he said.

"So, what's up?" she asked, stopping her pacing to lean back against the wall and cross one arm over her chest.

"I need my family to stop pressing me to get married."

She arched a brow. "To anyone?" she asked. "Or do they have bait?"

"High school sweetheart patiently waiting for my return," he said.

"For love or money?"

He paused. "Probably a little of both."

"But?" she asked, guiding him.

"I'm not ready to settle down. With her or anybody," he added, before she had a chance to ask.

"And if you loved her you would be ready."

"Right."

"So where do I fall in all of this?" she asked, although she had an idea of what his request would be.

But I could be wrong.

"I need the non-homosexual version of a beard."

I was so right.

Desdemona pinched the bridge of her nose. "I can't—"

"Just fly in for dinner, kiss a few babies, hug my mama, and then fly out with some to-go plates," he said.

"When?" she asked, squinting her eyes.

"Thanksgiving Day and then Christmas Day."

"Excusemesaywhatnow?"

"I'm willing to pay you extra," he said.

"You would have no choice," Desdemona scoffed. "It's the holidays and everyone wants to be with their family, open gifts, eat food, and pretend like their world is perfect because there's a turkey on the table or a decorated pine tree in the corner."

"You still hate holidays?" he drawled. "Maybe helping me out could change your mind."

"Who?" she asked in surprise.

"You," he responded.

"Uh . . . nah." Desdemona looked through the glass wall of the showroom at Patrice plugging in the tree.

"Triple rate. Think of it as a holiday bonus."

Desdemona felt conflicted. Not because of the money. She could easily pass on that. It was her awareness that Number One had introduced her to the world of wealthy and prominent tricks. He helped change her list from johns and tricks to her high-paying consorts.

And to think when I first caught his eye I didn't even know who he was. Only charged him a hundred. Who knew hot sex in a bathroom stall of a popular club would change everything?

"Listen, let me see if one of the girls can do it. It's last-minute. It's the holidays, but the extra money should sway one of them," she said, closing her eyes as she ran her fingers through her hair which was sleekly pressed. "And only double rate. Cool?"

"That's why you're the best, Mademoiselle," he said, his happiness clear in his deep voice.

"We'll see," she said before ending the call.

I hate the holidays.

Desdemona crossed the hall and walked into the showroom. "Patrice, go home with pay," she said. "Enjoy the rest of the week. You can get to this inventory after the Thanksgiving holiday."

"Really?" Patrice asked, clasping her hands.

Desdemona nodded, her mind already going through her list of paramours who were sans children.

"My husband wanted to drive to his parents in Georgia but I told him we had to wait because I didn't want to short my check by missing days," she said, already pulling on her wool coat and sliding the strap of her purse on her shoulder.

Missing days?

Desdemona could relate. There was a time being too sick to turn tricks had meant hunger.

"Enjoy your trip," she said, moving across the room to take the seat behind the large wooden desk.

"Thank you so much. I will," she said. "Bye, Ms. Smith."

Desdemona. Desdemona Dean.

"And Patrice, maybe we'll think about expanding your role here. If you want?" she asked, picking up a pen. "With a pay increase, of course."

Patrice paused in the doorway, her face filled with surprise and some other emotion Desdemona couldn't place. "I really, really need a chance," she said, her eyes filling with tears.

I've been there before.

Desdemona blinked to keep her own emotions from rising. "You've earned it," she said, giving her a reassuring smile. "Now go. Enjoy."

Patrice nodded and pressed her hands together under her chin in thanks before leaving.

Desdemona released a breath as she picked up her iPhone and scrolled through the contacts, deciding to try Olivie.

She placed the call. It rang twice.

"Mademoiselle," she said, her voice warm.

"Hello, Blue," she said, using her moniker. "Listen, I know this is last minute but are you available on Thanksgiving?"

"On Thanksgiving?" she asked.

"And Christmas Day," she added, raising her brows as she sat back in the chair and crossed her legs.

Desdemona explained the consort wanted a pretend girlfriend for the holidays. "Double rate for a weekend session for both days," she added.

"I don't know, Mademoiselle," she said, sounding doubtful.

Desdemona remained quiet. The decision was hers and she wasn't going to persuade her into it.

Olivie was tough about her money. She was a hair-stylist looking to save enough money to not just open her own salon/day spa but to own everything outright and do it debt-free. She also could be whatever she needed to be and, in this case, it was an adoring girlfriend.

Her silence continued.

"Hey, no pressure. Think about it and let me know within the hour. Okay? Okay," Desdemona said, ending the call.

Her eyes fell on the tree and its bright white lights. Never had she felt so lonely. "Shit," she swore.

Life was all about choices and hopes for no regrets.

She'd chosen not to have children and until lately she'd had no regrets. All she could think of was getting arrested and leaving a child behind without a mother.

Like I was.

She closed her eyes, hating just such moments when she wondered if she had made the right choices in life. With everything. Or had she been given a choice at all with the life her parents left her behind to live? Her world was not created for softness and love to reign.

I can hardly remember not being on guard.

"Shit," she swore again as tears rose and the pain she avoided was there to face.

She closed her eyes and released a shaky breath. "I was a kid. I was just a kid," she said in a harsh whisper. "So alone. I was so alone."

Desdemona covered her face with her hand and released a small cry that only hinted at the pain seeming to drown her very soul.

No child should know how it feels to be hated.

And she had.

Her shoulders dropped under the weight of her memories of being ignored and neglected. Living in a beautiful home and made to feel every day that she was a bother. Made to carry the shame of her parents' betrayal toward one woman.

Physical pain? No. Never. That would have left scars that people could see.

Desdemona tried to smile through the tears but failed as she took a gasp of breath and felt her tears roll down her cheeks. "I hate the fucking holidays," she said, sniffing back more tears as she used the sides of her hands to wipe away the wetness from her cheeks.

Cha-ching. Cha-ching. Cha-ching.

She cleared her throat and picked up her phone as she released a long and steady stream of breath through pursed lips.

A text. She opened it.

BLUE: I'm in. Send deets.
BLUE: $$$$$$$$$$$$$!

And just like that. Like many times before, more than she could count, Desdemona pushed aside her feelings and focused on work. On other. On forgetting. On not feeling.

Once the details were set and Number One purchased her costliest dress with the knowledge that the dress wouldn't be shipped until after Thanksgiving and he was to give the remaining cash balance to Olivie, the feelings resurfaced.

Even without formal education, stupidity had never been Desdemona's problem. She knew there was so much she had to face. Some painful truths and long-buried hurts. She'd seen enough of Iyanla Vanzant fixing lives to be aware that her past was imprinted on every aspect of her life. Every decision. Every viewpoint.

She was no fool.

The reasons behind avoiding love and being a mother were linked to her parents' deaths, her upbringing, and every horrible thing she thought she had to do just to survive.

She turned in her chair and faced her reflection in the full-length mirror lining the wall. Beneath the pretty face, expensive clothes, luxurious lifestyle, and organized businesses, she knew she was a catastrophe.

I am a beautiful mess.

She turned away from the mirror.

The truth is hard to face.

Desdemona pulled on her fox and picked up her tote. Her heels sounded like taps against the wood as she slowly walked to the door. She turned off the lights and looked back over her shoulder at the lit tree. She couldn't deny its beauty with its brilliant glow in the darkness.

She winced at a vision of a little girl of four sitting before the tree in her pink princess pajamas waiting for the strike of twelve to open one present as her mother looked on sipping from a cup of hot chocolate.

"O Christmas tree," Desdemona mouthed along with the vision of herself singing the carol in a sweet high-pitched voice.

It was a memory of the last Christmas she shared with her mother.

"I hate the dang on holidays."

With long strides, she crossed the room and unplugged the tree, casting the showroom into total darkness and causing the vision to, thankfully, disappear.

Knock-knock-knock.

Desdemona looked up from the book she was reading as she lay on her belly on the soft plush rug before her lit fireplace. She pressed the button on her iPhone to check the time. It was a little after seven.

Loren? Couldn't be.

She assumed their normal tutoring session was canceled for the holidays.

Room service? No. She'd gotten so lost in the book she'd forgotten to order dinner.

Who knew I was a reader?

Rolling over, she softly closed the book on her finger, marking her place as she rose from the floor and padded barefoot across the living room to the foyer. She checked the peephole, and her breath caught at the sight of Loren.

She leaned back from the peephole with her free hand still splayed on the door as she fought to recover from her surprise. She caught herself touching her curls to make sure they weren't too wild, but shook her head and smiled away her concern. With Loren—her friend Lo—she could always be herself. No pretense.

Desdemona opened the door, leaning against it as she

eyed him. "Something other than kicks? Surprise, surprise," she teased, taking in his bright orange V-neck sweater worn with a camel leather bomber, denims, and Timberland boots. His hair was braided and hidden beneath an army green skull cap. Spectacles ever in place.

He looked down at the book in her hand as he stepped inside the apartment. "Colson Whitehead's *Underground Railroad*. Surprise, surprise," he said, tapping the hardcover with his finger before he swung his designer book bag from his shoulder.

Desdemona clutched the book to her chest as she closed the door. "I have to look up some of the words but... I'm enjoying it," she said, ever surprised at how bashful she felt around him concerning her lack of education. "If our tutoring sessions weren't coming to an end I would ask you to read along with me like we did the Bradbury book."

Loren removed his coat. "You've come a long way," he said. "You don't need me. Plus, I've already read it."

"Figures," she said, reaching for his coat to hang in the closet before leading him into the living room.

"Well, this book of his, in particular, is exactly what I imagined myself writing when I got my undergrad history degree and then an MFA in creative writing," he said, removing papers from his book bag. "Now I'm pursing my doctorate."

Impressive.

"How do you jump from history to writing?" she asked, glancing back over her shoulder as she tucked the book under her arm and walked into the kitchen to grab two bottles of sparkling water from the fridge.

"I've always loved history," he said, taking both bottles from her to twist the caps off before handing her one back.

"Thanks," she said, sitting down on the couch.

"When most of my friends were reading comic books or playing video games, my head was stuck in books," Loren said, chuckling at the memory. "I loved books about history—

especially ancient Egypt and Africa. But a part of respecting history is being aware of it all—the good and the horrific."

She watched him, loving the conviction on his face as he spoke.

"But along with history my love for reading and books never wavered," he said, coming to sit down at the table. "In time I envisioned using my knowledge of history and layering it within a really well-written fictional story—entertaining and teaching all at once."

Desdemona sat back among the pillows on the sofa and eyed him, struck by the exuberance on his face and how he seemed to have an inner light of happiness and calm that was infectious. An urge to cross the room to be near him filled her, surprising her.

"You're a good person, Lo," she said.

He nodded in thanks. "I try to be," he said.

"You're so young, but you seem to have it all figured out," she said.

"Nah, definitely not," he said.

He turned from the dining room table and walked over to the window to look out at the New York night. His jaw was tight and his face troubled, unlike his normal self.

She continued to eye him.

With his hair braided back from his face, it was hard to deny his high cheekbones and fierce looks like a warrior.

"What?" she asked.

He glanced back over his shoulder at her. His face filled with questions.

"What don't you have figured out, Lo?" she asked, stroking her bottom lip as she assessed him and came to her own conclusion.

Am I right?

"Nothing," he muttered, before turning and walking back to the table to open his book bag. "Your test is coming up, and with the holidays we will lose a lot of time—"

"Lo," she said, interrupting him with ease.

He paused in his movements but didn't look to her.

She rose from the sofa and went over to him, covering one of his hands with her own. "You can talk to me. I'm a good listener," she said. "And I owe you so much more than you know for helping me start to see the world differently."

He raised his head. "Just trying to figure out what to get my girl for Christmas," he said.

Well, I was wrong.

Desdemona laughed. "That's all? That's easy. Jewelry," she said, moving away from him and dropping down on her sofa before she straightened the skirt of the kelly green long-sleeved wrap dress she wore. "And of course, sex along with the jewelry, especially while wearing the jewelry."

Loren remained quiet.

She looked up as she crossed her legs.

His eyes shifted away from hers. His discomfort was clear.

Her mouthed formed a little "O" in illumination.

Well, I'll be damned. I was right.

She rose from the sofa again and rushed over to his side. "Loren, are you a virgin?" she asked.

He cleared his throat and shifted away from the light hand she had rested on his upper arm. "Man, come on. Don't be ridiculous," he said.

She didn't believe him.

He was easily in his mid-twenties, handsome, with a tall and sinewy physique like a basketball player. Nerdy? Yes. Lacking boldness and confidence or the cocky swagger of most twenty-somethings whose penis got hard with the simple blow of the wind against their crotch. Sure. But a virgin?

"Can we just get to your lessons, Ms. Smith?" he asked.

"Yes," she said, respecting that he felt ill at ease and not wanting to embarrass him any more than she already had.

She reclaimed her seat. "Which subject are we tackling today, Lo?" she asked.

"I'm not a virgin," he said suddenly, slamming the sketch pad he held onto the top of the table with a *splat*.

"Okay," she said.

"Okay," he affirmed, withdrawing a thin stack of papers to walk over to hand it to her.

"Are you gay?" she asked, looking up at him.

He gave her a screwed-up facial expression. "No," he said, his voice hard.

"Okay, okay, okay," she said, taking the worksheets from his hand.

"For these last couple of sessions, I think we should focus on reading comprehension," he said, turning from her.

Desdemona nodded in agreement. "I agree. I'm pretty strong in math now and the reading is necessary for the other sections—"

"I want my girl to be happy."

She stopped flipping through the pages. "I'm sure the jewelry will be a good gift," she said, playing dim.

He gave her a sardonic look.

She bit the inside of her cheek to keep from smiling as she patted the seat next to her on the sofa.

Loren came over and took the seat, sitting with his legs open and his arms atop his knees as he hung his head.

Poor baby.

"Sex is an important part of a relationship, but if you're not ready—"

"I'm not a virgin," he stressed, his body tense.

Liar.

"Then what is it?" she asked, maintaining patience.

He remained quiet.

"How can I help you if I don't have all the relevant information?" she asked, extending her arm to rub comforting circles on his back.

"Help me? That's impossible," he said.

Is it now?

Desdemona eyed him. She could easily send one of her paramours to him to teach him tricks that would leave his girlfriend dazed and amazed beyond belief. That would be easy, but it would reveal more about herself than she was willing to share with him.

Besides . . .

Desdemona shifted her eyes to her hand on his back. "Maybe we can help each other," she said.

He looked back at her. "How?"

Her eyes fell to his lips. They were soft and full. "You tutored me for my GED," she began. "I can return the favor and teach you how to make love."

His eyes widened in surprise. "Ms. Smith?" he said, his voice strained.

The thought of being his first and leaving an indelible mark on his sexuality intrigued her.

"One good turn deserves another, Lo," she said, trailing her finger down the center of his back.

He shivered.

She chuckled.

He jumped to his feet. "I'm your tutor," he said.

She nodded. "And now I can be yours. Trust me, your girl will appreciate it. Happy girl. Happy world."

"Ms. Smith—"

She sighed. "I'm Ms. Smith. You're Loren. You're my tutor. Etcetera. We've been over all of that," she said. "Do you want my help? If not, let's get back to *my* tutoring."

"I started to have you do some questions from the app I had you download, but I think these questions are more difficult," he said as he walked back over to the table.

"Your loss," she said, as she picked up the papers.

"I thought we had kinda become friends," Loren said unexpectedly, turning to face her.

She glanced up at him. "We are. And we still would be afterward. Besides, who else makes love? Enemies?"

He remained quiet.

Desdemona read the directions. "Should I begin, Lo?" she asked.

Tap-tap-tap.

He was staring off into the distance and beating the eraser end of his pencil atop her dining room table. Just as he had the first day they met.

Nervous, huh?

"Lo," she called over to him.

"Huh?" he said, obviously distracted.

"Should I start?" she asked, feigning innocence.

He looked alarmed.

Desdemona rolled her eyes and held up the worksheets.

Loren visibly relaxed. "Remember to pay attention as you read. Sometimes the questions are tricky," he advised. "Utilize all of the tips I've taught you. If you get completely stuck let me know and we'll read it together. This is not the test so you can ask for help, so I can demonstrate again how to work through it. Okay?"

"Got it," she said, rising enough to tuck her bare feet beneath her bottom.

The room became quiet with only the subtle sounds from the lit fire and the sporadic scratching of his drawing pencils against the page of his sketch pad.

Desdemona's brows furrowed as she reread the passage before moving on to the multiple-choice question.

"What did you mean by we could help each other?"

She held up a finger to cease any further questions from Loren as she took the time to finish answering the next few questions. Finally, she looked up at him as she pressed the eraser of her pencil into her cheek. "I've been celibate for the past five years or better, Loren," she said.

His face was incredulous. "*Really*?" he asked in disbelief.

"By choice," she said.

"Of course."

They shared subtle smiles.

"And you want me?" he asked, his disbelief seeming never-ending.

"I *want* to help you," she explained.

"I don't want to cheat on my girl," Loren said.

"Okay," she said, turning her attention back to her work.

"But—"

"Loren," she said, almost snapping. She softened her hard tone with a smile.

Tap-tap-tap-tap-tap-tap-tap.

Desdemona sighed as she set aside her work and rose to walk over to where he sat. She took the pencil from his hands and snapped it in half. "Lo," she began, placing one hand on her hip and bending one knee that opened the split of her dress to expose her smooth brown thigh.

His eyes dipped down and then shot right back up.

"Lo, if you would like me to teach you how to make love to your woman—with no strings attached—then choose right now," she said, reaching to stroke his cheek.

Loren swallowed over a lump in his throat as he shifted in his seat.

She nudged his chin to lift his head, giving him a sultry smile that drew his eyes to her mouth. "The first lesson would be the art of kissing," she whispered down to him, softly running her thumb across his bottom lip.

He pressed his eyes closed and clenched his jaw.

"It is the *very* beginning of seduction, Lo," she said, pulling the string tying the wrap dress together.

"Damn, Ms. Smith," he swore, unable to look away from her naked body barely cloaked by the dress now hanging open at her sides.

She straddled his lap and pressed her hands to the sides of his face. "Yes or no?"

Loren dropped his head, resting it lightly against her cleavage. "Yes, please," he said, his will broken.

Desdemona raised his head; his eyes were closed.

"Look at me, Lo," she ordered softly.

He did.

"Eye contact is important. It connects you to your lover," she said, as she lowered her head to his without breaking their gaze.

"I don't have a condom," he said.

"Never break the mood with random thoughts," she instructed. "And we don't need one. Tonight's lesson is strictly kissing. Pay attention."

She placed soft kisses upon his mouth, shifting her head this way and that.

When he tried to plunge his tongue between her lips, she shook her head and leaned back. "Too wet, too forceful, too soon," she said, her eyes half closed.

He stiffened, turning his head.

"You have to be willing to learn," she said, repeating the words he once gave to her.

Loren smirked.

"Are you?" she asked, turning his head with her finger.

Their eyes met again.

"Not too wet, too forceful, or too soon," he repeated.

With a soft moan, Desdemona kissed him again, this time easing the tip of her tongue into the small groove in the middle of his bottom lip before lightly biting it. He swallowed just before he touched his tongue with hers. Lightly. With hesitance.

"Relax," she whispered before she sucked the tip of his tongue languidly.

He returned the favor with a small grunt of pleasure from the back of his throat.

"A little too much pull. But better," she said, stroking his neck as he brought his hands up to rest on her bare hips beneath the open dress.

For countless long minutes, they kissed. At times she whispered instructions to him. Other moments she got lost in him, shifting forward on his lap to press her upper body against his until her breasts were cushioned against his chest as she wrapped her arms around his neck and played with the ends of his braids.

She felt his hardness beneath her buttocks, unable to deny his length and width. And when his hands clumsily gripped her hips, she broke their kiss. "Much better, Lo," she said, rising from his lap and closing her dress before she turned from him and reclaimed her seat on the sofa.

"Huh?" he asked.

"Lesson over," she explained at his look of confusion with his eyes dazed from their kisses.

She picked up her workbook and tried to set her focus on her work, but she failed, lowering her pencil as she eyed him and stroked her lips with her fingertips, remembering the feel of his kisses.

Chapter Eight

Friday, March 5, 1999

I hate her too. I hate her more. I hate everything about her. I hate her in every way possible. In every word possible. H-ate. H-8. H-eight. HATE.

Desdemona sat up in the middle of her bed with her knees bent and her arms wrapped around her legs as she rested her chin in the groove. She looked at what should be proof of warmth and love but instead was a constant reminder of the life she used to have.

It was mocking.

The pretty pink princess bedroom was far too childish for a fifteen-year-old. And she felt like a prisoner. It was the only space in the house where her stepmother didn't make her feel unwanted, but it also isolated her. No friends. No family. No joy. No love.

"No TV," she muttered.

She rose from the bed and stood before the faded white dresser with bubblegum pink knobs to look at her reflection in the round mirror on the wall. She was tall and slender but her breasts, hips, and buttocks were developed, giving her a hint of an hourglass shape. She raked her fingers through her hair, frowning a little at the rough ends, thick roots, and haphazard curls as she did the best she could to do her own hair.

And wash her own clothes.

And cook her own food.

Thud-thud-thud-thud-thud-thud-thud...

Her eyes went to the closed door, frowning at the sudden noise.

By the time her stepmother got in from work, Desdemona had already done her homework, taken her bath, microwaved a TV dinner, cleaned the kitchen, and closed herself up in her bedroom for the night.

Thud-thud-thud-thud-thud-thud-thud...

Curious, she crossed the room and opened the door, looking down the dark hall at Zena's bedroom door. It was slightly ajar, leaving a sliver of light against the base of the wall and floor.

A feminine giggle and masculine chuckle sounded from the room.

Desdemona's eyes widened as she crept on tiptoes down the unlit hall, careful to miss the loose floorboard in the middle that always let out a loud all-too-telling squeak.

"Ssssh, before you wake her up," Zena said in a harsh whisper.

Desdemona pressed her back to the wall before peeking through the opening in the door. She frowned at the sight of Zena bent over the side of her bed with her dress up around her waist and her panties down around her ankles and Hervey Grantham—her father's attorney and best friend—pumping her from behind with his pants down around his ankles as well.

Her eyes widened in shock, and she covered her mouth with her hand and prayed the fast beating of her heart wasn't as loud as it seemed to her own ears. She turned to ease her way back down the hall.

Mr. Grantham and Zena?

That hurt. Desdemona knew her dad wouldn't like it.

"Hervey, it's been five years that I had to put up with her."

Desdemona paused in the darkness.

He grunted in agreement.

"Why can't I send her away to boarding school?" she asked.

Desdemona peeked into the room again, shaking her head at the bored expression on Zena's face while Mr. Grantham was sweating profusely and licking at his lips.

"You . . . can," he said, punctuating each word with a thrust. "But . . . the . . . money . . . will . . . go . . . toward . . . paying . . . for . . . it."

She looked back at him over her shoulder. "So, no kid—"

"No money," he finished with a deep bite of his full bottom lip.

It was Mr. Grantham's job to ensure Zena lived up to her obligations, and now Desdemona understood why she supplied the very minimum. She bought his complicity with sex.

Anger flamed inside her.

"I hate her. I hate her," Zena said.

I hate you, too.

"Just three more years," he said, his thrusts quickening in pace.

Three more years of this. I can't.

"What if she goes to jail or something? What happens to me?" Zena asked.

Jail?

Fear flooded Desdemona. What lengths was Zena willing to go to keep the money without being bothered with caring for her stepchild?

"The stipend would be put on hold."

Desdemona felt relief. Zena would not want that money to stop, not even to get rid of her. That she knew.

"And if she dies?"

That caused her heart to stop.

Would she? She wouldn't. Right?

It didn't matter.

She already killed my soul.

A tear rose and fell down her cheek. She didn't bother to wipe it away as she turned. "I can't do this no more," she mouthed.

Being sure to avoid the squeaking floorboard, she walked to her room and quickly packed a bag. There wasn't much to take that was meant for a teenager, but she was sure to jam her journals in with her things. With one last look back at the room, Desdemona closed the door and hitched her backpack up onto her shoulders.

Thud-thud-thud-thud-thud—

She looked down the length of the hall. For years there was so much she had wanted to say to the woman who made her life hell. She licked her lips, squared her shoulders, and gripped the straps of her book bag as she walked straight up the middle of the hall with quick and determined strides.

The floorboard squealed when she stepped on it.

Moments later she pushed the bedroom door open wide. It hit against the wall.

BAM!

Mr. Grantham stopped midstroke, and Zena looked at her with her eyes wide with shock.

"But my momma was the ho, right?" she asked with a sardonic shake of her head.

"Get out!" Zena roared, rising and pushing back against her lover.

"Hey!" he roared as he stumbled and fell backward onto the floor with his feet and moist erection pointed to the ceiling.

"You don't have to tell me twice. I'm gone," Desdemona said, turning to run down the length of the hall and across the living room to the front door.

An odd mix of fear and excitement were her adrenaline as she took off down the stairs and into the night.

Desdemona pulled her Maserati to a stop at the corner of depression and desperation. Once upon a time, the strip of three blocks had been her home. She released a heavy breath as she eyed the brightly lit liquor store on one corner with a long stretch of abandoned homes and vacant lots—dark and desolate—before a twenty-four-hour drive-through Chinese restaurant anchored it on the other end. For so many years her life had been walking the streets under the cover of darkness turning tricks to survive. Flashing fake smiles and far too youthful thighs in short skirts hoping to outshine her competitors—other lost souls—and draw the eyes and entice men driving by at a slow pace, choosing which of them they wanted to pay to please them.

She smiled, but it was sad, reflecting her heart. Those days, in cars or in the dark, abandoned halls inhabited by stray cats and rats, rain or shine, she had lost her innocence and her hope. Each stroke. Each grope. Each wet mouth on her privates. Each body's stench that almost made her puke. Bad breath. Bad screws. Bad souls.

Desdemona released a long breath as she eyed the dozen or so girls standing, walking, advertising under the cloak of darkness. The street lights were shot out each time the city repaired them and tried to bring light. There was no hope in that darkness. No shame. And for many, trapped by addictions or pimps, no escape.

I made it out.

But I never should have made it there.

She closed her eyes, surprised for her longing for a cigarette, knowing it wasn't a craving for the smoke and nicotine to fill her lungs but rather for the release. Any kind of release of the emotions flooding her, taking her back to days of which she knew she should be ashamed, but she wasn't.

I had no choice. I wasn't old enough to work. I was left behind in a house filled with hate, afraid that greed would cause my death.

Desdemona took an inhale this time—deep and slow—filling her lungs as she stiffened her spine in the driver's seat of her car. Bottling her emotions she was well practiced at. How else could she have made it through that house of hell, her days on the streets hungry and homeless, and then selling herself for food and shelter, and making the boldest and most defiant decision in her life to get away from being someone else's whore?

I did what I had to do.

She shook her head at a secret she would never tell. One she sometimes succeeded in forgetting.

Bzzzzzz . . .

Clearing her throat, she reached for her iPhones sitting on the passenger seat, choosing her personal one. The tip of her nail scratched the screen as she swiped with her thumb and opened the incoming email. "From Loren?" she said, her voice a blend of confusion and surprise, thinking he must be emailing her something to work on before their tutoring session the next night.

Her brows dipped as she read. "I feel you are more than ready for your GED test, but if you are in need of more tutoring I can recommend someone to you," she finished.

"Wait . . . what?" she asked, rereading the short email.

Loren quit as my tutor.

She rested her hand on her thigh as she held the phone and looked at her rearview mirror. She hadn't seen him since last week when she had offered him sex lessons and shared a kiss that even she couldn't forget.

"You're lying! Where's my money, yo?"

Desdemona focused her eyes across the street just as a tall and thin man swung and slapped a woman he was gripping around her throat. He slapped her again and again. She gasped with each show of violence. Her eyes dashed left and right, amazed at the people either looking on or looking away. No one helping. Cars slowing down to watch or record video. Someone yelled "Worldstar!" as they zoomed past.

But then amazement faded when she realized she was far removed from this life, but not enough to forget that she too had suffered plenty of hits and kicks.

When he flung the woman to the ground and kicked her like a football he was trying to punt for a long-range field goal, she balled her hand into her fist with her nails digging into the flesh as she wished she had a gun to grip. In her world guns weren't necessary, but this land of hard-to-ignore harshness was different. She tossed the phone onto the passenger seat and dug inside her tote bag for her baton instead.

"What am I doing?" she asked herself aloud as she put the car in drive and checked for oncoming traffic before she did a U-turn to the other side of the street. Her headlights shone on the man and woman just as he bent down to swing for more punches.

"What am I doing!" she squealed before she hopped out of the vehicle and flicked her wrist to extend the baton.

The woman's cries filled the air along with the sound of his hits upon her body.

WHAP. WHAP.

Desdemona swung her arm in an arc and brought it against the back of the man's knees, sending him down to the ground before she whacked him hard against his arms and head as his howls of pain pierced the night air. She eyed his victim. She was a teenager. No more than sixteen or seventeen. "Run!" she yelled, her stomach clenching from the blood and snot running from the girl's nose.

"I can't," she said, shaking her head. Her eyes filled with fear and her pain as she struggled to rise from the ground.

What am I doing?

She stepped over his body in her heels and grabbed the girl by the arm. "I will help you. Do you want it or not?" she asked, impetuously offering the girl the goodwill no one had dared offer to her.

The girl's eyes frantically shot to him and back to her before she nodded anxiously.

Pushing her roughly toward the passenger door of her car, Desdemona raced around the front of it to get in the driver's side just as the man began to rise with his hand pressed to the back of his head.

"Does he have a gun?" Desdemona asked.

"Hell, yes," the girl said, emphatic.

"Shit," Desdemona swore as he slammed one hand against the passenger window and reached behind him.

"Go!" the girl screamed, jumping back from him pounding on the window.

"Get out that fucking car!" he roared, extending his hand to point his gun at the window.

"He's gonna kill me," she whispered as she eyed the barrel.

Desdemona floored the accelerator, speeding away and having to control the sudden jerk of the wheel.

Pow!

They both shrieked at the echo of gunfire.

"What am I doing?" Desdemona yelled at the top of her lungs as she looked in her rearview mirror at him running full speed toward a black parked car. Within moments he was behind the wheel and speeding up the street behind them.

"Saving me, remember?" the girl said, her New York accent thick and her voice raspy.

Desdemona's hands clutched the wheel so tightly the skin over her knuckles was stretched thin. She eyed the rearview mirror as she kept up her pace, dodging in and out of traffic and taking side streets that she used to roam.

The girl looked over her shoulder. "I don't see his car."

"Good," Desdemona said, slowing down and releasing her grip.

What am I doing? Doing? Hell, what have I done?

"Thank you."

Desdemona looked over at her with a nod. "I couldn't take watching him beat on you like that," she said.

"I couldn't take it no more either," she quipped.

Desdemona was surprised by her humor and pleased to know she still held on to it after what she had just been through. "I know," she agreed, frowning a bit at the smell of sex rising in the air.

She turned down the heat in the vehicle, knowing it caused the smell of men left between the girl's thighs to rise.

"So, what now? He is not going to let me go that easy," she said.

"Food," Desdemona said, reaching for the only thing she knew she could provide for sure. "You hungry?"

I don't have a clue what I am doing.

"Not around here," she said.

"Definitely not," Desdemona agreed.

She took I-95 from the Bronx to Newark, New Jersey, pulling into the parking lot of a twenty-four-hour diner. Once they were settled in a booth and handed large plastic-covered menus, she finally took a good look at her new charge.

She was a bright-eyed cutie with a shortbread complexion in need of care. Her acne fought for prominence against her freckles, and her teeth needed a good cleaning, looking more buttery than white. Her hair was reddish brown and pulled back into a ponytail. She had already caught a whiff of her hygiene.

All signs that she was lacking proper guidance.

Her face said youth, but her body said full-grown woman. She had hips, boobs, and thighs for days and the long sleeved t-shirt and jeans with a hooded puffer jacket highlighted her assets without even trying.

"What's your name?" Desdemona asked, looking down at the girl's hands as she held the menu. Her fingernails were bitten down to the quick.

She looked up from the menu. "Portia," she offered.

Like my mom.

That took her breath away, and she blinked as her emotions were rocked to her core. *Was I meant to help her?*

"What you having, ladies?" the waitress asked, dressed in all black with a name tag reading Maxie.

Desdemona checked her own feelings and tuned in to

how tired the waitress seemed. "How are you doing tonight, Maxie?" she asked with a friendly smile, making sure to look her in the eye.

The waitress was taken aback. "Wore out, but the grind don't stop when the bills and my five kids won't either," she said with a weary smile as she tapped her pen against the order pad.

"More power to you, sis," Desdemona said, before turning her attention to her menu. "I'll have corned beef hash, bacon, and eggs scrambled with American cheese. White toast with extra butter."

"Okay, got you," Maxie said as she scribbled before looking to Portia.

But the girl's eyes were on Desdemona.

She's trying to figure me out. Ditto, kid. Ditto.

"Are you ordering?" Maxie asked her.

"Breakfast for dinner?" she asked.

"I love breakfast at a diner. Best thing ever," Desdemona said with a warm smile.

"I'll have the same thing," she said, her voice a little more proper.

Is she mimicking me? Is that how I sound?

"And your drink?" the waitress asked.

"What would *you* like, Portia?" Desdemona asked.

"Lemonade," she said, sounding unsure.

"I'll have the same thing," Desdemona said, taking her menu and handing both to Maxie.

"Be right back, ladies."

Desdemona settled back against the cracked leather of the booth. "What's your story, Portia?" she asked.

She shrugged one shoulder before removing her puffer coat. "Stuff I wish I could forget," she said.

"Like?" she pressed.

"Why?" Portia countered, her voice soft.

She sounds and acts younger than her years.

"Because I can't help you on your journey unless I know where you've been," Desdemona said. "What have I gotten myself into?"

"You? Me too?"

"Right," she agreed.

They fell silent as Maxie set their drinks on the table along with straws and retreated.

Portia removed the paper from her straw and dropped it in her drink. "Junkie mom. Deadbeat dad. Molestation. Rape. Physical abuse. Rebel. Runaway. Kidnapped. Pimped," she said, her voice monotone as if she separated her emotions from the memories.

"Beaten," Desdemona added.

Portia nodded and looked at her drink as she stirred her straw in circles. She looked distant. Her thoughts were elsewhere.

It was stories such as Portia's, and her own, that were why Desdemona never forced one of her paramours to do anything they didn't choose. She thought of her own pimp. Majig. Violence had been his best friend as well.

She flinched at the memory of one of his backhand slaps.

"So, he is all you have?" Desdemona asked, hating just how much she understood.

"*Had*," Portia stressed. "And yes. I lived with him because I'm not old enough to get my own place."

"How old are you?"

"Sixteen."

Still a kid.

"I'm not going back to foster care. Before I do I will go back to Papo and just recover from that ass whipping."

Desdemona was thankful their food arrived. She pretended to focus on eating as she tried to figure out her next step. This young girl was her responsibility now. But what to do with her?

Shit.

"What's your name?"

Desdemona looked up from pushing her hash around on her plate with her fork. "Ms. Smith," she lied with ease.

She had far too much to lose by letting this stranger too far into her life.

"And what's your story?" Portia parroted.

"Just a concerned citizen who wants to help," Desdemona replied, setting her fork down.

I just don't know how.

"You a social worker or something?" she asked.

"Far from it."

She didn't miss how the girl's eyes fell on her designer tote and the fluffy mink she wore. Was she impressed or scheming? Desdemona wasn't sure. "Finish your food," she said, picking up her fork to do the same.

She welcomed their silence, needing time to formulate a plan. No more flying by the seat of her pants when it came to this young woman who was too much of a mirror to her past. *Think, Desi, think.*

They finished their meal, and Desdemona rose, sliding on her fur and grabbing her tote before taking the bill. "Let me warm the car up," she said. "I'll flash the lights when it's ready."

"Okay."

She paid the bill at the register and scanned the restaurant until she saw Maxie coming out of the kitchen. She waved her over and pressed a crisp fifty-dollar bill into her hand.

The woman's eyes widened when she opened her hand. "Thank you," she stressed.

Desdemona knew what it felt like to be tired but too broke to rest.

She stepped out of the diner. The northeast winter air was frigid, causing her to rush across the parking lot. She used the key fob to crank the car and was thankful the seat was warm when she slid onto it. Glancing up, she eyed Portia looking out the window. She reached over to lock the glove compartment that contained her insurance card and registration, revealing her real name and address.

Get on point and stay on point, Desi.

She flashed the lights and turned up the heat, watching as Portia eagerly jumped to her feet and walked out of the diner as she pulled on her puffer coat. At that moment she saw an eager child wanting to be loved, and her heart ached.

Desdemona gave her a warm smile as she opened the door and climbed inside.

"Tonight, I'll get you a hotel room," she said, glancing at her before reversing out of the parking spot.

"By myself?" she asked.

Desdemona nodded, as she stroked the softness of her neck and focused on driving through the busy New Jersey traffic. When the silence was deafening and she had decided on her plan going forward, she turned on the satellite radio for the music to fill the air as she made her way back to Manhattan.

She pulled up in front of the hotel entrance of the building where she lived. She figured it was close enough for her to be near in case something went wrong, but she was still able to be in the comfort of her condo upstairs.

"I'm staying here?" Portia asked, peering out the window at the regal hotel with two uniformed doormen standing before the ornate double doors.

Desdemona put the crossover in park and glanced at her, seeing the amazement in her eyes. She looked at the front of the hotel again through the eyes of her sixteen-year-old self—homeless, desperate, never being close to anything akin to grandeur. She would have been just as stunned. "Yup. Home sweet home for a night or two," she said, opening the door as the valet rushed over to her.

She handed him the key. "I'll be back out in less than an hour," she advised him.

"Yes, ma'am," the portly blond man said.

Desdemona nodded at the doormen as one held the door open for them. She smiled at the wide-eyed way Portia took in the lavish surroundings. "Have a seat," she instructed her before continuing to the check-in desk as she pulled out her fake ID from her wallet.

"Good evening. How may I help you?"

"Good evening. One room. King bed. Please," she said. "Two-hundred-dollar daily limit on room service and pay-per-view. No outgoing phone calls at all."

"Yes, ma'am... Ms. Smith," the desk attendant said, reading her ID.

Desdemona glanced back over her shoulder to check on Portia. She nearly palmed her face to see the young woman and an elderly white man sharing a long look. "Excuse me," she said, walking over to the sitting area to stand in between them, blocking the man's line of vision.

His eyes met hers. "She's a kid," she said with an arched brow.

Portia laughed behind her.

The man's eyes bugged in alarm before he rushed to rise from his seat and move away from them.

Desdemona turned and tilted her head to the side as she looked down at her young charge. "Not here," she said, her voice low but stern.

The laughter stopped. "I just went into work mode. Sorry," she said, as she looked down at her hands before biting at what was left of her fingernails.

"I'm not bailing you out of jail," she said. "I *never* will."

Portia nodded in understanding.

"Come on."

As she led the young woman back to the check-in counter, that doubt lingered. *What am I doing?* she thought for what had to be the dozenth time.

She finished checking in, and they made their way to the

elevator. Desdemona handed Portia the key card. "This is the only key card. It's your room, Portia. All yours. If I want to enter I will knock," she said, just before the elevator doors closed.

That surprised Portia as well.

When they reached the door to the room, Desdemona held back, allowing Portia to unlock the door. She walked in slowly and looked around in wonder before rushing over to turn and fall back onto the bed.

"Tomorrow I'll bring you a change of clothes, and then we'll go shopping for all your necessities," Desdemona said.

Cha-ching.

She reached into her tote for her phone. An emoji of the strong arm appeared on the screen. "Cancellation. Family emergency," she mouthed as she read.

Denzin had a session at the mansion with Nicolette Lawson, a high-powered attorney with a proclivity for anal sex and verbal lashings while hogtied. Deposits were normally non-refundable, but she had been a steady and regular consort for the last five years.

"Portia, take a bath or shower while I make a few phone calls," she said, setting her tote on the chair before the desk.

"I don't have a change of clothes."

Desdemona glanced back at her. "There's a robe hanging in the closet," she explained.

Yet another surprise. Plush white robes with the monogram of the hotel were not to be found in run-down motels with musty rooms and scratchy carpets with doors leading directly to the parking lot.

She walked over to the closet and removed the robe and the folded disposable plastic bag, crossing the space to hand her both. "Put your dirty clothes in this bag to wash or to throw away. Your choice," she said, knowing how it felt to have very little and cherish it.

Portia nodded and took both before walking over toward

the open door to the bathroom. She paused. "Are you rich?" she asked, looking back at her.

Desdemona hated to lie. Even now she knew she might be setting herself up for a robbery if she wasn't careful. *More balls to juggle.* "No," she lied as she childishly crossed her fingers as if to hold off any punishment from God.

Just silly.

Portia entered the bathroom and closed the door.

Desdemona dialed Denzin's burner phone.

"Boss," he soon answered.

"Try to reschedule with her," she said, walking over to the window to look out at the city.

Movement was everywhere.

"Okay."

"Let me know the new deets so I don't double book," she said, turning from the frenetic view.

"Right."

"Did she say what the emergency was?" she asked, keeping her voice light.

Sudden changes or cancellations put her on alert.

"No, but she sounded really down," Denzin said.

She turned as the bathroom door opened. Portia extended her arm with the bag of clothes in her hand. "Okay. Keep me posted," she said, ending the call and sliding the phone into the pocket of her mink as she crossed the room to take the bag.

"I'll keep them," Portia said from the ajar door.

Lord.

"Okay. I'll bring them back clean tomorrow."

Portia closed the door.

She fought the urge to toss the bag in the small wastepaper basket by the polished wooden desk. Holding on to the clothes was a sign she didn't yet trust her, so throwing them away would really destroy any chance of that.

Trust is key.

She had learned that a long time ago. Broken trust had

scarred her. It was the reason she hated to lie. Nothing like being deceived to detest it.

"Trust me. I got you."

She closed her eyes and released a breath, hating the voice that suddenly replayed in her head and the memory that came along with it...

Desdemona paused in taking her clothes out of the backpack to look out the window at the rain pouring down on the city. The sound of it battered against the roof and windows of the laundromat.

If she hadn't found somewhere to sit out the rain she would have been sleeping in it. Again.

Twenty-four-hour establishments were her havens since she'd run away from Zena's house a month earlier. Emergency rooms. Train stations. Laundromats and restaurants. The secret she learned was to be clean and presentable and look like you belonged. Free lunch at school was sometimes her only meal when she couldn't beg up enough to buy something. She washed up at sinks and did the best she could with her hair.

She did the best she could with everything.

Pain radiated across her chest. Never had she felt so alone. So hungry. So lost inside her own head.

She was no fool. Her stepmother hadn't even reported her missing because she went to school every day without incident. No police or social workers arriving to see if she was there.

It's just me, myself, and I.

That was scary.

Some nights, when the twenty-four-hour joints didn't work, she languished between half sleep and fear in the park on a bench or on the back seat of a bus hoping the driver didn't notice her back there, worrying that she would be mugged or raped or worse.

And no one would care.

A tear raced down her cheek and landed atop the back of her hand as she gripped her bag in desperation and aching sadness. So much so that she wondered if she should have just stayed at Zena's.

"And if she dies?"

Desdemona winced at the recollection, reaching inside her front pocket to stroke her heart-shaped locket with her thumb. She was too afraid to wear it around her neck anymore. It was all she had.

"Whaddup."

She jumped in alarm as she turned, looking up at a man in his mid-twenties in a New York Giants jersey, jeans, and Nike Air Force 1s with a fitted hat tilted to the side on his head. Her eyes darted past him to the dark blue Ford Expedition with shiny chrome rims parked at the curb. She could just make out the sound of Jay-Z's "Money, Cash, Hoes" playing from his sound system.

Her eyes went back to him. Her heart pounded. They were alone, and she was afraid.

He smiled, revealing a gold grill on his bottom teeth. "You a'ight, shawty?" he asked, his voice deep and raspy.

She nodded nervously. "Y-y-y-yes," she stammered. "Just waiting on my dad. He went to get us food."

His smile broadened as he turned and hopped up onto the table. "Not true," he said. "Anytime you come here you're always by yourself. And you sleep here. By yourself."

Her eyes darted to the door.

He shook his head and held up his hand. "I'm not on no bullshit. You can leave. This ain't no stickup. Hell, you ain't got shit. I'm just tired of seeing you out in these streets alone. Hungry. Struggling. You too fine for that shit."

"Me?" she asked, taking in his caramel brown complexion and lean features.

"Hell, yeah," he said, reaching over to stroke her cheek.

She shivered.

He reached in the pocket on the front of his oversize jeans and removed a wad of money wrapped with a red rubber band. "You deserve somebody to look out for you, and I want to be that dude to take care of you," he said, smooth as ever.

"Why?" she asked.

"Because you're beautiful, and I want you to be my girl."

"Your girl?"

"Damn right," he assured her. "What's your name?"

He was cute. That she couldn't deny. But . . .

She gave him a smile as she walked past him and over to the door of the laundry. He didn't stop her as she stepped out onto the street. "Paper Chase" by Jay-Z and Foxy Brown blared loudly. The fact that he left his car running without a care about someone touching it earned her respect.

It meant protection.

She came back inside and walked back over to him and her bag of dirty clothes. "Desdemona," she finally answered, looking up at him and then shyly looking away.

"I'm Majig," he said, sifting through the wad of hundred-dollar bills to find and eventually remove a ten to hand to her. "Put your clothes in the machine and let's go eat."

Her hesitance showed.

"Trust me. I got you," he said, giving her a charming smile.

Desdemona shook her head at her naïveté. That night she moved into his apartment in the Hallmark on Hill Street and they made love to "Nothing Even Matters" by Lauryn Hill and D'Angelo. One month later her bliss was shattered when he requested to be repaid for all the money he'd spent on new clothes, hairdo, nails, food, and rent. And that night, when she understandably didn't have the money, he ordered her to sleep with men to work off the debt and locked her in a bedroom with a strange man she wished she could forget.

The first of many. More than she cared to remember.

And then she truly sold her soul to the devil when she decided to pull out every trick in her bag and seduce Majig into making her his in-house girl, figuring the devil she knew was better than any devils she didn't—especially when her days of streetwalking were over.

Desdemona jumped when a hand suddenly squeezed her shoulder. She whirled around and closed her eyes with a shake of her head at Portia standing there naked.

"I'm ready to thank you now," she said.

"Then just say thank you, Portia," she said, her voice hard as she shook off her touch. "Go put on your robe."

"But—"

"Go," Desdemona demanded.

The irony of the night she'd fallen into the clutches of a sex trafficker and her stepping in to help this girl of innocence lost was not missed.

When Portia stepped back into the room, Desdemona rose from the chair and turned to face her. "I'm sorry that life has taught you that no one will ever do something for you without demanding a piece of you in return, but tonight let me be the first person to teach you otherwise."

Portia dug her hands down deep in the pockets of her robe and hung her head.

"Hold your head up, kid, you have nothing to be ashamed of," Desdemona said, softening her tone.

She looked up.

"Did you drop out of school?"

Portia nodded yes. "But—"

"So, here's the deal. If you agree to go back to school and give up tricking, I will find you a small apartment, pay your rent, and give you a little money for your pocket," Desdemona offered. "You owe me absolutely nothing but keeping your word."

Portia's eyes filled with tears and confusion. "Why?"

"Because you deserve it." Desdemona came around the chair to stand before her and extend her hand. "Deal?"

Portia looked down at her hand before finally sliding her own into it. "Deal," she agreed.

"Okay, in the bed," she said, looking on as her charge crossed the room and slid beneath the comfy covers.

"We'll figure it all out tomorrow, Portia," she said, picking up the laundry bag and her tote.

"Ms. Smith."

Desdemona paused in the open doorway.

"Thank you," she said softly.

She gave her a reassuring smile and left.

Chapter Nine

Wednesday, January 9, 2019

Lonesome.

Desdemona and Loren stood on either side of the threshold and stared at each other.

"Hey," he said before releasing a breath.

"Hello."

More awkward silence.

She hadn't seen him since "the kiss" or since "the email." His appearance at her front door today was surprising. She couldn't imagine what he could want. She enjoyed his discomfort and did nothing to ease it as she eyed him.

"Can we talk?" he asked.

"About?" she asked, leaning against the edge of the door.

"Can I come in?" he asked.

She shrugged. "I don't know. Can you?"

He shook his head and shifted on his boot-clad feet, looking down the length of the hall and then back at her. "Look, are you mad at me?" he asked.

She took in his wild mane of hair and strong features before shifting her eyes down to the three-quarter-length hooded coat he wore over his denims and bright colored V-neck sweater. "Depends," she admitted.

"On?"

"Are you afraid of me?" she asked without hesitation.

His eyes shifted away.

"Awwww," she sighed, slightly mocking. "Poor baby."

He clenched his jaw.

"Come in, Lo," she said with a smile, stepping back and pulling the door open wider with her.

"Thanks," he said, glancing at her as he passed to step into the foyer.

"I don't think I've ever seen you without your Louis book bag," she noticed.

"Well, I'm not your tutor, so . . ."

"Right."

"Right," he agreed.

She invited him to the open living space with a wave of her hand in its direction.

"How'd your test go?" he asked.

"I rescheduled it," she admitted. "Life got in the way. It's all good."

Bzzzzzz.

Pausing her steps, she pulled her iPhone from the pocket of the floor-length casual dress she wore. It was a text from Portia.

PORTIA: Out of court. We won. I'm an adult.
MS. S: Congrats! I'll call you later tonight. U good?

Desdemona smiled at the praying hands emojis Portia text back. She slid the phone back into the pocket of her dress, pleased that her idea for Portia to file a petition for emancipation had worked. She was now legally able to make decisions for herself. Her allegations of abuse and the fact that she was technically homeless and in need of a place to stay helped her to push for an emergency hearing. Her parents not appearing in court and Desdemona locating and offering to pay the cost for a high-powered attorney also helped.

Best twenty grand I ever spent.

Now Portia could apply for a job and enroll in high school in September as a junior—all without Desdemona revealing her own identity or legally taking the girl on as her ward.

"Ms. Smith."

No. It's Ms. Dean. Desdemona Dean.

She looked at him. "Huh?"

"My girl and I broke up," he said.

Desdemona came over to sit on the sofa. "I'm sorry to hear that—"

"Because of you."

She screwed up her face. "How's that?"

He cleared his throat and licked his bottom lip. "I told her about the kiss," he said.

"Why?"

"I felt so guilty."

"But I kissed you," she stressed.

"And it fucked me up. It fucked my relationship up," Loren stressed, rubbing his hands through his wild hair before clenching the strands in his fist.

"I thought I did," she said.

He eyed her. "It wasn't fair to be with her and wish it was you," he said.

Their eyes locked.

Desdemona was taken aback, and her pulse raced. She bit her bottom lip. "Why are you here, Lo?" she asked, remembering the feel of his lips.

He sat back on the sofa with his head leaning against it,

exposing his neck and Adam's apple as he swallowed hard. He closed his eyes and shook his head.

Desdemona eyed him. She'd assumed she'd never see her young tutor again. At the moment his email arrived, she had been too busy with saving Portia to really evaluate just why he had canceled the last of their tutoring sessions. Between getting Portia settled and the Christmas holidays that triggered all of her woes about her past, Desdemona hadn't allowed herself to miss their friendship.

But when she did, it was with fondness and with regret that the kiss hadn't led to more.

She eyed him again. *I was curious. Hell, I still am. Is he a virgin? Can I teach him? Make him a better lover?*

Does he want me to?

"Live life with no regrets," she said to him, reminding him of his advice to her.

He turned his head to eye her. "Is it too late?" he asked.

"For?" she asked, giving him a beguiling smile.

"To teach me."

How sweet. And hot.

She had an itch of her own to be scratched.

"Are you back with your girl?" she asked.

"No."

"If you could, would you?"

"I don't know, because as much as I cared for her, if I was in love with her, you shouldn't have mattered," he said, and then looked startled. "Sorry. You know what I mean, right?"

Desdemona nodded. "I do," she said, beckoning him closer with a bend of her finger.

He actually pointed to himself as if to say, "Me?"

"Yes, you. No one else is here, Loren," she said patiently.

He was so nervous. So awkward. Unsure.

But handsome and filled with goodness.

This should be fun.

When he reached her, the warm scent of his cologne appealed to her, and her body responded to his closeness. Pulse racing. Heartbeat quickening. The sweet bud of her intimacy throbbing to life.

She removed his spectacles. "I want to thank you for teaching me to live, to enjoy, to explore more," she said as she set them on the coffee table. "You are—were—like a breath of fresh air to my stale life. My routine. My rut."

"You deserve it," he said.

She straddled his lap. "And you deserve this," she said, leaning in to capture his mouth with her own.

And so do I. The wait is over.

At first, the kiss was slow as their tongues lightly touched. She deepened it, welcoming the hunger she felt.

I need this.

"Sex is all about awareness," she whispered into his open mouth as their eyes locked and she reached for his hands to press to her hips. "You have to be bold enough to know you're a good lover, but sensitive enough to care if your lover is pleased, to be a great lover."

He shifted his hand to grip her buttocks.

Desdemona gasped in pleasure and surprise. "Very good," she said before leaning down to taste his mouth again before rising to her feet to ease her dress up over her head and stand before him naked.

"Damn," he swore, his eyes taking in every bit of her soft curves.

She twisted her hair up in a loose topknot. "Now what?" she asked.

He rushed to stretch his legs and dig into his front pocket. "I brought condoms," he said eagerly.

"Good, but there's plenty in between getting naked and

having sex, Lo," she said, taking the condoms to toss beside him on the sofa. "And you're not naked."

Loren jumped to his feet and began to remove his clothes in rushed jerks. She fought the urge to tell him to slow down and appear less eager, but like the first time he tutored her, she was assessing his skill level.

His body was lean but strong, and his erection was long and curved. And hard. So very hard.

"Damn, Lo," she said, looking up at him with appreciation.

He slowly grinned and massaged the length of his inches.

She stepped closer to him, tilting his dick upward to press between their bodies as she wrapped her arms around his neck and wove her fingers through his soft hair. "Damn," she whispered again against his lips before he dipped his head to kiss her as he massaged her lower back and buttocks.

Remembering to teach him and not get lost in her desire, she guided his head until his lips were on her neck. She did the same, suckling the soft dip above his clavicle and loving the race of his pulse against her tongue as he shivered. She pressed kisses across his hard chest and bent her knees a bit to circle one brown nipple with her tongue.

He cried out.

She smiled against his chest and did it again. And again. And again.

And when she leaned back from him, pushing her breasts upward, he held her securely around the waist and bent his head to do the same. Soft flickers. Deep sucks. Tender bites. Over and over.

"Nice," she sighed in pleasure.

"Huh?" he asked, raising his head.

"Don't stop," she said.

More suckling.

Yesssssss.

The urge to turn things up filled her, but she refrained. He was not ready for her to pull out all her tricks. Not at all.

One day, though.

She turned their bodies and sat down on the sofa. His erection was aligned with her mouth and she cut her eyes up at him. His eyes were wide with shock and hope, but again she refrained. He would climax in minutes without ever stroking inside her. She was that good.

Instead, she spread her legs wide and leaned back against the sofa as she stroked her own intimacy with her fingers and patted it lightly.

"Ms. Smith," he said in awe.

She smiled at that.

Loren dropped to his knees and leaned forward to press kisses against her cleavage as he fumbled his fingers below to stroke at her wetness. She arched her back and rotated her hips as he shifted to suck at one of her taut nipples. The feel of his middle finger sliding inside her pulled a cry of pleasure within her as she closed her eyes and stretched her arms out along the top of the sofa.

She gave in to her passion, reveling in mutual desire. Being wanted just for the sake of being wanted. Desire. Passion. Pleasure. And in those heated moments, her notice of his awkwardness faded as she let her body rule over her brain. What he lacked in skill they made up for in chemistry that shocked her.

Her entire body felt alive.

Awakened.

Were there things she needed to teach him about exploring more of her body, dirty talk, and slight aggression? Yes, but at that moment, as her throbbing clit ached relentlessly she didn't care. It was almost six years and even then, many years before where her pleasure had been forced and faked.

This was real and pure and good.

"Now, Lo, now," she cried out, needing a release.

As she writhed in pleasure, she could hear the tear of the condom's foil.

She was hungry for it. "You ready?" she asked, spreading her legs before him.

"Hell, yeah," he said.

When his probing of her missed the mark, she reached down and gripped him to guide his hardness inside her. With one deep thrust he entered her. She winced at the feel of her core adjusting to the feel of him. His length. His thickness. His hardness. That wicked curve.

Damn. Damn. Damn.

Loren wrapped his arms around her body and buried his face against her neck as he trembled. "If you feel like you're gonna cum, then stop stroking until it goes away to last longer," she said. "Okay?"

"Yeah."

His body was rigid and stiff for long moments that nearly made her mad, until finally—*finally*—he began to glide inside her. His thrusts were deep and fast. Hard and unrelenting.

She didn't tell him to slow down. She didn't want him to.

She twisted her fingers in his hair and jerked his head up to kiss him deeply as his sweat began to slicken the movements of their bodies against each other. He moaned in pleasure as she sucked his tongue with the same vigor that he sexed her.

What he lacked in skill he made up for in pure youth and strength.

Lord.

She admired the flexion of his muscles. His shoulders, arms, back, and buttocks. He was pure steel. His strokes glided up and down her walls. Her pleasure for him wettened her, slickening his moves.

Shit.

It was frenetic and kinetic. His pace was dizzying. Her mind felt scattered. Her senses were in overload.

Unable to deny herself, she sucked at his earlobe and whispered obscenities to him.

He paused.

She released a shaky breath, actually glad for the reprieve. Her heart was pounding so loudly she felt he could hear it as well.

He raised up to look down at her. "You good?" he asked.

"Hell, yeah," she said, her voice breathless.

She looked up at the fierceness on his face. The handsome lines of his face and the wildness of his hair. Desire and some level of crazy caused by passion gave his slanted eyes a bright light. He was beautiful.

He studied her face as well, and she wondered about his thoughts but didn't have a moment to ask as he began to stroke inside her again.

"So, you're not a virgin," she said.

He smiled a little. "No, I'm not."

"Next time I'll teach you about making love. *This* is fucking," she said, gripping his arms and being turned on by his muscles.

He paused midstroke. "Should I stop?" he asked, his eyes concerned that he was wrong.

Silly boy.

"Definitely not."

And it was on again.

Desdemona wrapped her arms around his neck and her legs around his waist and held on for the ride. Each furious piston-like stroke was like a jolt of pure electricity. And when he stiffened to keep back another rise of his climax, she shook her head where it was buried against his neck.

"Don't stop," she begged.

Loren roughly shoved his hands beneath her to grip her

buttocks as he pumped away furiously until his hardness was like that of a bat before it throbbed with each of his releases inside her.

She had to fight not to sex him back and drain him of every drop.

Next time, she promised herself.

With a few final thrusts that were fractured, Loren's body went slack atop hers.

She played with the curls of his hair as she released shallow breaths through pursed lips, waiting for her pulse and heartbeat to decelerate.

"What's my score?" he asked, lifting up to look down at her.

"You and the filled condom are still in me, Lo," she reminded him.

"Right," he agreed.

"Hold the condom while you pull out," she advised.

Loren chuckled. "I know," he said, doing just that.

She rose from the sofa and watched as he walked to the powder room in the hall. She made her way to her private bathroom and quickly washed up before she pulled on a lace robe. He was standing at the window in his boxers when she walked back into the living room. "No worries, kid, I give you a C overall," she quipped, moving to the bar to pour two glasses of wine.

He turned. "What will it take to get an A?" he asked.

"Not used to scoring lower than best?" she asked, crossing the room to hand him a glass.

"Definitely not; that's why I came for your help," Loren said.

She sipped her drink and ran her free hand through her hair, which had come loose in the melee. "Equipment is an A. Kudos for that," she said with a slight raise of her glass in a toast.

He shook his head as he chuckled. "And?" he asked before taking a sip.

"You rely on your size too much," she said frankly. "Just pumping away, but if your penis doesn't hit her spot she won't cum. I didn't. Not the big explosion that should have me on that couch still sticky from your sex and sleeping."

He frowned.

"Pay attention to her. Get her hot and wet. Caress her body. Kiss her everywhere—and I do mean *everywhere*," she stressed with a meaningful look.

"Nah, I don't do that," he said.

Desdemona eyed him. "Your loss," she said, chiding him as she reached up to pat his cheek. "There's nothing better than the taste and feel of a woman in your mouth. Stop denying yourself."

He fell quiet.

"Don't worry. I've only just begun to teach you," she said, raising her glass to him. "Here's to the making of a great lover."

Loren raised his glass to touch hers.

"See how he works his hips? In circles. Clockwise. Then counterclockwise. Not just back and forth."

Desdemona picked up the remote from the bed to pause the video on the television as she looked over her bare shoulder at Loren sitting on the bed leaned back against the pillows and her headboard, naked and beautiful with his member lying across his thigh, impressive even at rest.

He nodded and looked over at her.

She was as naked as he as she sat on her haunches with her heels pressing into her buttocks.

Desdemona looked back to the TV and continued the video. The lovers shifted their bodies so that he sat on the couch and she straddled his hips, reaching behind herself to hold his erection straight up as she slid down onto it. She bit down onto the tip of her finger as she watched them deeply kissing and whispering to each other as the woman rode him slowly as he thrust his hips upward off the couch.

She fell silent and enjoyed the show, feeling her fleshy bud throb against the plump lips of her womanhood.

"That's the thing about a good flick," she said in wonder. "You can tell when they're really feeling each other because they don't give a damn about that camera placement. This is one of my favorite flicks."

"Mine too now," he said.

She glanced back at him, but her breath caught at him now fully aroused with his erection casting an impressive shadow against the sheets beside him.

"Well, now," she sighed, tossing the remote aside and crawling on her knees up the length of the bed to reach him.

He sheathed himself with protection before she reached him and straddled his lap to take as much of his hardness as she could inside of her. He gripped her buttocks and deeply sucked a taut brown nipple as he pressed his face against the softness of her breasts. Her fingers gripped the headboard and she flung her head back until the ends of her hair teased the top curve of her buttocks.

Soon their cries of release and passion blended in the air with those from the video.

"Lo. Lo. Lo!" Desdemona gasped as he stroked inside from behind as she was bent over the coffee table with her breasts and hard nipples pressed against the chilly glass.

He stopped, his fingers gripping her fleshy buttocks before he slapped each cheek lightly. "More?" he asked, his voice thick with pleasure.

He really is a quick learner. Not perfect. But better. Shit.

She nodded eagerly, raising her face from the glass to look over at the lit fire as he pounded away again. "Slow it down, Lo," she advised. "And reach around me to play with my clit while you do."

He quickly obeyed.

She released a whimper and balled her hands into fists atop the glass.

Slow and with a devastating pace, Loren worked his hips to glide in and out of her. He bent his body over hers and licked at her shoulder and upper back.

A little too wet, but I'll tell him that later.

She arched her back, raising her buttocks and her core for him.

"Beautiful," he whispered.

"Put your thumb in," she gasped, wanting him to.

"Huh?" he asked, stopping his glide.

He's not ready, and that's low-level freaky.

"Nothing," she said, working her hips to pull downward on his hardness.

He moaned deeply.

Cha-ching. Cha-ching. Cha-ching.

She almost didn't hear her phone, and she almost wished she hadn't.

Damn.

"I gotta get that, Lo," she said.

"Fuck that phone," he said, stroking away.

She almost agreed, but there was too much at risk not to answer.

Cha-ching. Cha-ching. Cha-ching.

She pushed back against him with her buttocks to get room and then rose, feeling his hardness slide out of her.

"Ms. Smith," he moaned in disappointment.

She padded over to her phones on the charging station in the kitchen. She unplugged her business phone and walked toward her bedroom as she answered. "Yes."

"Mademoiselle, he slapped me. I don't know if he is high or crazy or what, but he hit me. He fucking *hit* me."

"Chelsea," she said, forgetting to use her moniker of Choc—short for chocolate.

Get it together, Desdemona.

She pinched the bridge of her nose and paced. "Choc, are you hurt? Where are you? Where is he?" she asked, her words rushed and almost colliding with one another.

The line disconnected. She called her prepaid phone back three times. No answer. She gripped the phone tightly and growled in frustration, feeling some of those metaphorical balls she kept in the air crash.

She headed back into the living space. She paused in the entryway at the enticing sight of Loren sitting on the sofa with the darkness broken up by the warm glow of the lit fire. She wanted nothing more than to rejoin him and claim the heated spot where they left off.

He looked over his shoulder at her. His surprise was clear. "Is everything okay?" he asked, rising to his full height.

No.

"I got an emergency with my business. Can we pick this up another time?" she asked, her thoughts on Choc's safety.

He immediately started getting dressed.

When he pulled on his coat and came over to her at the front door, she gave him a smile she hoped was filled with her regret.

"Is there anything I can do?" Loren asked.

She looked to him, surprised that this man nearly ten years her junior made her feel so damn safe at that moment. "I got it," she said.

"Let me know you got back in okay?" he asked.

Desdemona nodded. She looked up just before he gave her one last look and pulled his skull cap down over his wild hair before he opened the door.

"Lo," she called to him.

He turned in the open doorway. She walked over to him and wrapped her arms around his waist, holding him close as she rose up on her toes and pressed a kiss to the corner of his mouth.

With a playful smack of her bare bottom, he stepped over the threshold and left, closing the door as he did.

"Shit," she swore, using her iPad to send for her car before rushing to her walk-in closet to pull on a fitted sweater dress and thigh-high riding boots, topping it with a short leather trench and a fitted cap to battle the bitter January cold.

Rushing, she opened her safe and grabbed wads of cash and made sure her baton was in her tote before she finally left the apartment.

Cha-ching. Cha-ching—

It was Choc's consort with the hand problem. Number eighteen. She answered, squaring her shoulders as she continued down the hall to the elevator. "Complete violation of the rules," she said as soon as she answered the call.

"I know. I know. I'm sorry."

She paused before stepping onto the lift. His voice was odd. Slurring a bit.

Vic Lamonte was an Atlanta-based Grammy-winning record executive and producer favored by the top names in R & B and hip-hop. He was in New York working on a secret project with a diva pop star who hadn't released a new project in more than five years and was looking to make a comeback. He called Mademoiselle for a little relaxation time to get a break from the studio.

She'd known him for years.

"Are you drunk, V. L.?" she asked.

"Nah," he said.

She didn't believe him. Alcohol or pills—didn't matter. Both were prohibited. "Where's Choc?' she asked.

"Fuck her. Send me somebody else. Let me see. I want a, uhm, light skin dip with a big ass, Mademoiselle," he said.

She frowned. "You are not pulled up to the drive-thru window of McDonald's ordering food, V. L.," she snapped, stepping off the elevator. "Don't handle me like that. Besides, you're off the list. You're not new to this."

"What? You better send somebody to get this nut," he roared.

Desdemona frowned in distaste. "Call me tomorrow when you're sober," she said, feeling worn out from just dealing with him in his altered state.

This was not the fun-loving man with whom she was familiar.

"I'm not the one for you to play that way, *Ma-dem-oiselle*," he said disparagingly.

"Be clear with your intent and your words," Desdemona warned as she stepped out of the building and walked to the curb where her car awaited, already running and warm as she gave the valet a smile of gratitude.

"I'll fuck up your whole operation," he threatened.

She pulled to a stop at the red light and put her phone on speaker. "Let me be clear. I'm the best at what I do because I am the keeper of secrets, including *yours*. I will carry what I know and whom all I know about to my grave. But allegiance is paid for with the same loyalty. See, to protect those who deserve it I will absolutely handle a traitor. Even threatening me makes you that. Do you understand me? I will *absolutely* destroy you *if* you ever threaten me or mine again. I will give you that first hiccup as a show of my grace."

The line remained quiet.

The traffic light turned green, but she remained where she sat.

"Man, I'm tripping," he said suddenly with a little laugh. "Let me sleep off this drunk."

"It's been good knowing you, V. L. and if there is anything

I can do for you, outside of adding you back to my list, you let me know," she said before ending the call with a press of her thumb to the screen.

A car horn blared behind her. She accelerated forward, steering with one hand and dialing Choc's phone with the other. Still no answer.

Choc lived in Harlem, and Desdemona pulled up her address and fed it to her GPS before she headed in that direction, eventually hopping on the FDR Drive. With traffic, it took close to forty minutes to get there. She parked two blocks down from Choc's house, wishing she had used a car service to prevent anyone—even Choc—from getting her license tag number—a direct link back to her.

Another ball dropping.

The tree-lined street was clearly gentrified with white residents strolling up the block at a leisurely pace, with no signs of mom-and-pop corner stores to be seen for miles. Whether rent or a mortgage, it was all a sign that the cost of this neighborhood was high. Choc was pre-med at NYU—another costly expense and the reason for her work as a courtesan. How could she afford this as well?

Perhaps she's not alone.

Desdemona texted her this time. "I'm outside your house. Wanted to make sure you're okay. U home?" she said aloud as she typed.

She looked up the street at the brownstone. A shadow broke up the light in the second-floor window. She was glad for the dark pitch of her tint and that none of her courtesans knew what she drove; she usually made sure of that.

Cha-ching. Cha-ching. Cha-ching.

CHOC: Coming downstairs.

Desdemona waited until the shadow disappeared from the window before she climbed from the car and locked it.

She walked up the middle of the street where the snow had been cleared, creating a path. She was just approaching the brick porch with beautiful scrolled wrought-iron railings when Choc opened the ornately carved wooden door.

Everything sung "Money, money, money, money" like the O'Jays.

She took in the tall and elegant dark-skinned woman with the looks and grace of Lupita Nyong'o as she clutched her cashmere wool coat closer to her body and came down the stairs before Desdemona could come up.

"Are you okay?" she asked, studying her face.

The left side of her face was puffy, and her eyes were red-rimmed from tears.

"I'm done, Mademoiselle," Choc said. "I didn't sign up to be hit upon."

"I am so sorry. I try my very best, I promise you, to ensure that every consort is above this kind of behavior—"

"I don't blame you. I've . . . *serviced* him before and he wasn't like that the last time," she said. "But all I could think of was something going really wrong with him—or another one—and then what would I tell my fiancé?"

Desdemona didn't hide her surprise and looked up at the building to the window where she'd seen Choc's outline.

"Yes, he's home."

"Is this new?" she asked, wondering how her intel of the woman being single had been wrong.

"Just a few months ago. It was all whirlwind," she said.

Desdemona relaxed. Not wrong. Out of date. That she could accept. "If you're sure about your decision, then I'll cancel any upcoming sessions," she said, not even trying to convince her otherwise.

"I am," she said, her eyes sad. "It was a little fun before tonight and the money was so good, but I'll just have to figure something else out to pay for school. And maybe I should have done that in the first place."

She wasn't the first—or the last—to come and then go. In fact, Desdemona never wanted any of her courtesans to make it a lifelong career.

Then why are you?

Desdemona pushed aside her inner thought and reached to squeeze Choc's hand. The woman pressed her prepaid phone into it. "Goodbye... Chelsea," she said, turning to walk away.

The winter winds whipped through her coat without a care, and she shivered from the feel of it seeming to chill her bones, but she still paused in the street to turn and make sure Chelsea had gone inside. The outline never appeared in the window again before she continued and climbed into her crossover.

She took the battery out of the cheap flip phone and tossed both onto her passenger seat before cranking the vehicle and heading toward home. She rode in silence with the occasional blare of a car horn to break up the quiet.

Her thoughts were full, and her doubts of just where her life was headed continued to nag at her. What was the end game?

Live with no regrets.

She eyed her tattoo and smiled at the effect of Loren on her life. It had been five months since he'd become her tutor and just a few weeks since she'd become his teacher. Already his enthusiasm and positive outlook on life had made such an impact on her.

And the sex!

Each time he was getting better and better.

Were they meant for a love match and relationship? Definitely not—age and her secret life were just two factors—but she simply enjoyed him. Still, with her focus on her own happiness, it seemed her eye was off the business and things were slipping through the cracks. That was dangerous for her, her courtesans, and the clients.

She wondered if she would ever get the chance to do what made her happy when the responsibility of her paramours was all in her hands.

Desdemona released a heavy breath and pulled the Maserati to a stop at the side of the building with the entrance to the residences. The coat-clad valet was Johnny-on-the-spot, and she was thankful as she gave him a smile and made her way across the pristine sidewalk and into the building.

She paused at the sight of Loren sitting in one of the club chairs lining the wall. He rose to his feet at the sight of her. "You're still here?" she asked as she walked up to him.

"I wanted to make sure you got back home safely, but I didn't want to keep calling you, so I just waited," he explained, shifting his skull cap from one hand to the other as he looked down at her. "I was worried about you."

Desdemona's breath caught and her gasp was audible, seeming to echo in the air of the lobby. Emotions flooded her, and she felt foolish as she looked down at her boots and bit her bottom lip to keep the tears that welled from falling. She couldn't remember the last time someone had looked out for her. She was always the one constantly playing chess to protect everyone else . . . and herself.

"You okay?" he asked.

Nope. You just effed me right on up.

But she nodded and blinked rapidly to beat back the telltale tears before looking up at him. "Thank you, Lo," she said, clenching her fist to keep from reaching up to stroke his chiseled cheek.

"No problem," Loren said, tugging on his hat and zipping up his coat. "I'll see you next week."

Desdemona nodded, turning to watch his classic New York stride as he crossed the foyer to the glass double door.

A fly nerd.

"Lo," she called to him.

He stopped and turned.

Her heart raced as he looked at her. All of her alarms went off. She ignored them. "It's late. You want to stay over?" she asked.

His smile spread across his lean and handsome face with the smoothness of butter on a warm biscuit.

Chapter Ten

Thursday, January 31, 2019

Do I have the courage to walk away?

Desdemona's footsteps against the hardwood floors echoed as she walked around Loren's apartment and enjoyed her first chance to learn more about him. It was a small but neat studio apartment with a brick wall and tall, brightly lit windows. Books were everywhere. There was a drawing table with sketches in various stages of completion. And she loved that he had a khaki leather sofa that converted to a bed, giving him more room during the day.

"Thoughts," Loren said from behind her at the stove in his stylish but small kitchenette where he was making them homemade beef stew and corn muffins.

"Honestly?" she asked as she stroked the jacket of the hardcover edition of *Fahrenheit 451*—the book they'd read together as if in their own little book club. She was still touched by his offer to do so.

"Always," he encouraged.

"It's decorated really well. Good job," she said.

"But..."

"It's *really* small," she added with a wince meant to take the bite off her words.

He laughed. "Yeah it is, but it's all I need. *And* I'm a doctoral student. *And* I'm grateful. I cried because I had no shoes until I met a man who had no feet. Helen Keller," he added.

"I know," she said, remembering a time when even three hundred square feet would have been a blessing. "You're right, Lo. You're always right."

"Nah. Far from it. I'm just right about what affects me because I refuse to be unhappy. Life is too short to worry, and most times if you just ask yourself one question, you'll see things from a different point of view."

She came to stand beside him at the stove, giving in to the urge to ease her hand under his T-shirt to stroke his back. "And that is?" she asked.

"Or," he said simply, looking down at her over the rim of his spectacles.

Confusion reigned. "Huh?"

He turned and leaned back against the counter, crossing his bare feet at the ankle. "Let's say you meet this woman and she is always mad at you. Just mad. You should ask yourself: *Or* is she not mad at me but having a bad day? *Or* is she sick and grouchy in general? *Or* is she going through something and could use a friend? *Or*—"

"I get it," she said, holding up a hand.

He laughed and shrugged. "If you walk around not caring about others and making everything about you—like everyone and everything is out to get you—it will turn you into a miserable person."

"Is that why you are so damn happy all the time?" she asked, tilting her head to the side as she looked up at him. "*Or* is it just your youth and the world hasn't effed with you enough to dim the sunshine for you?"

His eyes were suddenly serious. "I'll always be this way, because everything you do, think, or feel is a choice, and I choose to be happy," he said. "Do you want me to change?"

Desdemona kicked off the leather booties she wore with a fitted cream cowl-necked dress of matte jersey with a skirt down to the floor. She settled her chin on his chest as she looked up at him. "Never," she promised him, wishing she had more of his optimism.

Avoiding jail just won't allow it.

Still, the time she spent with Lo made her life feel lighter, and she found herself craving more and more of it. He was the bright spot in a life once filled with struggle. He simply made her happy to be in his company. His joy was infectious.

When he pressed both of his hands to her face and bent to kiss her lips, she clutched at his shirt and extended the kiss with several of her own.

He winked at her before turning his attention back to stirring the stew.

She picked up her shoes and set them by the door before reaching in her tote for her phones to make sure she hadn't missed a call. She was relieved to find she hadn't. She had five courtesans out at the moment. She wasn't a doctor, but she was on call.

Desdemona turned to look at Loren again, taking in his burnt orange V-neck shirt, khaki cargo shorts, and bare feet with his hair pulled back into a bushy ponytail. "Who braids your hair?" she asked, suddenly in need of that information.

"One of my homegirls," Loren said, putting a lid on the pot and wiping his hands on a black kitchen towel before draping it over the sink. "I need to call her. I washed it this morning."

"Nah," she said, mimicking his style as she sat on the sofa and pointed to the spot on the floor between her legs. "Sit."

Loren looked doubtful. "You can braid . . . with those?" he asked, eying her nails.

"Nothing elaborate like old girl but definitely two cornrows," she said, lifting the skirt of her dress to drape over her thighs. "Bring a comb, brush, and hair grease if you have it."

He did, retrieving everything from his bathroom before sitting down on the floor between her open legs. "Hand me the remote?" he asked, taking it from her when she did and turning on the large flat-screen on the wall.

They watched a marathon of *Martin* as Desdemona took her time and greased his scalp before she brushed his hair until it gleamed. Using the end of a rattail comb, she parted it down the middle and then took her time capturing the mass of hair in two straight cornrows. The ends of them were past his shoulders and automatically curled. "There," she said, twisting the cap back on the pomade before setting it on the floor beside him.

Loren reached up with his large hands to feel his hair.

"You could just go look in the mirror," she said.

Loren shook his head, turning around between her legs to get on his knees. "Now what fool would leave from between your thighs?" he asked, before bending to press hot kisses to her thighs.

Desdemona cupped the back of his head and rolled her hips. "Don't start nothing you scared to finish," she warned, opening her legs wider.

Loren cut his eyes up at her with his lips still pressed to her leg. "Maybe it's time I see what the fuss is all about," he said, his words blowing against her smooth inner thigh and evoking a shiver of anticipation.

"Uh oh," Desdemona said, playful and flirty, as she wiggled her brows—and then she was amazed that he created a space for her to be that way—playful and flirty.

Loren pressed her knees up and out, causing her lips to spread and expose her bud like it bloomed.

"Do I need to walk you through it?" she asked.

He shook his head. "I've been watching more flicks," he admitted with a wink before licking the tip of his tongue against her flesh.

She cried out, and her legs wanted to snap closed, but his hands kept them held open wide. "Lo," she gasped, wishing his hair was free so she could pull on it as he pursed his beautiful lips and sucked the quivering bud into his mouth.

And with a steady one-two motion broken up only by gentle licks he brought her to a climax so strong that she tried to back away from his unrelenting pressure, but the couch wouldn't allow it. And when he finally freed her, hearing her cries that she was near passing out, he kissed her, and she tasted herself on his lips.

"Grade, please?" he asked, his slanted eyes twinkling.

Her breathing was harsh, and her legs still quivered as she eyed him with her hand pressed to her pounding heart. "B-b-b-b-b-b-b-b plus," she said with effort.

He chuckled. "I'll get that A next time," he promised.

She could only muster enough strength for a thumbs up.

Cha-ching. Cha-ching. Cha-ching . . .

Desdemona pulled on her bright pink leather gloves before she checked her personal phone as she left the coldness of some random corner in Tribeca to climb into the back of her Lux Black. She was glad the gloves were made for touchscreen as she swiped and answered the call of her number one.

"Hello, there," she said.

"Whaddup, whaddup, whaddup," he said.

"Congrats on another win," she said, having watched the game with Loren at her condo, trying not to be amused by his near worship of the man she knew all too well.

"That's what we do," he bragged jokingly.

"Looking to celebrate?" she asked, careful of her words.

"I'm home. My girl got that," he said. "But I didn't call about that."

Her "spidey sense" tingled as she went on alert. "Okay," she said, hearing her own hesitation.

"Nothing like that," he said, laughing. "I didn't know you and V. L. had an issue."

She still didn't relax. "And how do *you* know?"

"V. L. assumed I already knew from you."

"I didn't see a need to share our personal issue with anyone. That's not what I do and that's why I am who I am for y'all. Right?" she asked.

"He wants back on the list."

She shook her head, looking out the tinted window at the Manhattan streets that were no less crowded with the light snow that had begun to fall. "No."

"Dammmmmmmn," he said. "What happened?"

"What did he say?" she asked.

"He didn't. He just said you were trippin'."

Her left eye twitched in annoyance. "Let me just say this as I ride in the back of this Lux Black—and no, I didn't mean to drop a rap bar," she teased. "Please let your boy know that it's best he just walk away from this situation and put it behind him and refrain from bashing me in any way or I will tell you and everybody else just what he did to get booted. Right now, he is still in those graces I told him about, but my patience is as thin as his receding hairline. Cool?"

"Cool. We good?"

"It would take heaven and hell merging for me and you to *ever* fall out, Number One," she said. "On some realness. I owe you too much."

"Nothing owed but friendship," he said. "And don't worry about V. L. I got that handled. Thank you for your loyalty, yo."

"'Til death," she promised, before ending the call.

"How are you today?" she said to the driver, sliding the phone into her Louis Vuitton tote.

He just eyed her in the rearview mirror and said nothing, like he was pissed.

Or...

Desdemona shook her head at Loren's influence.

"Excuse me, Paul," she said to the middle-aged man with flecks of gray in his hair. "Is everything okay?"

He eyed her again. "I'm sorry," he said. "My baby girl is sick, but we got bills and I have to work. So, I'm out here, but I rather be at the hospital. You know?"

"What's your little girl's name?" she asked, surprised because she usually hated a talkative driver, but here she was stirring the pot.

"Amiyah," he said with tears brimming in his eyes.

Tears from a man were a hard thing to see, but not as hard as it was for him to allow them to fall.

"Father God, bless Amiyah with your mercy, your grace, and your healing," she said, unable to remember the last time she'd prayed and how good it made her feel to do so.

"Amen," he said, roughly wiping each eye with the back of his hand.

They rode the rest of the way in silence. She was busy thinking Loren would enjoy her story of "Or..." when the SUV pulled up outside the extended-stay hotel she was renting for Portia until she was approved for an apartment of her own. Desdemona opened the door and came around the truck to stand at the driver's door. He lowered the window.

"Go to the hospital and be with your family," she said, handing him a stack of hundred-dollar bills.

Paul pushed it back to her with a shake of his head. "No, ma'am. I can't take that. The man in me won't allow me to take that," he stressed. "What means more to me is that prayer."

"But—"

"I have to be able to look myself in the eye every day as a man," he repeated.

"You're stubborn, but my father probably would have done the same thing," Desdemona admitted. "But what if it's a blessing and not about male and female, but just one good heart giving to another."

"Thank you but no thank you," Paul said.

"Okay," she acquiesced, stepping back from the vehicle. "I'll be thinking of your daughter."

"That means everything," he said, before waving and pulling off.

Stubborn but commendable. She admired him for his conviction.

Desdemona dropped the money back in her tote and looked at the boutique extended-stay hotel where Portia lived. The renovated seven-story townhouse on the Upper West Side housed 120 studio spaces with a community kitchen and laundry. Its brick face was charming with the neighborhood offering a good mix of people, style, culture, and convenience. The tree-lined street never bustled with too much activity. The rate for the very small studio and private bath was inexpensive in comparison to five-star hotels. So far, Portia's apartment rental applications had been rejected because she had no credit, work experience, and because of her age—even with her emancipation by the courts.

She entered the building and crossed the art deco lobby to the stairs, avoiding the elevator that was small and reminiscent of the house's first days as a home and not a hotel. She reached the second floor and walked down the tiled hall with its pale-yellow paint to knock on Portia's door at the end.

Desdemona frowned at the muffled sounds coming through the door and leaned in to listen more closely. She knocked again. Her room was no larger than a walk-in closet and there was no way to miss a knock.

Moments later the door opened.

"Hi, Ms. Smith," Portia stammered, running her hand through the tangled lengths of her Pocahontas-styled weave.

Desdemona gave the young woman a look. "Hello, Portia," she said, taking in the long robe she was holding closed with her hands. "I just came to see how you were doing. Can I come in?"

"Uhmmmm." She hesitated with a quick look back over her shoulder. "Sure."

Slick self.

Desdemona walked into the room as Portia stepped back and opened the door wider. There was just a queen-size bed with colorful linens, a modern space-saving desk with a chrome chair in the corner, and the flat-screen television on the wall. It was clean, and for that she was grateful. Teaching the young woman about hygiene and neatness had been an early struggle she thought they would never overcome.

But in the air was the smell of sex.

She walked over and opened the window, thankful for the breeze, even though it was crisp and cold. "You don't mind, do you?"

Portia shook her head as she sat down on the foot of the bed. "I was just about to call to check on the job applications I put in at the mall—"

Desdemona held up her hand and shook her head. "Boyfriend or trick?" she asked, with a heavy breath.

Portia feigned confusion. "Huh?"

Desdemona arched a brow and turned to lean over and open the bathroom door just as Portia jumped to her feet. Sitting on the commode was a half-naked white man of middle age with balding head, pot belly, and thin legs. "Trick," she decided. "Get dressed, please."

She swung the door shut.

WHAP!

Portia slumped back down on the bed. "Ms. Smith, I—"

Desdemona held a gloved finger to her lips demanding silence without saying a word. And they remained silent until the man left the bathroom fully clothed and scurried around the large bed to leave the room.

"I'm disappointed," she began, tucking her hand inside the leather trench coat she still wore. "My goal that night was to save you from your pimp and yourself. I wanted you to want more for yourself, but if I want it more than you, then I am a fool. I don't like being a fool. Explain to me why? Free rent not enough. Money every week, not enough? Clothes. Hairdo. Nails. All of it not enough?"

Portia hung her head and bit at her bottom lip as she shivered from the cold breeze tumbling through the open window.

Desdemona turned to close it.

"I am so grateful, Ms. Smith, and I still don't know why you help me so much after all this time. All of *that* stuff is enough," she said.

"Are you on drugs?" she asked, looking at her body and eyes for any telltale signs but seeing none.

"No."

"So what isn't enough?"

"It's all I know," she admitted, looking up at her. "It's familiar because everything else for me ain't."

Desdemona frowned.

"Maybe it's like a drug for me," she said. "It felt good to get his eye, work out the money, and bring him back to my room. It felt so good to me. Not him. Not the sex. I just zone out for that, but all of the rest of it. Maybe tricking is my drug because sometimes, like today, I feel like I can't stop."

"You have to find your worth in something else," she said, saying the right words but feeling like a hypocrite because she sold sex every day.

But she's not a grown woman making a conscious decision. She's a kid. She was abused and pimped. I want to save her.

How could she if she no more had the will to walk away from being a madam than Portia did to walk away from prostituting?

The commonality between them and their connection to sex work disturbed her. Desdemona headed for the door.

She paused at the door with her gloved hand on the handle. "I won't bail you out of jail," Desdemona repeated her warning from the first night they met.

"I know."

"Your rent is paid through the month and I'll give you one more, but then I'm done," she said, not looking back at her as she spoke. "You continuing to sell yourself wasn't a part of the deal."

The bed squealed as Portia jumped to her feet. "No, Ms. Smith. I'll stop."

This girl was a liability. Desdemona had never ever been arrested. Not once, and she wasn't looking to break her track record and ruin the lives of her consorts and courtesans if she was exposed by the decisions made by a reckless little girl in need of—

Help.

Desdemona shook her head. *I have too much to lose.*

"Ms. Smith, please. I won't do it again. *Please.*"

When she looked to her she hated that she saw glimpses of herself. "Find a job, Portia, and an apartment in the price range we discussed. This is my last attempt to help you," she said and just left the room, quietly closing the door.

Desdemona was in the bath with the water lapping against her body, her arms splayed and hanging over the sides as she tilted her head back.

"I feel like I can't stop."

"I feel like I can't stop."

"I feel like I can't stop."

"I feel like I can't stop."

She winced at the words echoing in her head, before sliding her bottom across the slick floor of the bath until her knees poked above the water's level and her head dipped down beneath it.

"I feel like I can't stop."

She emerged, uncaring of the water that overflowed to the heated marble floor, as she ran her hands back over her head to stop the flow of soapy water into her eyes. She wrapped her arms around her knees and settled her chin in the groove between them.

Pussy runs my life. The desire of it and for it. My mother's inability to think beyond it. My father's desire of my mother and his lack of respect for his wife's. My pimp's controlling of it. And now my control over others.

"Pussy, pussy, pussy, pussy," she said aloud softly. "I'm sick of it."

What was most troubling was not her guilt over no longer helping Portia, or her fear of leaving behind the successful—albeit illegal—business she had grown, it was that she had no one with whom to share her thoughts, her fears, and her guilt. No one who knew Desdemona "Desi" Dean.

She thought of calling Loren, but that would just be a diversion from her reality, and with Denzin discussions of her even thinking of quitting might lead to a power move on his part. She trusted no one.

No, I trust Lo. It's me that he *shouldn't trust. Plus, he's studying tonight.*

She climbed from the tub and selected one of the dozen white towels neatly rolled and stacked on the counter beside the Jacuzzi tub. She wrapped it around her nudity and grabbed another to twist around her damp hair like a turban.

For the rest of the night, Desdemona kept busy. She called and checked on Portia, who was working at a retail store in the Manhattan Mall. She rescheduled her GED test for April. Got the receipts for the dress boutique together to take to her accountant to file her taxes. She checked on the new stock Patrice wanted to order for the boutique and checked on the status of a dozen orders in queue. She ordered room service and picked over her meal of seared tuna with Asian slaw but devoured the dessert of New York cheesecake with raspberries, even raising the plate to lick at the sweet glaze. She depleted her supply of her favorite wine and turned up the music as she flung her towels away and danced around her apartment naked and carefree.

"Living my best life!" she sang along with Lil Duval as she ran down the length of her couch from one end to the other.

When Whitney Houston's song "I Will Always Love You" came on, she grabbed a lighter and sang along with her. "Oh, Nippy!" she wailed in drink-induced grief before the heat of the lighter singed her thumb.

"Shit!" she swore emphatically, dropping it and then furiously kicking it away to spin across the smooth hardwood floor.

It was Marvin Gaye's "Sexual Healing" that led her to call Loren.

"Whatchu doing, Lo?" she asked, her words slurring.

"I'm studying, remember. I have a quiz in the morning."

"I got that feeling. I want sex-u-al heal-ing," she sang with a body roll. "Come heal me, Lo. Heal me."

"Alisha?"

"Who's that?" she asked with a twisted facial expression.

Oh, that's right, he thinks that's my first name. Hell, everyone does. I'm Desi. Desdemona Dean. Thankyouverymuch.

"You okay?"

"Sex-u-al," she said, slowly winding her hips as she stood in front of the window.

"Are you drunk?"

"No! Are you?" she snapped, looking down at her phone as if he could see her as she frowned. "Come. Heal. Me."

"This is hilarious and sad all at once," he drawled.

"Your ass," she snapped before dropping the phone onto the floor and walking away in a haphazard pattern until she fell face-first onto her couch with her limbs spread.

Knock-knock-knock-knock.

Desdemona jerked her head up from the sofa and winced as every part of her body ached as she turned over.

Knock-knock-knock-knock.

Her mouth tasted sour, and the brightness of the overhead lighting hurt her eyes. Clear signs of sleep. "How long?" she asked, her throat dry and her voice raspy.

"I feel like I can't stop."

"Not that again," she said, sitting up on the sofa.

"I feel like I can't stop."

Desdemona sighed, running her hands through her hair. It was already dry. That surprised her.

Knock-knock-knock-knock.

She looked over her shoulder at her front door before rising and walking over to it, feeling weighed down by a thousand pounds. She opened the door wide.

"Hey! Ho! Hey! Hold up," Loren said, stepping inside to cover her nudity as he closed the door. "You naked little drunk."

He swung her up in his arms.

"Loooo," she sighed breathily.

He frowned and turned his head. "Whoo. That breath on fiyah!" he said.

She covered her mouth with her hands and then giggled. "My bad," she mumbled from behind her fingers.

He carried her down the hall to her bedroom and laid her down atop the bed before covering her with the soft cashmere throw at the foot of the bed.

She snuggled down under it and clutched a few soft pillows. "Lo, I love your hair braided like that," she said, opening one eye to look up at him.

"We'll talk about that later," he said, sitting on the edge of the bed and smoothing her hair back from her face. "Sober up."

She nodded, enjoying the feel of his hand and not knowing when she again slipped into slumber.

Desdemona opened her eyes, and the darkness of her bedroom startled her. She flung back the covers and sat up in bed, swinging her legs over the side. She remembered Lo carrying her to bed after she overindulged in wine. Everything before that was a blur.

Still cloaked by darkness, she remained still and enjoyed the quiet.

"I feel like I can't stop."

"So do I," she whispered into the ebony. "So do I."

The halls light turned on, and she looked to the door just as Loren leaned against the frame. "You're up," he said.

She reached over and turned on the bedside lamp, casting the room in a soft glow of light. "Just thinking through some things," she said. "I have a lot of decisions to make."

He stepped into the room, pausing to pick up her robe from the bench at the foot of the bed. "Is that what the drunkfest was about?" he asked, opening the robe to drape over her shoulders.

Giving him a smile of thanks, she eased her arms into the robe but let it hang open on either side of her body.

"You want to talk about it?"

She leaned over to lightly knock her shoulder against his. "I'm thinking about leaving my business behind," she admitted.

"Wow," Loren said in surprise. "Why? It provides you a good living."

"Just too many burdens to keep it going," she said truthfully, and feeling such sweet relief to say it. "It feels like it's weighing me down."

"Are you secure enough—moneywise—to leave it or sell it?"

Sell it? I wish.

"Yes," she said, thinking of all the money she had squirreled away over the years.

"Then take the money you've made and run toward some kind of happiness," he said as if it were all that easy.

Is it?

"What time is it?" Desdemona asked.

"Two."

"In the morning?"

He chuckled. "You went down the first time for an hour. I came over after you dropped your phone when I wouldn't come to give you some sexual healing."

She grimaced, remembering it now. "Come heal me, Lo," she mimicked herself, shaking her head and hiding her face in her hands.

"So that was an hour you lost by the time I got here, and you opened the door butt-ass naked."

"And you've been here all this time."

"Studying... and cooking dinner, or is early breakfast now?" Lo asked, rising to his feet and holding out his hand to her.

He looked good in a navy blue V-neck sweater and distressed denims. Something in her, deep in her, that she didn't want to face caused her soul to warm as she slid her hand into his and let him pull her to her feet to follow behind him.

"You do know that robe open on you like that is sexy as hell, right?" he asked without looking back.

"Absolutely," she stressed with a laugh.

Chapter Eleven

Thursday, February 14, 2019

Drugs are and will always be the devil...

"A'ight. All done. Whatchu think?"

Her hairstylist turned the chair, and Desdemona looked at her hair in a bob that flowed above her shoulders when she turned her head left and right. "Love it, MiMi," she said, running her fingers through the silk-pressed strands.

The tall and full-figured beauty with a shaven head and beautiful lips coated in red matte gave her a wink as she removed the embroidered cape. "You needed a good cut, and this fits the shape of your face so well," MiMi said, still running her fingers through the layers.

It was MiMi who had revitalized Desdemona's hair after the damage she had done to it when Zena gave up on fixing it for her. And that's why years later, wealthy or not, Desdemona still made the trek to the small Harlem salon. MiMi's skills, the soul music playing in the background, and the abundance of sisterhood and good conversation were addictive.

"Did y'all see the Grammys?" someone asked.

"Girl, *did* I?" someone else answered.

Desdemona smiled as she stood and played with her own hair in the mirror as she eyed the women laughing together. "I saw it, too," she said, reaching into her leopard print Yves Saint Laurent crossbody bag to remove the cash to pay and tip MiMi.

"See you next week," MiMi said with a smile, sliding the money into the black cape she wore before motioning for her next customer to sit in her chair.

Cha-ching. Cha-ching. Cha-ching.

Desdemona was laughing at one of the customers imitating a performer from the awards show, but she stopped as she reached in for her phone. Number thirteen. He was supposed to be having an afternoon delight with Plum at the Riverdale mansion. "Hello," she said, grabbing her wool cape and rushing from the shop, leaving behind the smell of sweet-scented spritzes, chemicals, and hot curling irons pressed to curling wax on hair.

"She's dead."

She paused on the street, causing the crowd of people to bypass her as they continued at a fast pace. "What?" she snapped, her heart hammering.

"I'm out of here. Leave me out of it."

Boop.

He hung up.

"Shit," she swore, rushing down the street, dodging people and street vendors selling everything from food to books and artwork—even surrounded by the frigid air of winter.

Desdemona reached the side street where she had parked, hating that her hands were shaking in fright as she climbed behind the wheel and started her keyless ignition. "Shit," she swore again.

She dialed Denzin, hating the tremble that caused her to

miss and hit the wrong number and have to back up and start again.

Keep it cool, Desi. Calm down. Gather yourself and keep it cool.

She released long, steadying breaths and continued to do so as she dialed him successfully.

"Hey, boss."

"I need you to go up and check on Plum. I got a call that's she's dead in the house," she said, putting the phone on speaker and setting it on her lap.

"What?!" he exclaimed.

"Go check," she said, surprised by her calm voice even as her heart pounded fast and hard.

"She's dead."

"I'm getting too old for this," she muttered as she turned the corner and eased into traffic, gripping the wheel to help steady her hands.

"Plum!" Denzin shouted. "Plum!"

She heard slapping noises.

"Come on, Plum, Wake up. Wake up," he said, his voice frantic.

"Denzin," she called out.

He didn't respond.

He must have put the phone down.

Desdemona heard a commotion and then a splash of water. She bit her bottom lip as she drove in and out of traffic trying to get to Riverdale as soon as possible, feeling helpless and hopeless.

"Boss," he said into the phone suddenly. "She's alive."

"Oh, thank God."

"She almost overdosed."

"Plum?" she asked in disbelief, thinking of the young Latina with the brightest and most infectious smile and warm disposition that made you love her on the spot. To Plum, everyone was "love" or "mama" or "baby." Everyone.

"There's heroin in the room, boss."

Desdemona came to a red light and was thankful for the chance to close her eyes and let her heart ache. Drugs. Addiction was tough. It was an illness. It was hard to kick. It was a whole new pimp. A different master.

No, Plum.

A vision from the past that left an indelible mark on her life flashed, and she shook her head to free it. To forget it. As she had done for years. As she had had to for years.

"Plum," she mouthed, feeling overwhelmingly sad at the battle the young woman would have to fight to overcome heroin.

"I'm on the way," she said softly, barely above a whisper, her eyes filling with tears as she ended the call and lowered her head to the steering wheel.

The long and steady blare of a car horn—or a few—behind her caused her to raise her head and accelerate forward. It took her twenty minutes to make it to Riverdale. She gathered herself during that time and calmly pulled her car into one of the spots inside the garage, closing and locking it behind her before she climbed out and entered the house through the side entrance.

Her steps echoed in the quiet of the house as she made her way down the hall and to the right to the elevator. What came next would not be easy, but she had prepared herself for it and was sticking to her guns.

"Hey, boss," Denzin said solemnly, leaning against the railing with his arms crossed over his bare chest, wearing nothing but sleep pants.

She gave him a smile that didn't reach her eyes as she walked up to him and squeezed his hand. "I'm responsible for y'all, you know," she said softly.

"We appreciate you, boss. Trust me," he stressed.

Desdemona looked to the open door. "Leave us alone, okay?" she asked.

"No problem."

She let her hand trail across his arm until it fell to her side as she walked away from him and into the room, closing the door behind her. Plum was sitting on the side of the unmade bed, still in a barely-there black teddy, with her hands covering her face, leaving nothing in view but her shoulder-length hair dyed her trademark plum color.

Her eyes fell to the heroin packet on the floor. There was still a bit of the drug in the corner of it.

The devil.

"Hi, Plum," Desdemona said, deciding to leave it there.

The beautiful Latina, who resembled Cyn Santana in looks and body, looked up at her. Even her ruined makeup couldn't detract from her beauty. Nor could it hide the glassiness in her eyes.

How did I miss it?

Desdemona walked over and hugged her tightly to her side. "I'm thankful you're okay, Plum," she said earnestly.

"Me too," she said.

"I honestly love you, Plum. Out of all my girls. I love you," she said, biting her lips as she felt her composure begin to slip. "You are the sweetest person I know."

The woman's shoulders began to shake.

Desdemona reached for her chin and raised her head. "*That* shit will change you," she said, twisting her head to make her look down at the heroin packet. "I would hate for it to change one single thing about you."

Tears rolled down her plump cheeks as she closed her eyes.

"I've never met *anybody* that everybody loves, Plum, except for you," she stressed with conviction. "You walk into a room and everybody smiles, *but* you gotta see your own light. There is nothing but darkness and death in that shit. You hear me?"

Plum nodded, looking at her and then looking away in

what she assumed to be shame. "I messed up," she said, her Dominican accent present.

Desdemona wiped her tears away with the sides of her thumb. "Throw that shit away, Plum," she requested, stepping back from her.

Plum eyed it and then her and then stared at it again.

With longing. With love. With hate. With reservation about breaking its hold on her.

Fight it, Plum, she silently urged from the sidelines of the battle between addiction and a desire for sobriety.

Patiently, Desdemona stood there. She lost count of the minutes that passed. She didn't rush her. She'd seen this fight before...

Desdemona danced around the apartment to Destiny's Child's "Independent Woman" as she opened all the windows and set about cleaning up the empty liquor bottles, containers from take-out food, ashtrays packed with cigarettes, and even a few used condoms. Majig's Friday night parties were infamous, making her Saturday morning cleanups a task she didn't look forward to.

But it was a part of her duties—her many duties.

Whore. Maid. Punching bag—verbally and physically. Drug mule. Flunky. Footstool. Fool. Etcetera, etcetera.

She placed her hands on her hips in the frayed denim skirt she wore with a fitted white tee with "NO BUSH... in the White House or between your thighs!" Everything was back, polished and in its rightful place. She couldn't deny that Majig had good taste. The black décor with colorful accents and chrome tables was dope.

A beautiful prison.

She hated it.

Not the amenities, clean surroundings, and never walking the streets again trying lure tricks, but the confinement. She only left the apartment once a week to run errands; other than that she was here. With him.

She looked over her shoulder and eyed the door to his master suite.

It was hell never knowing when she would get a slap, kick, or be cursed with venom. And she still turned tricks in her own room, with him charging her for half the bills. She didn't think she would ever be free of the debt or of him. When she thought of how he had lured her with lies of love, she used to ache with the pain and betrayal.

Now? After three years, the pain had faded and was replaced with her fear of him. Her slow simmering hate of him.

For the hitting.

For the tricks.

For the other young girls she watched him woo into prostitution the same way he did her.

There were moments when she felt numb—either from the neck up or the waist down. Whatever it took to survive the particular moment.

From one devil to another, *she thought, thinking of her stepmother and her early days living on the street after she ran away.*

I will never forgive her.

Knock-knock.

Desdemona looked across the space to the front door before closing in to check the peephole before opening it. "Hey, KeKe," she said to the petite woman with the fuchsia weave she wore down her back long and straight. It matched the Baby Phat jumpsuit she wore with gold heels.

"Where Jig?" she asked, before setting off a string of pops of her bubble gum.

"In his room," Desdemona said as she dropped onto the black leather sofa and used the remote to turn on the fifty-two-inch plasma television mounted on the wall.

KeKe sat on the other end of the couch, opening her Guess purse to pull out a prerolled blunt and a lighter. "You in?" she asked as she lit it.

Desdemona had enough battles she was fighting without taking on addiction of any kind.

She just shook her head and continued flipping through the channels.

"I need to talk to Jig," KeKe said before releasing a stream of smoke.

"He's in there . . . if you want to wake him up."

KeKe looked at her like she had three heads. "Last time I did I wound up with a bruised rib and bust lip. So that's a no."

Humph. Been there. Learned that painful lesson.

"What you need?" Desdemona asked.

"I want to get at some bigger fish," KeKe said, rubbing her fingers together and causing her long acrylic nails to hit against each other. "More money."

Desdemona eyed her. Over the years Majig had grown his ring from streetwalkers to call girls and escorts. He didn't take lightly shifting a girl up to the next level. "You think you're ready?" she asked.

"Hell, yeah," KeKe said with enthusiasm. "I know my pockets are."

They shared a laugh.

KeKe had been tricking for Majig for two years and usually worked Desdemona's old stomping ground between the liquor store and the Chinese restaurant. Her money was consistent. Never late. Weed was her strongest vice, and she was funny.

"I'll tell you what," she said, following her gut. "There's a party tonight at that strip club on Vine."

"I know the place."

"Good. Go there. Look for a dude named Gary. Tell him Majig sent you, put in that work for free, and let's see what he thinks of you."

KeKe took a deep inhale before she released the smoke and looked at her through squinted eyes. "Damn. You running shit up and through here now?" she asked.

"Definitely not. I just help him out here and there when he's busy, but this is Majig's ship. I just crew. You know?"

Busy meant high. What started out as something he did to help party and relax had become more of a problem lately.

KeKe looked skeptical. "Right," she said, sounding unsure.

She was right to feel that way.

The last five months Majig had taught her the ins and out of running his prostitution ring. She took to it like a fish to water, even making changes that further protected Majig, increased his income, and weeded out bad call girls and clients. With each day he was releasing more and more of the control as the drugs gained the power over him.

"You in?" Desdemona asked.

"I'm in," KeKe said, releasing another thick stream of silver smoke before she pulled out a bankroll to toss into Desdemona's lap before she stood, retreated to the front door, and left.

Desdemona twisted the money in her hand as she rose and walked down the long hall to toss the money inside a glass bowl on a small table outside his door. By the end of the day, it would triple.

Desdemona was walking back up the hall when she heard a crash. She stopped and turned in alarm. Her eyes were on the door. Knocking on it when he was in the wrong mood could lead to hits and kicks that would leave her in pain and bruised—if not worse. There were times she wondered if he would kill her during one of his tirades. She literally scratched her scalp as she debated checking on him before she turned and took a few steps.

What if he needs my help and blames me because I didn't?

She paused.

Lately, if he wasn't raging, he was stumbling or nodding off from his heroin high. What had started as recreational use had turned into an addiction. Every day his grasp on the drug weakened, and it overpowered him. It was why he entrusted her with so much of the business: most days he was too high to care.

She ran her fingers through her hair as she walked back to the door. With a lick of her lips, she lightly knocked. "Majig? You up?" she asked, hating the fear that sped her heartbeat. Hating that she was already flinching from the thought of him opening the door and backhanding her; she took a step back.

But there was no answer.

Maybe he's in the bathroom.

Or maybe he fell.

She turned the knob and eased the door open slowly. She saw his feet first. He was on the floor. Pushing the door open wider, she stood in the doorway and gasped at the sight of his naked body on his side with his arm extended and a syringe still in his vein. He grunted. It was so soft she barely heard it. His eyes were dazed and staring off. His lips were tinged blue. He was sweaty. His breathing was raspy. Drool stretched between his mouth and the floor.

He was overdosing.

She took a step forward.

Wait.

Desdemona paused. She felt like she could hear the pounding of her heart dominate the quiet as death neared. She blinked as moments of his abuse, control, and manipulation came back in a rush. To save him was to continue to enslave herself.

His breathing slowed.

Help him.

"No," she answered herself.

She thought of other young women falling prey to his lies and getting entrapped in a world of sex for money when they thought they were getting love.

I thought I was getting love.

Three years had passed since that night at the laundromat. How much more time in her life did he believe belonged to him? How many more bust lips, black eyes, bruised ribs, broken arms were in store for her? How many more rapes? How much more disrespect?

This is my escape.

A tear raced down her cheek. In truth, it wasn't for him, but for herself. The very fact that her life now was at a crossroads, choosing his death or her freedom, was pathetic.

With a rush she stepped out of the room and closed the door, turning to press her back to it as she covered her mouth with her hand and looked up at the ceiling. Frantic. Unsure. Guilty. Panicked. Afraid.

She slid down the door and sat, drawing her knees to her chest.

Instinctively she reached to her throat for her heart-shaped locket. It wasn't there. He had snatched it from her neck years ago and hid it away, knowing it meant the world to her.

She thought of her parents.

Neither would want this life for her, but would they agree with letting a man die?

Help him, Desi.

She scrambled to her feet and opened the door.

Too late.

He lay still. There was no breathing. His eyes lacked life.

I'm free.

She covered her mouth with her hand again, flooded with guilt at that thought. She stepped into the room, and her eyes scanned the room for the cordless phone. In the middle of his bed was a small safe that was open and unlocked. She gave his body an anxious look before stepping over his feet and moving over to the king-size bed, peering down into the metal box.

There were some money and a notepad. As she opened it, her eyes widened at the list of names and phone numbers she found. His client list for the escorts and call girls.

She turned and picked up the cordless phone, calling 911. The entire time she reported the apparent overdose of her "boyfriend" in their apartment, her eyes were locked on that safe.

He owes me.

After ending the call, she picked up the safe and left the room, giving his dead body one last look before closing the door. The weight of the safe in her arms was nothing to the weight she now felt on her shoulders.

Desdemona reached for her locket on her bracelet. Most times she repressed that memory of her death-filled last moments with Majig. Looking on as Plum struggled with her own heroin addiction brought it all back home. She didn't want her to lose the battle, but she had to want it for herself.

Like I did. It was my freedom or his power over me.

Choose yourself, Plum. Please.

Plum released a long, heavy breath as she rose to her feet. She smirked. "When it's good I love it. When it's bad I hate it, but I need it to stop feeling bad," she admitted, casting Desdemona a brief look before fixating on the drug again. "Chicken or the egg, you know?"

She remained quiet.

Plum stepped over and stooped down to pick it up. "You almost killed me," she said, stroking the clear bag with her thumb as she walked over to the bathroom.

Desdemona looked on as Plum raised the bag to her mouth and kissed it before dropping it into the commode and flushing it away. She felt flooded with relief. *There's hope.*

Plum continued looking down into the commode. "Something in me wishes I could dive down there," she said.

"That's your brain," Desdemona said, walking over to her. "You have to reprogram it not to crave it."

The woman's eyes shifted up to the mirror over the commode.

"You're fired, Plum," Desdemona said, forcing firmness into her voice. "But I will pay for you to go to rehab—ninety days or more—to get rewired so you don't *think* you love it."

Plum's face crumbled with her emotions, and she covered it with her trembling hands.

"And when you get out, I will give you the same amount of money you normally make in three months to help you get on your feet," she finished, eyeing her reflection. "But you'll never work for me again, and I don't think this line of work is for you anymore."

"I wanna go," she whispered through her fingers.

"Tonight," Desdemona stressed.

She nodded.

"Okay, I'll be right back. Stay here." Desdemona walked across the room but hesitated and turned. "How'd you beat the drug test?"

Plum gave a slight smile. "I used to wait to get high until after the monthly test," she said.

A flaw in her plan.

"Just that simple," Desdemona admitted.

Plum shrugged one shoulder.

She turned and left, leaving the door ajar.

Denzin had waited and turned as she entered the hall.

"Stay with her. I'm going to try to get her in a ninety-day program tonight," she said to him softly.

He nodded, his eyes troubled. "I will."

As soon as he was back inside the room with Plum, Desdemona allowed her knees to buckle a bit as she gripped the railing and looked down at the foyer below. She closed her eyes, hating that she so clearly recalled Majig's dead pose.

It was a secret she shared with no one how she had stepped in to claim Majig's throne. Instead, she focused on changing the game, in how she treated the women who *chose* to remain working for her. But it took a long time for her to accept and reconcile that she had done what she had to do.

Remembering that, she stiffened her back, squared her shoulders, and locked her knees. There was no shame in choosing herself.

As soon as Lo opened the door, Desdemona stepped into his embrace. She didn't care how it looked or how he interpreted it. She wanted—needed—to be wrapped in his goodness. His sweetness. His kindness. Everything.

"Awww," he said, pressing a kiss to her temple as he walked them back into his apartment to close the door. "Bad day?"

"Horrible day," she said, snuggling her face against his neck. "That's why I'm so late."

Plum was finally checked in to a ninety-day program in Connecticut. Desdemona had driven her there herself, never once leaving her side. Now all she could do was hope—and pray—for the best.

"Heal me?" she asked, tilting her head back as she rose up on her toes and kissed his mouth.

He rocked their bodies back and forth. " 'When I get that feeling, I want sexual healing,' " he sang near her ear. It was deep, low, and on key.

Desdemona leaned back. "Is there anything you don't do well?" she asked teasingly.

"You tell me," Lo said.

"Not a thing," she said. "You're *almost* ready for your finals."

"Almost?" he balked, backing them over to the sofa bed that was pulled out and made.

She straddled his lap after he sat down. "The Perfect Lover is a weighty title, you know?" she asked, with a smile she tried to hide as she playfully massaged his shoulders.

"So is claiming to be a woman perfect enough in bed to teach him to be the Perfect Lover," Loren countered, chuckling as he snaked his hands under her dress to cup her soft buttocks.

"I haven't even taught you all my tricks, lightweight," she teased, removing his glasses to toss onto the bed as she studied his eyes with her own.

They're beautiful.

"What more is there?" he asked.

Oh, you beautiful innocent.

"We'll get to that," she said, deciding not to overload his mind.

"Okay," Lo acquiesced.

Desdemona smiled at him as she dug her fingers through his wild and curly Afro to stroke his scalp.

He reached to pick up a small wooden box from a wooden slab serving as a shelf on the brick wall behind the sofa. He removed a prerolled blunt and a lighter.

"You smoke?" she asked in surprise.

"To relax. Maybe once a week, sometimes not at all," he explained, lighting the end of the blunt. "Only weed. No lacing. No chemicals. Only quality herb."

"Every time I think I have you figured out you peel back another layer, Loren Palmer," she said.

He took a long toke and then released the silvery smoke through his nostrils before offering her the blunt. She shook her head. "I don't partake," she said.

"Cool," Lo said. "I got something for you to relax to anyway."

He reached across the bed for a remote and pressed a button. Moments later, the first sweet refrain of Chopin's "Nocturne, Opus 55, Number 1" began to play.

She gasped and then smiled sweetly in surprise. "You remembered me telling you I love this?" she asked.

He nodded as he took another toke. "It's pretty dope, actually," he said.

Desdemona closed her eyes and gave in to the music, not even caring that his smoke surrounded her head as if she were in a cloud as she wrapped her arms around his neck and leaned back. "It's so haunting. So delicate. Hopeful and sad all at once," she whispered. "It's like the pianist is barely touching the keys. Barely stroking them. So gentle. I just love it. And then the middle—this part right here—is like a beautiful storm that sudden erupts as he pounds the keys a little harder and picks up the pace. Do you hear it?"

"I hear it," he agreed.

The music ended, and she released a satisfied breath as she eyed him through the smoke and shook her head. "Play it again," she requested. "Please."

He did. Several times.

She enjoyed the music and he his blunt as they embraced or kissed or just stared at each other.

* * *

Lo closed his eyes and moaned. "So, we're just pretending it's not Valentine's?" he asked, opening one eye to peek at her.

She tilted her head back and looked up at the ceiling, avoiding his look. "Yes," she said lightly. "I have never celebrated V-Day before and I don't plan to."

"You've never had me in your life before."

The feel of cool metal on her chest and his warm fingers at the back of her neck caused her to look down at the necklace he had just fastened around her neck. Dangling from it was a small but beautiful 3-D butterfly charm. She stroked it with her thumb.

"Don't think of it as a Valentine's—"

She gave him a meaningful look.

"V-Day," Lo stressed, correcting himself. "Don't think of it as a V-Day gift. I know you're not my girl and never want to be. We're friends and I'm grateful for your help. There are different kinds of love to be celebrated this day, even friendship. So happy V-Day, *friend*."

"Thank you for my very first V-Day gift ever," Desdemona said with meaning, locking her eyes with his as she pressed her hands to his face and leaned in to kiss him. "*Friend*."

They laughed together. Softly. Warmly.

He kissed her. "With benefits?" he asked, his words touching her lips.

She reached for the hem of her dress and pulled it over her head. "Oh, yes," she assured him.

"Good."

"Good?" she asked.

"Great," he said, sucking her bottom lip.

She shivered. "I agree."

They laughed together and kissed as Loren turned his body to press hers down onto the bed. He left her just long enough to slowly remove his clothing as he eyed her body stretched out on his bed. When he pressed a knee to the bed between her legs, she spread them long enough to welcome his weight down atop hers, her heels digging into the flesh of his buttocks and her hands twisting in his hair. The streetlight outside illuminated them as he entered her smoothly and swiftly. She gasped into his open mouth at the feel of him stroking against her walls with a slowness that was addictive.

Their breaths were panted.

Their eyes locked on each other.

Their hearts pounded wildly.

Stroke by stroke by stroke.

She circled her hips and matched his rhythm. "Lo," she sighed, lightly biting his shoulder.

"Say my name again," he demanded, raising up to look down at her, the rapture on her face like a wild animal's with the intensity of a hunter on its prey.

"Lo, Lo, Lo, Lo, Lo," she moaned, biting her lip as she met his stare.

Their chemistry was off the charts, and nothing at all what she had expected as they shared kisses and whispered praises as they made love. Slowly. Deeply.

And when the anticipation of their rising climaxes quickened their moves, they clutched at each other's bodies, quivering and gasping as they gave in to the white-hot pleasure of release. Together. It seemed endless. They didn't rush it. Slow stroking to one climax that left both shaken, spent, and speechless.

Chapter Twelve

Monday, March 4, 2019

The only difference between "hoes" and "whores" is not the number of lovers, but whether you charge or not . . .

Desdemona stood at the full-length mirror and stroked her butterfly charm as she looked at her reflection. It was delicate and beautiful. And troubling.

The last thing she wanted was for Loren to expect more from their liaisons. She was teaching him, and he was fulfilling her sexual needs. That was it.

Beautiful, thoughtful gifts were a complication to a simple plan.

"Come back to bed."

She smiled at Loren in the reflection as he stood behind her and wrapped an arm around her waist to lightly jerk her nude body back against his. She felt his growing hardness nestled against the divide of her buttocks and reached up to stroke the side of his face as he kissed her shoulder and brought his hand up to warmly cup her breast and lightly stroke the taut, brown nipple.

Desdemona shivered, seeing her desire heat her eyes in the mirror. "I wanted to take a shower," she said softly. "You were sleeping."

"I could get lost in the scent of you," he said. "Do you smell this good everywhere?"

"I guess so," she said, biting her bottom lip.

He came around her body and kneeled, lifting one of her legs over his shoulder as he nuzzled his face against her clean-shaven mound. He kissed it before tilting his head back to look up at her. "Madam, may I?" he asked, his voice deep and sexy.

Desdemona's body went stiff as her eyes widened. "What? Huh? W-w-w-what did you say? Huh?" she asked, jumping back and then falling backward when she forgot her leg on his shoulder.

She landed on the floor on her back with an *umph*. She closed her eyes in embarrassment as some pain radiated across her body.

"What happened?" Loren asked. "Are you okay?"

She opened her eyes, and his closeness, as he stood between her sprawled legs looking down at her, was startling. *Breathe, Desi, breathe.*

He extended his hand and she took it, letting him help her to her feet.

"Why did you call me that?" she asked, trying to sound aloof.

"What? Madam?" Lo asked, his handsome face filled with his confusion.

She nodded.

"I didn't want to call you Mother," he explained. "You know the game 'Mother, May I'? My bad. I was trying to be playful."

Her mouth widened in understanding, and she felt herself

relax with relief. "Oh," she said, drawing it out as she lightly touched his chest. "I get it."

Loren relaxed as well. "Besides, I wouldn't disrespect you by calling something so lowlife as a madam," he balked. "That's a female pimp out there selling souls and not caring. All for the sake of money."

Her steps faltered, and she squinted at his judgment. If he felt so strongly, he might even call the police. "You don't feel a woman has a right to do what she wants with her body?" she asked, knowing a heated debate might lead to her slipping and revealing her truth.

His judgment stung, whether he knew he was insulting and degrading her or not.

Well, damn.

She turned and walked into her bedroom, leaving him with her question as she pulled on a black silk robe.

"Of course I do, but there are a lot of women who believe their worth lies between their thighs and twice as many being forced into prostitution via sex trafficking," Loren said, coming into the room behind her and walking to his side of the bed to retrieve his glasses. "Not to mention the kids in the middle who think they're in control of their bodies and foolishly don't realize they are being used and demeaned. No one should be paid for sex. It's revolting."

Desdemona was brushing the tangles from her soft hair. She paused as she looked across the width of the bed at him as he searched under the covers for his discarded boxers. She bit the inside of her cheek but failed to hold back her thoughts. "Prostitution is the world's oldest profession, and you don't feel women played a powerful role in any of that."

He stood erect with boxers in hand and then jerked them on. "There were African tribes who helped sell their kinsmen into slavery and that damn sure didn't make it right," he said, seeming to be annoyed. "Complicity isn't the ultimate co-sign that something is okay."

At the moment she felt intimidated by his intelligence and unable to piece together a solid argument against his opinions. "I just think men shouldn't tell a woman she has to do whatever he chooses with her body," she said, turning and leaving the room with a quick pace toward the kitchen.

Her body felt warm with embarrassment, shame, and anger. She poured herself a large glass of wine and took a sip.

"You do understand that the ones who agree to prostitute themselves and give off this ridiculous notion of empowerment help to create a culture where men think all women or gay men want to be sexualized?" Loren asked, his face incredulous. "Thus, leading to assholes willing to trick, kidnap, or brutalize someone else into selling themselves. One begets the other."

Desdemona thought of her own story, Portia's, and so many more. She felt overwhelmed. Her thoughts were muddled. She refused to believe she was no better than Majig and so many other brutal pimps. It wasn't the same.

One begets the other.

"Never mind, Lo. Just let it go," she said, sounding—and feeling—weary.

He crossed the kitchen to take the wineglass from her for a sip.

Desdemona eyed him and how comfortable he was in her kitchen. In her life. He denied it constantly, but she knew he wanted more from her—even if it was more time—and she had to bring it to an end. Their conversation really brought it home that she could never be more with him. *He doesn't even know me. The real me. My name. My profession. My background. How I make my living? How I try so very hard not to be what Majig was to me?*

He came over and hugged her close, setting his chin lightly atop her head as he rubbed her back.

Desdemona closed her eyes and allowed herself to enjoy the feel and smell of him. She tilted her head back, and he kissed her mouth. All of the sensitive spots on her body pulsed as if charged with a bolt of electricity.

"You're beautiful," he said, low in his throat, as his eyes—those damn sexy, slanted eyes—studied her face.

"Thank you," she said, her voice barely above a whisper.

As she looked at him she felt sad, because she knew it was best for them both to end it. Things had gone far beyond what she had planned. And in truth, it wasn't just Lo. She had begun to see him as familiar. Wanted. Needed. That was scary.

There was no room for him in her world, and in his, there was no space for her past. Not with acceptance and understanding.

"My GED test is coming up next month," she began.

"You still ready?" Loren asked, combing his fingers through her hair to press his fingertips to her scalp

Even that tingled from his touch.

Bananas.

She shrugged one shoulder. "I think I've done all I can for you," she said, hating that she was unable to meet his eyes. "So now I can focus on me for a little bit and get ready . . . on my own."

Desdemona felt him stiffen against her before he stepped back, breaking their hold.

Loren nodded a few times as he looked around the kitchen at anything. Everything. "I get it, Ms. Smith," he said, reverting back to formality. "Thank you."

"You're very welcome," she replied, deserving an Oscar for her performance of indifference.

"I better get dressed and get out your way," he said, failing at keeping the stiffness from his tone.

She remained stoic. It wasn't easy, but she did not fail.

Not long after, he strolled into the kitchen in his jean jacket over a dark blue T-shirt, matching denims, and throwback Jordans. He stopped in the entry and looked across the distance at her. "Good luck on your test," he said, looking at her.

"Thank you, Lo," she said. "And good luck with your final in a couple of months."

He raised his eyebrows and nodded his head like "Oh, it's like *that*. Cool." His handsome face was cold, his jaw square and his eyes fiery. He gave her nothing else but a head nod before he turned and left.

The door closed. It seemed to echo.

She covered her face with her hands. Waves of emotions flooded her, weakening her knees and unsteadying her hands. The very thought of never seeing him again sent her to the floor with her back pressed to the cabinets. It was hours before she finally rose and crawled into bed, pulling the covers over her head.

Two weeks later, Desdemona knocked on the front door of the four-story Upper East Side townhouse as she held a pile of dresses in bags across her arm. As she awaited an answer, she took in the home's street-level garage, ensuring easy access by vehicle without having to give up privacy. She shook her head at the cleverness of a scoundrel.

The door opened.

Desdemona turned and eyed the beautiful redhead standing there completely surprised. "Well, hello there, Red," she said.

"Hi, Mademoiselle," she said, casting a nervous look over her shoulder.

"Tell Mr. Garrett I'd like to speak with him, please," she said as she pressed the dresses to the woman's chest and stepped past her inside the house.

Red struggled to keep them from sliding down her body to the polished hardwood floor. "Mademoiselle—"

"I don't have all day, Red," she said gently, walking over to take a seat on one of the sofas that helped to make up the

French country design. She set her tote on the floor beside her feet.

"Please don't do this," Red pleaded, draping the dresses over the back of the opposite sofa.

"Do what?" Desdemona asked. "You don't even know why I'm here. In your new home. And new life."

"Who was at the door?"

Both women turned to the entryway as Hunter Garrett, ultra-conservative Republican pundit and new host of his own show on cable, entered the room. He was shorter than Red by nearly a foot and desperately in need of a toupee or a full-on haircut to finish what nature started. He was almost as red as her hair as he eyed her sitting there.

"Mademoiselle, what are you doing here?" Hunter asked, buttoning the monogrammed sleeve of his shirt as he continued into the living room.

"Your phone seems to have stopped working, Hunter," she said. "And we need to settle up some business. Alone."

Desdemona and Hunter shared a hard stare. Red looked from one to the other.

"Red, I would love some bagels for breakfast," he said, not breaking their stare.

Another look between the adversaries was cast before Red picked up her purse and keys from the sofa table and left the townhouse.

Desdemona waved a hand to the sofa across from where she sat.

He chuckled and shook his head at her taking the lead in his home as he came to claim the seat.

"Respect is given where respect is earned," Desdemona began, crossing her legs in the black-and-white-striped Valentino dress she wore, with its flared short skirt's stripes in a different direction from the top.

His eyes dipped to her exposed legs as if invited by the move.

He was mistaken.

"And you find it respectful to come uninvited to the home of—"

"*Your* concubine," Desdemona inserted smoothly, tilting her head to the side as she crossed her hands and set them atop her knee. "*My* former courtesan."

Hunter crossed his legs as well. "Her choice."

"By your invitation...and that's fine, but that leaves a debt to be paid," she said. "Because neither of you handled this appropriately. There was no respect for me, my business, my time, or my financial stability because you two want to play house in your silly little townhouse that your even sillier wife knows nothing about... *yet*."

He stiffened in his seat. "Are you threatening to blackmail me?" he asked, his voice hard.

Desdemona offered him a smile. "Definitely not who I am. It has always been my job to protect my clients, and that doesn't end because a wolf like you stole one of the chickens from the coop. I'm here to prove to you that you are not slick or being smart or protected by this move. I found you. Others can. She may. That's all."

Hunter nodded as he adjusted his tie. "What do you want, Mademoiselle?"

"What I'm owed for the miles you are about to put on Red's pussy for free."

He held up his hands, motioning about the room. "Does any of this look free to you?"

"No, it just looks temporary for Red," she countered quickly. "The place to stay and pretty clothes and fancy food and accepting being hidden away... until you're tired of her."

He smirked.

"And until you pay me what you owe for the privilege of meeting her through me, then yes, it's free," Desdemona assured him.

"And if I don't pay you?"

"Then you're no longer just my ex-consort but also a thief, and thus no longer have access to my protection of your secrets," she said, arching a brow as she tilted her chin up a notch and eyed him with an unrelenting stare. "Fifty thousand should do it once and for all."

Another stare between them. This one more hostile.

He released a heavy breath as he rose. His steps echoed against the quiet.

"And Hunter?" she said, reverting to his first name as a clear show of equality.

He paused.

"Betrayal cannot be met with loyalty."

She could count to ten before his steps resumed.

Desdemona looked up at the sound of his footsteps nearing. For a brief second, she imagined him nearing her with a gun in his hands instead of cash.

Pow!

She blinked, finding him handing her the money instead. She removed her portable cash counter from her pocketbook, giving him a smile as she fed it the money and verified the amount. "Thank you," she said, then rising from the seat to walk over to the rear of the other sofa to select two dresses from the stack. "I already charged the card you had on file for those two dresses. C.Y.A. all day. Right?"

He just clenched his lips so tightly that the skin around them blanched.

"Your info will be deleted today, and you will never see or hear from me again, Hunter."

"Good," he mumbled.

The front door opened, and Red entered, looking warily between them as she held a small brown paper sack.

"Red, can I talk to you for a second to say goodbye? Alone," Desdemona said.

The ginger looked hesitant before giving Hunter a look begging his permission.

Hunter threw his hands up in exasperation. "Get it over with and get her the fuck out of here, Red," he said before leaving the room with short, angry strides.

"I had every right to quit," she began. "You said anything you did for us was a gift and not something to be repaid or held over our heads."

Desdemona nodded. "Absolutely true, Red," she said. "Or should I call you Kevna now?"

"I'm still Red to him," she said with the hint of a smile.

"And to you?" Desdemona asked. "Who are you? Or have you given up on your dreams of selling luxury real estate? Because sitting here waiting for him at his whim and his wife's allowance will lead to you taking your eye off the ball."

Red looked down at her feet as she continued to hold the bag of bagels. "I'll get back to it one day," she said, not sounding like she believed it herself.

"And he is giving you a stipend while you quit work?"

"It's not like that with him, Mademoiselle. I love him," she said earnestly.

Good grief.

"Never forget that you matter, Kevna," she said, intentionally using her real name.

The woman looked up at her.

"Any person entirely relying on someone else for money is foolish," Desdemona said, reaching in her tote for the money. "Since I failed in teaching you that, little girl, I decided to look out for you."

Desdemona removed five thousand dollars from the stack to keep as a finder's fee and crossed the space between them to drop the rest atop the bagels in her bag. "That's forty-five thousand I just convinced your great love to pay me for stealing you from my roster. I only did that to ensure your naïve behind has a nest egg tucked away for the day he decides he's just as tired of you as he is of his wife," she said, walking over to bend the rest of the dresses over her arm. "Or if you decide you're ready to leave and want a little something to help you do it. Either way, never contact me again."

Desdemona retrieved her tote and headed to the front door.

Red reached out and grasped her wrist. "Thank you," she stressed.

She nodded. "Going forward, be smarter," she advised before taking her leave.

Desdemona pressed her fingers to her mouth and then touched her father's side of the standing headstone. She clung to it, looking down at his name engraved in the marble. It had been years since her last visit to his gravesite. Her reasoning was twofold. Coming there brought home to her that his body looked nothing like it did when he lived. Then to top it off, seeing that the other side of the headstone was still empty meant his wife—Zena—was still alive somewhere in the world.

She hadn't seen her since the night she ran away and was perfectly fine with keeping it that way. Dead or alive, Zena was of no consequence to her. On her twenty-first birthday, she had strolled into the office of Hervey Grantham and staked a claim to the balance of her father's estate. She used it to expand her business and truly elevate from streetwalkers and call girls to her paramours once Number One gave her the co-sign and the wealthy consorts started calling.

She rarely thought of the woman who had made her life hell, and hated the reminder that she wasn't skidding on her own path to literal hell yet.

To hell with her and her coordinates. I'm here for my daddy.

Of late, the painting on her mantelpiece didn't suffice to feed her hunger for her parents, so a visit was warranted. It was her father she remembered most.

"I'm tired, Daddy," she whispered, still stroking his headstone. "Not the 'I'm tired and I'm ready to off myself and see you in heaven' level of tired, but just ready for a change. Newness. Other. You know?"

She gave the marble one last pat before walking along his grave to sit on the marble bench she had added to the foot of his grave years ago. Crossing her ankles, she tilted her head to the side. "I do wonder if you are proud of me, even though I know you wouldn't be. You're not. I'm sure you're somewhere in heaven frowning, but no one is perfect. Not even you and Mama, but I love you both so much anyway, so I can only hope you both have the same grace for me."

The spring winds blew her hair back from her face, and the scent of the graveyard's gardens filled the air. She allowed herself a moment to enjoy both, closing her eyes and inhaling deeply.

"Is Loren right? Am I a part of the bigger problem?" she asked in a whisper, giving life to the seeds of doubt he had planted that last day they shared in her home.

"One begets the other."

"Whatever," she muttered.

I'm good to people. Even when they aren't good to me. Even when life hasn't been good to me, Daddy.

A beautiful multicolored butterfly fluttered up to her before landing on her knee. She smiled. It was the first she'd seen of the creatures since winter finally began to thaw.

A symbol of change.

She stroked the tattoo on her inner wrist when the insect rose and flapped away. Live with no regrets. Lately, she felt she had plenty.

Cha-ching. Cha-ching. Cha-ching.

She crossed her legs and reached for the phone from the side pocket of her Vuitton bag. Number thirty.

"Hello," she said, forcing lightness into her tone. "I haven't heard from you in a while."

"Work has kept me busy, but now I need to unwind," Jason Reedman said.

"Absolutely. The whole weekend, like always?" she asked, shifting her eyes up to the sky.

He chuckled. "Yes, the wife is away for the weekend, so it's time to play," he said, sounding amused.

She opened her mouth to say something cute and flirty, but the words would not come, and the aversion to his glee about cheating on his wife was new to her.

Is helping a husband cheat on his wife my fault, too? How, when he would just get to someone else? He chooses to cheat. He chooses to love the beauty of a woman with a stiff dick. I don't make him or any of the others disrespect their vows.

She rolled her eyes heavenward, enjoying a rather comical image of choking Loren until his head popped off his neck and floated away like a balloon. His effect on her thoughts and beliefs, even subconsciously, was more far-reaching than she ever imagined. It had been two weeks since she had sent him out of her life, but his imprint remained.

Damn it.

"Mademoiselle?"

"Yeah? Yes," she said, softening her tone as she stroked her brows. "I'll get it all set up and call you back with details."

"Perfect."

Desdemona was glad when they ended the call. Nothing was perfect. Not this deal. Not life. Not love. None of it. She learned early that every situation was a series of making the best out of it as possible. "Y'all taught me that," she said, looking down at the ground beneath which her father's body lay. "And so have all of the people I have met over the years. So many people trying to improve their lives in the best way they think they can, and I try not to burden them with the brutality or coercing or disrespect that I got. All of the women—and some men—who went on to live better lives with better careers. People who are happier than they were when I met 'em. Hell, like Franco, who wants to save up the money for gender reassignment surgery. There are two sides to every story, and on this side of it, I did my best to make people happy, Daddy. Doesn't *that* matter?"

I should have said that to Loren, but no, I couldn't. Not without revealing a piece of my life closed off to him.

"Why is a woman who chooses to prostitute of her own free will any worse than women who plot to marry wealthy men or those who have numerous lovers because it feeds their ego? So, a woman who freely fucks is more honorable than one who charges?"

It was always easy to argue with someone after the argument was done. She had all the proper responses for Loren now. *It doesn't matter. It's done. We're done.*

Desdemona looked around at the many graves surrounding her. "Daddy, I *really* gotta get some friends," she muttered with a little chuckle and self-deprecating shake of her head.

Desdemona tapped the end of her sharpened pencil against the page of the GED prep workbook as she looked out the windows at her view from where she sat at the dining room table. She was finding it hard to ignore just how much time she and Loren had spent in the very same spot—she studied and he sketched.

This absence was so different from the time he ended their tutoring sessions through an email. What had once been missing a fun person in her life was a longing for a lover. And her hunger for him—the all of him—was a hundred times worse under her very own roof.

Memories of him were everywhere, left behind like a haunting spirit. Tempting her. Making it hard to forget him.

"Shit," she swore, dropping the pencil and raising her reading glasses to press the bridge of her nose.

Her life felt like that Deborah Cox song because she

wanted to know how he got there when nobody was supposed to be there. Not love. But definitely in her life, filling the man space so easily that now she missed him. That wasn't a part of the plan.

She got up from the table and walked across the space and down the bending hall to her bedroom. The bed was neatly made, but sitting on the bench at the foot was a pillow. She picked it up and pressed her face into it to inhale deeply of the scent of him that still clung to it. She hadn't washed the pillow since the day he left. Same pillowcase and all.

And sometimes, late at night in her bed, or in a bath, she remembered him stroking inside her with ferocity and brought herself to an explosive climax that made her want him—in her bed and her life—even more. She still had so much to teach him about making love.

And he could have kept pushing me to live life to the fullest. To smile, laugh and be carefree.

Desdemona put the pillow down and went to her walk-in closet, opening the top drawer of the island. There atop the velvet lining with her expensive jewelry lay the necklace Loren gave her. She stroked the butterfly, loving the thoughtfulness behind his gift but dismayed that it reminded her of him, making the longing more intense.

My first V-day—Valentine's Day—*gift at thirty-five.*

She closed her eyes with a soft grunt at the love they made that night. The Chopin and weed smoke blended in the air above and around them as they slow-stroked to one small climax after another until the final explosion that left them both shivering and weak.

I want to feel that way again.

Desdemona closed the drawer and hopefully memories of Loren.

In the kitchen, she poured a glass of Rieussec. In the dining room, she reclaimed her seat at the dining table and tried to resume her studies. When they failed to hold her attention, she made her way back to her bedroom and pulled up his Instagram account on her iPad.

Most were pictures of his sneakers with the hashtag #sneakerhead or of his different hair designs. Funny memes. Black history knowledge. Anti-Trump retweets. Covers of books he's reading. Motivational quotes. A few big-butt beauties as his women crush Wednesday. Very few selfies.

She stopped at one of him in a suit and tie with his ankle crossed over his knee showing off his patterned socks and dope hard-bottom shoes. His hair was wild and his glasses were thin and gold, making the picture even more savage and sexy. "Future professor," she read his caption, then smiled at all the women dropping heart-eyed emojis and kisses in the comments.

She wasn't mad at him. He was irresistible.

And then she spotted the baby pic he had posted for throwback Thursday. "Awww," she sighed. Every bit of it was adorable, from the massive curly Afro to his plump cheeks as he laughed, showing off one tooth trying to break through his gums. "I would love a little boy that looked just like . . ."

The rest of the words faded as she sat up straight, surprised at even a moment of imagining herself with a child. A mother? Me? A child? For Loren?

He would be such a good father.

Desdemona gasped at that thought. "What is wrong with me?" she asked herself, her eyes wide as something so unfamiliar to her tugged at her. A longing for that forever love between a mother and a child. She envisioned Loren holding her from behind with his hands splayed on the round belly carrying their child.

She pushed it away. "Nah, I'm good, love. Enjoy," she said, but the longing still lingered.

Desdemona hurriedly scrolled some more. "The biggest

mistake you can make is holding on to someone who has already let you go," she read the meme he retweeted from @feeling.forgotten.

Her heart skipped a beat as she looked at the date. March fourth. "Oh, Lo," she said, feeling her heart melt. "I wish I *could* forget you."

She went back to the post of him in the suit and pressed her finger and thumb against the screen, spreading them to enlarge the picture. She pressed her bare lips to the screen and shook her head as she accepted that somewhere along the line Loren Palmer had made a way into her heart, and she loved him.

Chapter Thirteen

Tuesday, April 23, 2019

Have I sold my soul . . . and if so, did I charge enough?

Desdemona fed the cash counter another stack of bills as she smoothed the hair that slipped from her loose topknot, more from habit than necessity. She eyed the television, taking in the lone occupied bedroom of the mansion as she sipped from a glass of wine.

On the second level, in the master bedroom, she eyed Liam Franks and Paulette Reeves talking as he massaged her shoulder and pressed a kiss to her nape when she lowered her head. They made a beautiful couple physically.

Liam was tall and in good shape, with dark hair and piercing blue eyes. Paulette was a tanned and shapely size twelve with every bit of it in the right places.

It was one of her consorts who had referred Liam to her, speaking of the forty-five-year-old's desire to gather enough funds to make a comeback after being disgraced as a stockbroker, fired after being investigated for insider trading. Paulette, a well-known lesbian actress and high-profile activist for gay rights, liked to be sexed by a man twice a year and came to Desdemona for the privacy to do so—never wanting the same man twice.

They were both single and had really good chemistry. If not for his current career and her inclination toward a serious relationship with women, they would have made a good couple.

She turned the volume up on them.

"Dildos are hard but not hot, and I like the heat of a stiff one sometimes," Paulette said in her raspy voice as she turned to reach for Liam's crotch.

She closed out the screen displaying them just as he roughly snatched her body to his and kissed her like he was hungry. She didn't watch or record the sexual activities or conversations of those who trusted her—unless it was a part of their kink.

As the shuffling of the money in the machine came to an end, she looked down at yet another stack in her hand and then the bundles of cash on the desk. She thought of the money in safe deposit boxes in banks and the safes in her home. Those spread out across prepaid debit cards and the one valid banking account connected to her online boutique and showroom.

She had nearly five million dollars tucked away, not including the value of her condo and furnishings, her vehicles, the inventory of her dress boutique, her diamond jewelry collection, furs, and designer items.

When is enough enough?

The money was good, but not easy. Juggling never was. There was no part of her life that felt complete. A little time here and a little there. Spreading crumbs of herself but never a full meal. Feeling as if she cheated herself. Not enough time. Not enough sleep. Exercise. Sex. Joy. Fulfillment. Freedom.

"I need more of all of it," she said aloud, leaning forward in her chair to reach for her glass of wine.

"Security alert. Front gate."

She sipped her wine and set the glass down while she fed the counter and looked to the television screen showing Yolanda "Tasty" Norton entering her visitor code to unlock the gate.

She put the cash counter back in the drawer and dumped the bundled cash into her tote bag before closing the hidden door to the fireplace. She replaced her heels and double-checked her hair and makeup in the mirror over the pedestal sink in the adjoining bath. With one last look around her haven, she reclaimed her seat behind the desk and watched via the security screen as Denzin ended his run on the treadmill in the exercise room in the basement. He made his way upstairs and to the front door.

Bzzzzzz.

She looked at the three iPhones on her desk. One for business, one for personal usage, and the last for Portia. She picked up the one in the bright pink case. A text.

PORTIA: Have 2 cancel dinner. Picked up eXtra hrs @ work. #SchmoneyGang

Desdemona smiled at the cash emojis as she simply replied with the "ok" emoji. She'd been trying to spend more time with Portia, but if work called and she chose to answer, there was no fault to be found in that. She was fighting like hell to ensure Portia stayed out of the pussy game.

Knock-knock-knock.

She set the phone facedown on the desk along with the rest and cut off the television. "Come in," she said.

Tasty and Denzin both entered. He claimed a seat on the edge of her desk and she stood before it. Desdemona eyed the shortbread cutie with wide eyes and pug nose with a dimpled chin whose short hair perfectly framed her round face. "Hello, beautiful people. What's up?" she asked, sitting back and crossing her legs in the burnt rose gold dress she wore with matching metallic heels.

"I wanted to tell you in person that I'm done. Probably one more session should do it, and I will be graduating from law school next month debt-free," she said, smiling and revealing the gap in her teeth that worked for her cuteness. "I'm ready to focus on taking the bar and getting to work as soon as possible."

Desdemona gave her a warm smile. "Your regulars will miss you, but I am happy for you," she said, rising to come around the desk and offer her a hug. "You got in, reached your goals, and now you're getting out."

Tasty returned the hug.

"Now hopefully I will never need your legal expertise, Miss Solicitor," Desdemona joked as she came back around her desk.

Denzin chuckled as he eyed them both. "I told her the same thing about me," he said.

Tasty's eyes became serious. "If there ever was an issue, Mademoiselle, I'd be there for you *for free*," she said.

Desdemona shook her head. "No, you wouldn't, because I would not let you. It would bring too much attention to you and a possible connection with me," she explained, rising again to walk across the room to her closet for two wineglasses and two fresh bottles of her favorite wine.

She paused, thinking of her GED test coming up that weekend. She truly admired the woman finishing law school, especially when she had no clue what her next step would be *if* she passed. "Let's toast to you," she said, walking back into the room to hand the unopened bottle to her. "This one is for you to take."

"Wow. Thank you," Tasty said.

Desdemona set the glasses on the desk next to her half-empty one and used the open bottle to fill their glasses before handing them each one. "Congratulations, Tasty, may you kick ass in every court in which you show up with your extraordinary black girl magic," she said, a twinkle in her eye.

"Hear, hear," Denzin agreed, lightly tapping his glass to each of theirs.

"Now, to make sure you have all the study time you need and to send you on your journey as soon as possible," Desdemona began, sitting down and removing a stack of money from her tote under the desk. "You are done as of today. I will reschedule the session you have for tomorrow and set you free."

She set the money on the desk and slid the five thousand dollars with one pointed fingernail toward her.

Tasty's eyes widened as she set the glass down and picked up the money. "This is enough to pay my final law school bill, Mademoiselle."

"Good. Go be great, Tasty," she said, finishing her wine in one deep swallow before picking up her phone and pretending to open emails. In truth, she wanted to avoid any back-and-forth of pleading with the woman to take it.

"Thank you," she stressed.

Well, that was easy.

Desdemona looked up from the phone in surprise and amusement. "*Go*. Be great," she repeated.

Tasty nodded with enthusiasm before quickly coming around the desk to hug her again before doing the same with Denzin and then taking her bottle of wine and cash before she left with one last wave.

"Man, boss, you some black girl magic your damn self," he said.

Desdemona felt truly happy. "You know what, Denzin, I fucking agree," she said, allowing herself to finally feel proud that she was willing and able to dole out good will.

"To you," he said, raising his glass in a toast.

"To *change*," she corrected before they toasted.

* * *

"Hello, neighbor."

Desdemona paused in unlocking the door to her condo. She turned to find a thirty-something woman with the kind of curls and complexion that made her heritage difficult to place. "Hello," she said, before turning back to her door.

"Actually, I'm new in the building and thought I'd introduce myself."

Desdemona looked pensive for a moment before straightening her face and turning again. The woman now stood behind her with the door to her apartment ajar.

"Melissa Colbert," the petite woman said, extending her hand.

Desdemona Dean.

"Alisha Smith," she said, sliding her hand into hers. "Nice to meet you."

"I've been seeing you in the elevator and going in and out of your apartment, but I decided to work up the nerve to finally introduce myself," she said, taking a comical little bow as if proud of her accomplishment.

Desdemona chuckled. "Are you new to New York?" she asked, forcing herself out of her comfort zone of not mingling with her neighbors unless necessary—and so far, to date, it hadn't been.

She splayed her fingers and motioned her hand back and forth a bit. "It's been three years since I moved from Boston, but I'm brand-new to trendy Tribeca," she said. "I'm in advertising."

Oh? Me? I'm in the procurement of sexual pleasure. Isn't that interesting?

"You'll love Tribeca," she said, pushing aside her unease at the line of questions that normally followed after a first-time meeting. Husband? Kids? Career?

Desdemona looked past her neighbor to her door being nudged open by a nose. Moments later a small French bulldog with a beautiful fawn coat sat in the doorway with its tongue wagging and an adorable pink collar with a bow around its neck.

Melissa looked over her shoulder and then smiled. "That's Frenchie. I won her in my divorce earlier this year," she said, turning and bending. With a soft clap of her hands, the dog came trotting forward.

"Adorable," Desdemona admitted, looking down as the woman stroked her.

"Are you afraid?" Melissa asked, looking back at her. "I didn't think to ask."

"No, I'm not."

Melissa picked the dog up into her arms. "She's ready for her walk," she said. "Listen, maybe we can do dinner. Let me know. My mother thinks the divorce broke me and I need a friend. She's mistaken about the divorce, but maybe she's right about the friend."

"We'll see," Desdemona said, shying away.

There was a shift in Melissa's eyes—a wariness—even as she smiled. "Let me know," she said with a shrug before turning to cross the hall and enter her apartment.

Desdemona turned to her own door, finally undoing the lock with her key before entering. She paused and stared at the door across the hall. She felt so weird having never had a friend. Not in school, where she struggled to find herself without her father, and not during her streetwalking days, when she grappled with the truth of the change in her life. The control levied upon her by her fear. And not as a high-powered madam, constantly juggling balls and finding friendship the one thing she could afford to never pick up.

Closing the door behind herself, she locked it before she set her bag and keys on the table in the foyer and kicked off her flats. Removing the pin that secured her topknot, she ran her nails over her scalp and shook out her hair as she turned on the lights as she made her way through the apartment. She drew a bath, lit candles, and used the remote to turn on the television in the mirror over the double sink that she hardly ever used.

She undressed and stepped into the tub, enjoying the feel of the heated water as she lowered her body beneath the depths until her chin dapped the surface and sent rings out in the water. She looked around at the beauty with the sound of the Eyewitness News in the background. "Lonely is *not* the business," she said, arching a brow when her words seemed to echo.

"The search continues for a missing thirteen-year-old girl in the Brownsville section of Brooklyn. Local police are asking for any information regarding the disappearance of Ayanna Lewis, who never made it home yesterday evening after school."

Desdemona turned her head to eye the cute black girl with sideways cornrows the younger girls called "Lemonade braids" after Beyoncé sported them in the video of the same name.

"She is five foot, three inches tall and weighs one hundred pounds. She was last seen wearing a black T-shirt, jeans, and black sneakers with a black hoodie. Anyone with information on Ayanna should call the police."

Desdemona prayed the little girl was somewhere safe and not in the clutches of a man looking to trade her innocence for money. "Be safe. Be smart. Be vigilant. Get home, Ayanna," she said aloud in prayer. Sex trafficking was an all too real epidemic in America, and she knew that firsthand.

"One begets the other."

"Get out of my head, Loren," she drawled.

She didn't linger as she normally did and finished her bath, pulling on a red robe of soft lace that stroked the floor as she moved. "I need work. Work is good," she said, sitting on the couch and picking up her laptop. "Work is distracting."

But it didn't work.

Plum was in rehab. And fired.

Red was living her temporary dreams on the Upper East Side. And quit.

Tasty was steps away from being a lawyer. And resigned.

Her roster was short by three, and it was nearing a year since she'd even interviewed a new courtesan. She thought of Jann's unenthusiastic lay with Denzin and winced as she closed the laptop. There was a time she would have been pressed to replace them, but she wouldn't. She didn't want to.

Three less people to worry about.

These days she was feeling like less was definitely more.

Even the mansion in Riverdale was a burden she was considering letting go. The multiyear lease was up for renewal in six months. No monthly rent. No upkeep. No weekly cleanings. No worries over raids.

"I think I better let it go," she sang in baritone, making herself chuckle.

Maybe it's time to let it all go.

The thought of that made her feel light-hearted.

If not now, when? If not me . . . then let someone else do it.

Plum left it to get clean.

Red left it to get a man—even part-time.

Tasty left to follow her dreams.

And so many more had come and gone over the last seventeen years for one reason or another. And still, Desdemona remained. She wondered if and when she would have the courage to walk away from the business. The money was good, and the work was far easier than when she was streetwalking.

I'm only thirty-five and love my lifestyle as is. Five million won't last me for the rest of my life.

Desdemona drummed the tips of her fingernails against the laptop as she tilted her head to the side and looked up at her family portrait above the fireplace. She squinted as a reality settled upon her. "The hell," she said, sitting up straight.

Both of her parents died young. Super young. She had outlived her mother by a couple of years and was closing on her father's age in the next five years. She frowned. Deeply.

Desdemona pressed her fingertips to her pulse but dropped her hand, realizing how silly that was.

Am I going up yonder early like my parents? Then what will happen to the money, the house, the clothes, and all the other material things she cherished and was afraid to lose?

"I am *so* confused," she whispered, still eying the painting.

With a breath, she laid her back against the couch and looked up at the high ceilings. She became pensive, remembering how it felt to skydive in Vegas. Schedule to take her GED. Think about college. Make love to Loren. Travel more.

Any time she stepped out of her comfort zone she had found nothing but bliss.

The power of "Or."

I could keep living and making money just as I am, or . . .

She was uneducated but far from dumb, and she knew there was a middle ground—a compromise between where she was and where she knew she would one day be, out of the game. "No extension on the mansion lease. No new courtesans or consorts. Wean the service hours down to just the weekends," she said, ticking each off on her fingers. "Less business. More pleasure. Live with no regrets."

Loren.

Desdemona closed her eyes and saw the face of her biggest regret. Loving Loren. She loved him. The very thought of him made her warm, her heart swell, and her stomach fill with flutters likened to a million butterfly wings. Still, she had accepted that she could not have him. There was no way. There was no Loren and Desdemona. No happily ever after.

No chubby babies with wild curls and beautiful eyes smiling up at me and saying "mama."

She jumped to her feet, pushing aside longings that she never before had.

It was time to get some of Bobby Brown's prerogative and do what she wanted to do. Taking on Portia had put the kibosh on Desdemona's momentum to travel and explore. Her ward was working and saving money as she built up more time on her job to qualify for a decent apartment. She didn't need as close guidance as she once did.

Desdemona looked over at her front door before coming around the sofa and striding to the foyer to open and leave it ajar. She crossed the hall just as a door down the hall closed. She paused with her fist near the door to find the couple down the hall standing there staring at her—the husband a little more than his wife.

"Albert!" she exclaimed, her face reddened with anger.

Desdemona looked down at her lace robe and shrugged. *People are so weird about the human body.*

She ignored them as Becky, or Emily, or Susan pulled Albert down the hall to the elevator at the end of it.

Knock-knock.

She gave them a wave just before the elevator doors closed on the wife scowling and Albert smiling.

"Hello again, neighbor."

Melissa's eyes dipped down Desdemona's body and then back up again. "Uhm, Alisha, I can see nipples, dear," she said dryly, her eyes twinkling with amusement.

"Okay. They're probably not very different from your own or what you see on television. Just nipples," Desdemona said, liking that the woman was more amused than horrified. "I thought about it. Let's go get dinner. Tonight, if you're free… and I promise to put the nipples away."

"Thanks," Melissa said. "And explain to me how I am supposed to enjoy a great meal and wine with all of this inspiration to work out in front of me. A little cruel. Just pointing that out."

Desdemona laughed. She was funny. Good. "Ready by seven?" she asked.

"That'll work," Melissa said.

Desdemona turned and walked across the hall to her own apartment.

"And now I can see your buttocks. The split and everything," she called behind her.

"It's just a butt, Melissa," Desdemona said before stepping inside and closing the door with a chuckle.

Two hours later the women were seated at the bar of Smith and Williams, a converted carriage house that was small and intimate with a rustic and unique décor of muted shades of green that gave it character.

"I just want to toast your ownership of a bra," Melissa said lifting her cocktail.

Desdemona inclined her head and raised hers as well. "Next we'll work on panties," she said.

The bartender laughed. "I'll toast to that *not* happening."

Desdemona gave him a playful wink before sipping her drink. "Another round of oysters," she said over the chatter of the crowded space.

He nodded and turned to Melissa in question. "Chicken meatballs, please."

"Coming right up," he said, before walking down the metal-topped wooden bar.

Melissa leaned over closer to Desdemona. "And your number," she whispered.

"Seriously?" she asked, eyeing him.

"No. After my divorce I am enjoying some me time and not immersing anyone's energy with my own," she said.

"A break is good. Unpack the baggage," Desdemona said.

"What about you?" Melissa asked, sucking the juices from the orange slice in her drink.

Here we go. Husband? Kids? Career?

"I had a little something with someone special but I

ended it," she admitted, thinking of him and feeling that same warmth spread across her chest.

When will my love for him fade?

"Why?" Melissa asked.

"Huh?"

"Why'd you end it with the special guy?"

"He's too young, and we're too different," she said.

Her face was expecting more and became exasperated when Desdemona offered no more. "Okay, so my hubby of the last fifteen years—who was working on his music career while I held down the job and the bills—was sleeping with my assistant and using my money to fund the bullshit."

Desdemona eyed her. "I'm sorry you had to go through that," she said.

Melissa turned her lips downward and shrugged. "I miss my assistant more than my husband. That slut was *really* organized," she said before chuckling.

"You missed your mark with comedy," she said, sitting back as the bartender set the plate of oysters on the half shell before her.

"I laugh to keep from crying." Melissa eyed the plate of meatballs topped with slices of crusty bread that was set before her as well.

Desdemona squeezed lemon and dashed hot sauce across the oysters. "Whatever it takes," she said.

"I agree."

They fell silent as they enjoyed their food.

She wondered what this stylish and smart ad executive, who probably had a degree from Wharton or the like, would think about having dinner and cocktails with a high-school dropout, former prostitute, and high-end madam.

"Good sex?"

"Huh?" Desdemona asked.

"The younger guy. Was the sex good?' Melissa asked.

She had a heated memory of him gripping her hair as he

stroked her from behind until she was clutching wildly at the sheets, sweating like a fiend, heart racing, and crying out with her explosive release.

"Whose pussy?" he had asked.

"Yours," she had moaned before capturing the sheets between her teeth.

Desdemona pressed her thighs together as the bud nestled between the lips of her intimacy throbbed to life. "Great sex," she said.

I taught him well.

"Give the kid a chance," Melissa said, swiping at a crumb of bread from the corner of her glossy lips. "If the worst he has going for him is he's younger than you, then enjoy the ride until the wheels fall off."

"It'd be easier if I didn't love him," Desdemona said, surprised that she admitted that to this woman who was just a little more than a stranger to her.

"Ohhhh," Melissa said, drawing it out in understanding.

Desdemona took a sip of her drink.

"Well, you gave up yours and somebody took mine, but we found each other across the hall," Melissa said. "So, here's to friendship."

Desdemona smiled, raising her glass to hers. "To friendship," she agreed, liking the sound and feel of that.

Cha-ching. Cha-ching. Cha-ching.

Over the rim of her reading glasses, Desdemona eyed her phones where they were charging. She was taking a timed practice test ahead of her actual GED test the next morning, but couldn't bring herself to turn off her phone. She regretted that.

For once she just wanted to put herself and her needs first. And she needed to study because she needed to get her GED. Attending college was her next goal.

But old patterns were hard to break.

Cha-ching. Cha-ching. Cha-ching.

To hell with new sessions being booked. That she could overlook. But what if someone was in trouble? Safety was her obligation to those women and the few men who worked for her.

"Shit," Desdemona swore, closing out of the test and removing her spectacles as she rose and crossed the living room to pick up the phone. Number three. She wished Denzin had been available to be her safety net that night as well.

She set the phone back down but remained standing there as it continued to sound off.

Cha-ching. Cha-ching. Cha-ching.

The testing would take nearly all day, and in preparation for it, Denzin was handling any emergencies that arose, but she wasn't taking on any new sessions and overwhelming him.

But Francis McAdams and the sadness of his wife's condition tugged at her heartstrings. She was so tempted to answer him, but she was intent on setting boundaries. She had to put herself first sometimes.

Cha-ching—.

She felt heady from the relief she felt when the ringtone ended.

Releasing a breath, she turned and made her way back to the table. *Should I start over or just do some workbook?*

She picked up the can of peach-flavored Perrier she was sipping through a straw.

Cha-ching. Cha-ching. Cha-ching.

Her shoulders drooped, and she felt like a noose was around her neck pulling her back to the phone. The steps across the room felt weighted. The obligation was tiresome.

"Hello there," she said, forcing kindness into her tone as she crossed her arm over her chest in the oversize Versace tee she wore as a dress.

"My Kimber left me."

His wife had passed. "I'm so sorry to hear that," she said, knowing his struggle with his wife of more than forty years slipping into a coma after a burst aneurysm nearly two years ago.

"She's at peace, but I'm not," he said.

"Well, Red is no longer with me, but I have someone else in mind," she said. "I'm just not scheduling any appointments until the weekends now, and I'm booked until next Friday."

"A whole week?"

"Yes," she said, feeling it dragged from her like someone breaking up two people fighting to the death.

"Mademoiselle," he began.

She shook her head. "There's nothing I can do, Francis," she said. "I'm sorry."

He began to weep.

Desdemona tucked the phone between her ear and shoulder and held up her hands in exasperation—at herself, not him. Guilt and her inane desire to come to people's rescue led to that boundary she set evaporating. "For when, Francis?" she asked.

"Tonight."

Well, damn.

"Let me see what I can get set up for you."

"Thank you, Mademoiselle."

Pushover.

She ran through the list in her head of all the courtesans booked for the night—be it work or requested personal time—but paused. She really didn't feel like it, and she was beginning to feel more and more like that every day.

Push through, Pushover.

It took less than five minutes to line up a four-hour session with the Swedish twins. The notification for his dress order came through. Patrice would ship it Monday. The twins would collect the cash once they met at a luxury boutique hotel in Midtown known for its discretion.

Double his fun. Half the grief. For four hours, anyway.

"Now," Desdemona said, clapping her hand. "Back to *me*."

For hours she studied and then completed the practice test in good time with a solid score. It wasn't until then that she stripped off her clothing as she made her way to her bedroom and went to bed—not bothering with a bath or the à la carte dinner of Ossetra and Kaluga caviar on warm brioche followed by a dry-aged rib eye with caramelized garlic and a side of swiss chard.

She was asleep as soon as her head hit the pillow. Not even dreams of Loren proclaiming his love for her before they ran away together could stop her from jumping up as soon as her alarm sounded at six o' clock.

Her one and only focus was her test.

It's time to right a wrong.

She felt like it was the first day of school. Nervous and excited. Childlike.

Once dressed and in the back of her Lyft Black, Desdemona stroked her tattoo, played with her diamond butterfly bracelet, and played with the necklace and charm that Loren had given her, which she wore for good luck.

"I am such a cornball," she said.

"What's that?" the driver, Yusef, asked.

"Nothing. Just talking to myself," she said. "I've been doing a *lot* of that lately."

"As long as you don't answer yourself you'll be okay," he said.

"That's good to know," Desdemona said before falling silent.

As the vehicle turned onto West 125th Street, Desdemona clearly recalled how much she used to love going to school and learning. Even when she ran away and was homeless, she had made her way to school. And even after Majig had her working the streets at night, she went to school during the day until her humiliation sent her running from her education for good.

Until now.

"Thank you," Desdemona said to the driver as he pulled to a stop in front of the towering building in which the SUNY Manhattan Educational Opportunity Center was housed.

She climbed from the vehicle and squared her shoulders before crossing the sidewalk to reach its front doors, thinking that for the first time in nearly twenty years her parents were finally proud of her.

Desdemona turned her head this way and that as she studied her reflection in the full-length mirror. Everything about the night was extra, including her appearance. Full-on makeup beat with smoky eyes and pale glossy lips. She wore all of her diamond jewelry, including necklaces of varying lengths and thickness. The jewel-neckline dress she wore had a full, dramatic skirt with the layers barely concealing the black thong she wore beneath it. The northeastern April air was still chilly at night, and she loved the short fur she wore that looked like a fur ball. Her purse, which she treated herself to today once she finished the seven-hour testing, was a Judith Leiber Couture Collection in the 3-D shape of a butterfly with gold, white, and black crystals.

Desdemona felt as good about the test as she did her look.

Time to celebrate.

She double-checked her glitzy purse as she walked down the hall and eventually left her apartment. Melissa was about to walk into her apartment with Frenchie in her arms at the same time. Her eyes widened at the sight of her, and Desdemona did a turn this way and that before wiggling her shoulders playfully. "You like?" she asked.

"Yes!" Melissa said, clapping her hands as best she could

with her French bulldog in her arms. "Where are you headed?"

"To the Met," she said, after a pause during which she considered inviting her but decided against it. "I have a love for Chopin, and there's an opera based on his music."

"I'm not an opera type of girl, but you look amazing," she said as they began walking down the hall together.

"It's my first time going, so I'll see if I love it or fall asleep," Desdemona admitted. "I better get going. I called a Lyft to avoid the parking."

"Stop by when you get back and we'll have wine while you fill me in on your night of glamour and classical music and I'll regale you with my poop-filled adventures in dog walking."

Desdemona laughed. "I definitely will," she promised before picking up the hem of her dress and rushing down the hall on her Louboutin heels at the sound of the elevator's arrival on the floor.

She joined an elderly gentleman in a beautiful linen suit with a paisley ascot. "Good evening," she said, inclining her head.

"Same to you," he said, tapping his cane on the floor.

She recognized him as her neighbor but had no clue as to his name.

"I overheard you're headed to the Met," he said.

Desdemona nodded. "Yes. I'm celebrating, and I honestly couldn't think of any other place I'd rather be tonight," she said.

"Enjoy and congratulations," he said.

"Thank you."

And later, when she sat in her parterre alone, having purchased all five of the seats in the pseudo-private box, she was very clear and proud of her personal growth. To think of fifteen-year-old Desdemona—Desi to her parents—struggling to live on the streets and fight off both hunger and danger now a woman sitting in the Metropolitan Opera about to watch a performance made her proud.

I been through it and today was huge for me. Huge. And now I sit here, feeling beautiful, feeling a little bit more whole, doing something I want, alone and okay with that.

"Hello."

Desdemona looked to her right to find a tall, slender, brown-skinned man with salt-and-pepper hair and goatee. "How you doing?" she asked, seeing several of the people in the parterre with him looking at them with open curiosity. "Hello, everyone."

He chuckled and moved from his plush velvety maroon seat to the one next to the low-slung partition. He cleared his throat and crossed his legs, adjusting the hem of his tailored suit pants. He motioned with her head for her to move closer to the partition as well.

He was mid-forties and fine. And rich. She could tell. The cut of the suit. The subtle jewelry and Piaget watch.

She eyed the closed curtains as she set her purse on the seat to her left and shifted over to the seat on her right next to the divider. The scent of his cologne reached her. Nice. Warm. Subtle.

But not Loren.

"How can I help you?" she asked, crossing her legs as well.

"Trevor King," he said, extending his hand.

Desdemona shook it with her own. She wanted so badly to present her real name. Step into her own identity once and for all. "Alisha Smith," she offered instead, feeling a little of her black girl joy dim.

"This is a work function for me, but I would like to exchange info and take you to dinner," he said, speaking only for her ears.

Fresh breath. A plus.

Her hand was still in his and it felt warm, not offensive. But not Loren.

This same touch from him would have me palpitating, light-headed, and weak. Our chemistry was dizzying, and my love was lasting.

She eyed this grown man, already established in the world, and wondered if he was the next to help her get over her ex-lover. *Maybe he is just what I need.*

"Your card, please," she said, loving how refined she sounded.

He reached in his inner pocket and removed one from a gold metal container to hand to her between his index and middle finger.

"Okay. Smooth," she said teasingly as she took it from him. "I'll be honest—"

The lights dimmed.

They both looked to the stage.

"I'm not sure if I'm looking for anything—even a date—but if I change my mind I will definitely call you, Mr. King," she said. "Cool?"

The conductor took his spot before the orchestra.

The audience welcomed him with applause.

"Cool," Trevor said with a warm smile.

She moved back over to her seat in the center of the parterre and dropped his card inside the leather interior of the bejeweled butterfly as she focused her intention on the music of Chopin now swelling in the air around her.

Chapter Fourteen

Wednesday, May 15, 2019

I'm done. Madam, may I . . . live my life?

"Does this make me a stalker?" Desdemona asked as she sat down on her sofa and handed Melissa a glass of her favorite wine.

Melissa tilted her head to the side. "Eh. A little," she admitted with a shrug. "But I'm here with you. Your Samoan sister in stalking."

"Oh. Samoan. Like the Rock. I've been wondering," Desdemona admitted as she made the live stream play on her laptop in full screen.

Melissa frowned. "I should go to work and leave you stalking your ex alone."

"He's not my ex."

"Your sex then," she countered.

Desdemona remained quiet, but she was amused. That was commonplace in her friendship with the woman. She was brilliant and pretty and nice but above all funny with quick wit. She had no regrets welcoming the petite woman with the big sense of humor into her life.

"And what will Trevor think of this?' she asked.

"Considering we're only dating, he should think nothing of it," Desdemona said. "Ssssh. They're calling them up for the hooding."

Loren had successfully completed his doctorate in creative writing, and the university was livestreaming the convocation.

"How do you know about all of this?"

She side-eyed the other woman. "He posted about his graduation on Instagram and I looked up the info on the university's website. I intended to go, but there were no tickets available."

"That good, huh?" Melissa asked.

Desdemona arched a brow and nodded.

"Celibacy sucks," she muttered into her glass.

"Six months? That's a cakewalk. Try *five* years," Desdemona stressed.

"Five?" she repeated. "Maybe he's not that good and you were just that horny."

"Perhaps," Desdemona agreed, taking a sip of wine as she eyed Francis McAdams standing on stage next to the podium in his black robe and cap as the president of the university. He appeared happy. She was glad to see that. His night with the twins had been his last. They reported back how his grief that night had prevented much of anything from happening.

"We will now recognize candidates who have officially met the requirements for a doctorate in the creative writing program."

They both fell silent and settled back against the sofa as each candidate was called up onto the stage of the Theatre at Madison Square Garden with the seated professors and deans, all dressed in their academic regalia of caps and gowns with their hood color or trim signaling their degree or discipline.

One by one each candidate walked across the stage, shook the hand of the university's president, and then stopped before the dean of their school to be hooded and pose for a picture.

"We've been watching this for over an hour," Desdemona said, touching her fingers to her lips. "Do you see how few doctoral candidates of color there are across all disciplines?"

"PhDs so white . . . and Asian."

Desdemona offered her a weak smile. "No, seriously, I am so proud of him," she whispered. "I *really* am."

Several more candidates crossed the stage.

"Loren Marc Palmer. Creative Writing. Supervisor, Gregor Polk."

Desdemona's heart set off at the pace of a racing greyhound as Loren stepped onto the right of the screen, handed his hood to Francis, who opened it and handed it to the dean to place around Loren's neck before he turned and posed for a photo.

Melissa leaned forward to pause the live stream capturing Loren as he smiled.

"Okay, maybe it was him," she drawled.

"Perhaps," Desdemona said softly.

Loren was as tall and handsome as ever, of course. And her reaction to him had not lessened. She blinked and took a breath at a heated memory, but also accepted the ache in her soul from missing his wisdom, fun nature, and hopeful attitude. He was the impetus for her change.

"Oh, wow, you love him," Melissa stressed. "It's all over your face."

Desdemona nodded, not willing to deny it.

"Poor Trevor," she added.

Desdemona cut her eyes at her. "Right," she agreed begrudgingly as she leaned forward to take the live feed off pause. The screen went black for a moment and reappeared with Loren already gone.

"Does he love you, too?"

"I don't know. I've wondered that myself sometimes, but

it's all good," she said, rising to collect their glasses and carry them into the kitchen to place in the sink.

Desdemona ran her stiletto fingernails through her curls.

"You good?" Melissa called from the living room.

When will the love fade? There was no future for them, and her brain was ready to move on. It was her heart that held on to him.

Desdemona moved back into the living area. "Yeah, I'm good," she said. "Thanks."

Melissa rose, smoothing her hands over the crisp and stylish red blouse and slacks she wore. "I'm headed to work," she said, walking to the front door in her matching patent leather heels. "What am I going to do when you're on super-vacation?"

"I don't leave for weeks," she reminded her, coming over to the foyer as well.

"Too soon," Melissa quipped.

"Eh. A little."

She held up both hands. "Off to work to stare at my assistant's butt and pretend not to do so," she said before taking a bow and leaving.

Desdemona closed the door and leaned back against it. Today was the first day of the rest of her life. She was done. Mademoiselle was preparing to take her final bow, and the thought of that made her smile.

No fear. No doubts. Just a sweet relief and joy for moving on.

When she gave herself time to live Monday through Thursday, she began to enjoy life more. She partied a little. Traveled. Enjoyed hanging with Melissa and dating Trevor. Took up hobbies. Enjoyed not being tied to that business phone. And the more she reclaimed of her life, the more she wanted. A door inside her had been opened, and she decided once and for all to blow it off for good.

There had been some pushback from her regulars, but the more they refused to let her be, the more she realized that she had created these foolish expectations they had of her. She had set the boundaries far too late. She stayed in the game far too long.

Desdemona wasn't letting the balls drop, but she couldn't wait to safely and carefully set them aside.

"It's time," she said, moving to the living space and cleaning up from the breakfast of fresh fruit and pastries she had ordered for them to enjoy as they watched the convocation. "Going out on top and in my own way."

She had passed her GED and was looking forward to applying to college next year—once she decided on a major and took an extended vacation to see the world. Africa. Italy. Paris.

First things first.

Desdemona retrieved her business phone and sat on the sofa with her feet tucked beneath her. She dialed Number One and clicked her nails against each other as she awaited an answer.

"Whaddup, Mademoiselle?"

"Nothing much. Congrats on the win last night," she said. "I'm sure you and the team will get the championship this year, so congrats on that in advance."

"You sound like we won't speak again before that."

Her eyes went to the windows. "We won't," she said.

He fell silent.

"You there?" she asked.

"I'm *off* the list," he said, his deep voice incredulous.

"No, no, no, no," Desdemona said. "I am. I'm done. I'm out."

"Wow," he said, his surprise obvious. "You good?"

"I am fucking great," she said. "Just going out on top. That's all. I've been at this for more than half of my life. Time to try on a new coat. You know?"

"You about to shake the game up," he said. "Is this on lock or spread the word?"

"I'm calling the entire list today, so I'm sure shit is about to get mad hectic," she said. "I'm calling you first, though."

"You know what, Angel?" he asked, reverting to her old alias. "I'm happy for you. I'm not judging, but you're a dope girl and still young as hell, and you deserve more than lining up pussy for us knuckleheads and keeping all our secrets."

"Thanks for that, and please know those secrets will remain locked away, and you can let everyone know that I will *not* sell my list," she assured him, rising up enough to untuck her feet from beneath her.

"Damn. No more Mademoiselle."

"That hoe dies today," she said, chuckling. "Angel, too."

"And the phone?"

"Clean and burn," she said. "Cover me like I have covered you all these years."

"Got it. Clean and burn."

They fell silent.

"I hear someone coming," Number One said. "I gotta go, but I feel like I don't wanna let you go yet."

"I will take that as a compliment, Champ. Goodbye," Desdemona said before ending the call.

One by one she made her calls. The morning shifted easily to late afternoon by the time she was done. Celebrities. Athletes. Politicians. Heirs and heiresses. Even royalty. Most took the news with the same nonchalance as learning orange juice instead of apple juice was being served for breakfast. Some tried to buy her back in. A few were angry. Many wished her well. Over the years they had cultivated an odd but necessary relationship with trust at its very core.

She grabbed her keys and slid on her dark, round-framed shades, leaving her apartment behind. During her drive to Riverdale, she put Cardi B's "Best Life" on repeat and danced in her seat as she drove, feeling light-hearted and happy. "I made a couple M's with my best friends, turned all my L's into lessons," she sang along to the chorus, lightly pounding her fist against the steering wheel.

When she finally parked in front of the sprawling home, she was happy to see Denzin's motorcycle parked by his side entrance. She couldn't deny the apprehension she felt. "Now or never, Desi," she said before climbing from the car with her keys in hand.

She paused and took in the warm weather and sun shining.

"Whaddup, boss?"

Desdemona turned her head to find Denzin standing in the now open doorway in just a towel. "Just the man I wanted to see," she said, walking toward him.

Denzin stepped back, pulling the door open wider before she entered and strolled into the foyer.

The scent of his soap, deodorant, or cologne was nice. It reminded her of Loren.

"I have some good and bad news," she said, turning to face him as he closed the door and crossed his muscled arms over his broad chest.

"Okay," Denzin said, eyeing her in open interest.

"Good news. I am closing down the business," she said, reaching to clasp his arm. "Bad news. The month-to-month lease is up in five months, but I would like to give thirty days' notice and clear out of here."

Denzin nodded in understanding. "Two questions," he began, holding up two fingers. "One. Does that mean my regulars are up for grabs? Two. If I no longer work for you can I now beg you for some pussy?"

He dropped his towel and stood there naked before her with pride in his eyes.

"I wish you and your dick happy fucking with any and all of your regulars," she said, dropping her eyes to his impressive inches. "I've seen your penis far too much to be impressed anymore. Plus, I've seen bigger. Hell, I've *had* bigger."

With a grunt she pushed aside an image of Loren in the shower surrounded by steam with his erection hanging from his body like a third leg.

"Well, damn, boss," he said, sounding offended as he bent to pick up his towel and wrap it back around his waist.

"How long have we worked together, Denzin?" she asked as she walked over to the elevator.

"Four or five years," he said.

"You don't seem surprised I'm leaving it all behind," she said as they stepped onto the lift and closed the metal gate.

"I've seen it coming. You've changed, and I could tell especially the last few weeks with asking me to step in and then you shut it down to just weekends," Denzin said. "I didn't know it was coming this quick, but I knew it was coming. Oh, a brother definitely started making alternative plans so I'm good, boss."

"Like?" she asked as the elevator slid to a stop on the top level.

Denzin opened the gate and stepped off to hold it for her. "Buying a house for sure," he said as they walked down the short hall to her office. "Living rent-free for four or five years has its advantages. So, thank you."

"You're welcome," she said, unlocking the door and walking inside.

The sun beaming through the window was welcoming, and she walked over to stand in its warmth.

"I have to do something with all this furniture in the house," she said. "Do you want it?"

He frowned. "Honestly?" he asked.

"Always," she encouraged.

"I'll pass. I have seen way too many things go down on all of this furniture. Don't forget I was present and working for the big orgy of 2015," he said with a shake of his head. "No offense."

"None taken. Why do you think I don't want any of it."

"Have it cleaned and donate it all to Goodwill and let someone without the history of the furniture enjoy it."

"Right," she said.

They shared a laugh.

"I'm thinking of starting a catering business," Denzin added.

"You can cook?" She balked in disbelief as she kicked off the wedged heels she wore with a short-sleeved jean mini dress that showed off her solid, well-shaped legs.

"I graduated from Le Cordon Bleu in Atlanta," he said. "See? Not friends."

"Le Cordon Bleu? Atlanta? Oh, my God, Denzin, who are you?" she asked, laughing as she scratched her scalp.

He chuckled as well. "I'll tell you what. Our last night with the house I will make you a huge meal—my treat—and we will say goodbye to each other with good food and good wine."

"Awww," Desdemona said, walking over to the desk. "I would hug you, but I know you will get hard."

"Would I," he agreed.

They shared a look that was part sadness and part happiness—like the last day of school.

Denzin closed the distance between them. "I'll be good," he said, pulling her close for a hug and pressing a kiss to her temple. "I always wanted to know your story. What led to you being the—in my estimation—the top madam of the east coast and beyond. I never asked."

"No need to now. It's all in the past," she said, finally feeling like it was getting smaller and smaller in her rearview mirror.

"I'm gonna miss you," Denzin said, sounding sincere.

"Same," she agreed. "Same."

They continued to hug until Desdemona felt the weight of his erection press against her leg. "Denzin," she said sharply, stepping back and breaking the embrace.

He held up his hands. "That motherfucker got a mind of his own," he said, before turning to leave with one final look back over his shoulder.

"Security alert. Front gate."

The security alarm system.

"I'm taking my television," Desdemona said, opening the top desk drawer to remove the remote to turn it on.

She eyed Franco entering the visitor code of the security gate to open it before he drove forward in his black Honda Accord. When she first took Franco on as a courtesan he had a beautiful vintage Benz that he eventually sold to put the money toward his gender reassignment surgery.

In continuing with her preparations to close up shop, Desdemona had called some of her courtesans the night before to inform them, but there were some she wanted to talk to face to face. Like Franco. She had every intention of him leaving the Riverdale mansion with the remaining balance he needed to have his surgery.

Desdemona wanted to bless so that she could be blessed, including offering Patrice partnership in the online dress boutique as she took it completely legitimate and allowed her showroom manager to take on even more responsibility.

Everything just felt right, and with every ball she had been juggling properly set aside, the weight of her world was lessening on her shoulders.

Later that afternoon, back in her apartment, which was freshly cleaned by housekeeping, with the windows open and letting in the summer afternoon breeze, Desdemona poured herself a full glass of wine before sitting cross-legged on the floor before the fireplace. The entire apartment was chilly even with the windows ajar. She had turned up the air-conditioning to counter lighting her fireplace in May.

She looked up at her parents' faces in the portrait and

raised her glass in a toast to them. She loved them. They made her. They also imprinted on her life in ways she was sure they would regret, but her love far outweighed any regrets or judgment she had. Adulthood had taught her that life was all about doing the best you can with what you have and, unfortunately, she didn't know their backstory or what events imprinted their lives and affected the decisions they made as adults. That left her open to forgiveness and understanding.

Who am I to judge?

Taking a sip of the wine before she set the glass on the raised hearth of the fireplace, Desdemona picked up the first journal on the stack. She rubbed the cover and opened the pages to touch her words. Her feelings. Her experiences. Journaling had made her feel closer to her mother and the memories she had of her writing away in her own little book.

There were no logs from the days she was homeless and then under Majig's rule, but she found comfort in journaling again when she began her reign as a madam. The one from the years after her father's death remained in her safe, but within the pages of this stack were veiled references to some of her consorts over the last seventeen years. It was time to be free of the burden of keeping those secrets.

And so as she listened to Chopin and sipped her wine she tore the pages from the journals to toss into the fire, claiming her freedom once and for all.

Knock-knock-knock.

Desdemona's nerves were shot until the moment the door opened and Loren was standing before her. Fine as ever. Sans glasses. Hair wild. Smelling delicious. Dressed in nothing but basketball shorts. "Hello, Dr. Palmer," she said, giving him a smile.

He took a step back at the sight of her as his face became incredulous. "What are you doing here?" he asked.

She looked past him into his studio apartment. "Are you alone?" she asked, before shifting her eyes up to his.

"What are you doing *here*?" Loren repeated.

Desdemona licked her lips and slid her hands inside the pockets of the T-shirt dress she wore with heels. "We never said goodbye the right way," she said, soft and hesitant.

He shook his head. "I didn't say goodbye, you did, Alisha."

Desdemona.

"Right," she agreed.

A door opened and closed on the floor above him, echoing down the stairwell. Next, there were footsteps. They fell silent as a heavyset dude with dreads came down the stairs and passed them with a head nod to Lo as he continued down the last flight of stairs and out the door.

"I watched your graduation's—sorry, your doctorate convocation's—live stream today. Congratulations, Lo," she said, reaching over to lightly touch her fingertips to his chest.

It was bare, and the goose bumps she gave him were visible.

He closed his eyes and tilted his head back as he covered his face with his hands. "Yo, you killing me," he said, his voice strained.

She held up her hands. "It's okay. I'll go," she said, turning from him to walk down the tiled hall.

"How did your GED test go?"

Desdemona stopped. "I passed," she said, looking back over her shoulder.

Their eyes locked.

She felt warm from his very look and heady from being in his presence again. *I love him so much.*

Loren leaned against the doorway with his hand over his mouth as he studied her. He shook his head and laughed a little. "Just when I'm starting to get my shit together. Here you are."

Desdemona turned and leaned against the railing of the

landing. "Here I am," she admitted, her voice just a tad more than a whisper.

"For?" he asked.

"I needed to say goodbye to you better than I did, Lo," she admitted. "You meant way more to me than what I showed you that day, and you didn't deserve that."

"No, I didn't," he agreed, looking down at his bare feet and then over at her again.

Their eyes locked again.

"Do I get a chance to redo it?" she asked, giving him a beguiling smile.

His eyes dipped down to her thick thighs exposed by the short hem of her T-shirt dress. "Is it still goodbye?" he asked.

She nodded. "Yeah, it is, Lo," she admitted.

His eyes never left hers as he extended his arm to open the door wider in invitation.

Desdemona pushed off the railing and walked over to him, slowly letting her hand trail across his rigid abdomen as she passed him to enter the apartment.

He closed the door and reached to pull her body back against his with one strong arm.

"Yes," she sighed, turning in his embrace to entwine her fingers in his hair as she kissed him with a slowness as he eased his hands down her back and buttocks to raise the hem of the dress.

She gently sucked the tip of his tongue as he cupped her buttocks in the black lace thong she wore. She moaned and crushed her body against his until her soft breasts were flattened against the soft hairs of his chest. "Lo," she sighed into his open mouth in between kisses. "Oh, Lo."

He bent his legs and wrapped an arm around her waist to lift her body up against his with a strength that made her weak. He reached his sofa and turned to sit down with her straddling his lap. His hands cupped her buttocks before gripping her flimsy lace thong into his fist and tearing it away from her.

She gasped.

He pulled her dress over her head and flung it away before he pressed his face against her cleavage and planted warm kisses there.

She shivered.

He shifted his head to the left and licked at her nipple.

She cried out and arched her back, gripping the soft tendrils of his hair as he pleasured her from one taut brown nipple to the other and back again, stoking a heat inside her that seemed to warm her from her head to the tips of her toes. "Lo," she sighed.

"Damn, look at you," he moaned, sitting back to do just that.

She raised her hands high above her head as she watched him, enjoying how sexy he made her feel with just his heated gaze. "Look at this," she said, bending over backward and spreading her legs before him as she pressed her hands to the hardwood floor.

"Shit," Lo swore.

He shifted his body and then bent down to blow a cool stream of air against her intimacy.

Her thighs shook, and she bit her bottom lip as she winced.

The first feel of his tongue stroking against her swollen bud buckled her arms. And when he sweetly sucked her clit between his pursed lips, he moaned in pleasure and gripped her soft inner thighs before sliding his hands across her belly and down to massage her breasts.

Well, damn, Lo . . .

He was both passionate and methodical with his wicked movements, between sucking and licking at her clit with perfect timing.

"Cum for me," he whispered against her.

She released a shuddering breath as she began to circle her hips, bringing her core up against his tongue.

Loren wrapped his arms around her upper thighs, locking her in place as he felt her body tremble with her release. His moans echoed her own as he tasted her on his tongue.

He released her and slapped her buttocks before she rolled over onto her stomach and then moved back between his open legs on her knees. He gripped her face and kissed her deeply as Desdemona jerked the elastic waist of his shorts down to free his hardness. "Oooooh," he softly roared into her mouth at the feel of her hand stroking him from root to tip. Again and again. Slowly and then quickly. "Shit."

With one hand twisted in his hair, she jerked his head back to free her mouth from his so that she could lower her head and take him into her mouth, adjusting herself to fit him to the back of her throat.

Loren's legs shot out straight on either side of her, and he fell back against the sofa as he thrust his hips upward with a savage cry that seemed torn from his gut.

She pleasured him with well-acquired skill as she eyed his face and enjoyed the feel of his hardness against her tongue and lips, drawing shivers and moans and looks of shock and pleasure. She circled the smooth tip with her tongue before taking his top inches into her mouth to suck until her cheeks caved and a little of his release shot from him to coat her tonsils.

Desdemona sat back with a lick of her lips as she worked his hardness with both her hands.

"Don't. Make. Me. Cum. Please," Loren begged, his eyes wild and fiery as he looked at her.

She rose up on her stiletto heels. "I needed this, Lo," she admitted as she straddled his hips and reached between them to hold his heavy hardness upright as she slid down onto him inch by inch.

His mouth formed a circle.

"And I want you to remember that this is my dick," she said, slowly lowering herself up and down on his rigid inches as she bit her bottom lip. "Even when you're with someone else or even married, it will always be *my dick*. Right?"

"Hell, yeah," he agreed, digging his fingers into her soft hips as he looked down at their union. "And that's *mine*. Right?"

Desdemona sat down on his strong thighs, taking all of him into her with a soft grunt. "Always," she promised.

Right along with my heart.

Her emotions tightened her throat as she leaned in to kiss him. He encircled her with one arm across her back and the other cradling her quivering buttocks as he worked his hips in sync with her.

Back and forth.

The base of his hardness slickly pressed against her clit, and before long she was quivering with another aching release. She sucked at his lips as she looked down at his face. "Lo," she gasped, her climax drawing tears. "Lo."

Loren massaged the back of her as his eyes searched hers. "I'm a fool to love you," he admitted, his voice low and deep. "And an even bigger fool to tell you that I do."

They stopped the lovemaking and stared at each other. Hearts pounding. Pulse racing.

She nodded. "I love you, Lo," she said with every bit of emotion she could pour into her words. "I love you so much."

He tilted his chin up to capture her mouth with his own. "But it's still goodbye, isn't it?" he asked in between the sweetest kisses.

A tear raced down her cheek as she pressed a kiss to the corner of his mouth and buried her face against the hollow of his neck as she nodded again.

He comforted her, massaging her back. "It's cool. At least I know what love feels like for the first time."

She raised her head. "Me too," she admitted.

They made love with a fierceness that both frightened and excited them. Slow and steady. Fast and furious. Going still to hold off their climax, neither wanting their connection to end. And then, when they could no longer deny themselves, giving in to their passion they climaxed together, feeling the ultimate high. Riding the waves. Enjoying the splendor as they clutched each other tightly with their mouths locked in passionate kisses.

Long after the ride was over, they still clung to one another.

"Stay the night," he softly demanded, pressing a tender kiss to her shoulder as he rubbed circles on her back.

"Okay," she agreed, closing her eyes and inhaling deeply of his scent as if to capture it within her.

"So goodbyes in the morning?" he quipped.

They shared a laugh.

But the night was not for sleeping. Twice they made love, once in the shower and then again in his bed just as the sun was beginning to rise above the city. He rested on his elbows looking down at her face as he slowly stroked them to another climax.

"We can do this, you know," Loren said, his eyes imploring hers, revealing his heart's desire.

She kissed his mouth and held his face with her hands. "There is so much you don't know; please believe if I thought we could find forever in this I would never say goodbye to the man—the *only* man I have ever loved," she stressed. "You have to trust me on this."

"Trust you while you break my heart . . . again."

Desdemona rose from the bed and pulled her dress over her nakedness and stepped into her heels. The torn panties she left behind on the floor.

"Ali—"

She rushed over to kiss him again, ending him saying that name that was not truly hers. "Tell me you love me one last time and say goodbye," she pleaded with him, her eyes soft. "Please, Lo."

"No," he said, even as she saw the emotion brimming in his beautiful slanted eyes.

"I love you, Loren Palmer," she said, placing a kiss on each corner of his mouth. "Goodbye."

She rose from the bed again and picked up her keys from where they had fallen on the floor before making her way to the front door. Her steps were hurried but only because she was afraid she would never leave him.

His hand on her shoulder surprised her.

She turned and looked up at him as he pulled her close and kissed her. "I love you," he spoke against her mouth. There was a long pause before he finished. "Goodbye."

Desdemona smiled, reaching to stroke his chiseled cheek one last time before she turned and did the hardest thing ever in her life by leaving.

Epilogue

August 2020

"Okay, this is me."

Desdemona shifted her leather sack on her shoulder as she opened the door to the classroom and entered. The size and setup of the room surprised her, with the seats and desks aligned in semicircles in descending levels before a large whiteboard. People passed her by with more confidence, claiming seats that weren't already occupied.

I can do this. I just traveled the world alone for a year. College won't be the end of me.

Taking a breath, she moved down the steps and eased past people seated at their desks to claim one in the middle of the row. She opened her messenger bag and removed a notebook, pen, her book, and the case holding her reading glasses as she crossed her ankles.

There wasn't much chatter in the large theater-like room as she looked around and smoothed her topknot. There were easily a hundred students in the class and less than a few who were older—or at least looked to be older.

She picked up her pen and doodled on the lines of the

blank page of her notebook. Remembering she had dinner plans with Melissa, she withdrew her one and only phone to text her.

DESI: Dinner @ 8?

When Desdemona got back from her last trip of the past year—a two-week cruise to the British Isles, Iceland, and Northern Europe—they had slipped right back into their friendship . . . and Desdemona had even admitted that her real name was Desdemona Dean. She explained her previous desire for anonymity in the big city and was glad when laid-back Melissa accepted the explanation. It had not been easy pulling back the façade but necessary. For her, there was no coming back from being addressed as Desdemona or Ms. Dean during her travels over the last year.

No more Alisha Smith. *That hoe finally dead.*

MELISSA: Perfect. Locanda Verde?

The thought of the restaurant's excellent Italian cuisine made her empty stomach grumble.

DESI: Yesssss!

She set the phone down.

Bzzzzzz.

Desdemona picked up the phone again.

MELISSA: Not too late, though. Benji is staying over.

She smiled at the eggplant emojis at the end of the text.

DESI: Jealous. Days of celibacy: 455.

Melissa texted her the praying hands emoji.

The door on the left side of the room opened, and Desi sat up straighter as she looked down at the professor entering the room. She gasped.

Loren.

Her entire body went on high alert as she eyed him. More than a year later. Still handsome. More confident.

Still deeply planted in her heart.

Damn.

Four hundred and fifty-four days since she'd seen him last, and nothing had changed. He was still in her heart, still imprinted on her soul, and still her life's biggest regret.

"Good morning, class," Loren said, looking handsome in a lightweight linen suit with his hair pulled back and wire-framed spectacles in place. "I'll be stepping in for Professor Warren this semester. He has a health matter that warrants his attention at this time but no fears or worries. You will leave this—my class—more proficient in English and even in storytelling."

Should I leave? Would he want me to? Do I want to?

She stayed. Hunkered down. Took notes. Tried her best not to remember just why she had denied herself happiness with him. They had fallen in love.

And I still love him. Easily. So very easily.

And when the class was over and they were given their reading assignments before their next class two days later, Desdemona took her time gathering her things into her satchel until she was the last student in the class. "Great class, Dr. Palmer," she said, rising from her seat and coming down the steps toward where he cleaned the whiteboard.

He froze.

She smiled as he looked over his shoulder and over the rim of his glasses at her walking up to his desk. He was just as surprised at her as she was at seeing him. He clutched the eraser tightly in his grip before setting it down and turning to face her.

"Were you in this class this whole time?" he asked after clearing his throat and removing his glasses.

She nodded.

"Your name is not on the register," he said, looking down at a paper on his desk.

"It is. You just don't know my real name," she admitted before she extended her hand. "Desdemona Dean."

Loren took a step back in surprise. "Oh, so when you said there was so much I didn't know, that was an understatement."

She gave him an encouraging smile as she eyed him and accepted that there was no exit when it came to her love for him. "I didn't know you were teaching this class," she said, stepping close to him.

Loren looked down at her, and their eyes locked. That crazy kinetic energy was there. Pulsing. Vibrating. Taking them back to the familiar.

"Desdemona?" he asked.

She nodded as she reached up and stroked his chin. "My name sounds so good on your lips."

"And do you still think I am not man enough for you?" he asked.

"Not anymore," she admitted. "I have never stopped loving you, and this is fate saying stop denying this. Be happy."

"With me?"

"I'd like to try. Flaws and all," Desdemona said. "I can't reveal everything to you. A lot of it has to stay in the past for us to make it, and you have to be okay with that."

Loren turned his head and kissed the palm she had pressed to his cheek. "My love for you will help make me okay with it," he said. "I just know this last year has been some real bullshit without you, *Desdemona*."

"I love you," she whispered up to him as he placed a hand

to her back and pulled her close. "I am so tired of fighting this."

"Then don't," he said in that hotly anticipated moment before he pressed his mouth down on hers.

They swayed back and forth a bit as they kissed.

"Madam, may I love you?" Loren asked, teasing at that quip he had tried all those months ago that had gone horribly wrong.

This time she stroked the soft curls on his nape as she gently nodded. "With all that you have."

Jessa's Intro

Where do I begin? How do I tell the story? Our story. His and mine.

He was my lover and her husband. You would think that wasn't possible—like saying dry rain or cold heat—but it was true. She had the ring and the license... but I had him. From that first heated moment in their kitchen when his strong hands reached beneath my skirt to grab my soft, bare ass, I knew I had him.

I don't recall the specific moment when our lust turned to love. When our time spent together became about more than just fucking, more than just rushing through electrifying sex that left us both panting, sweaty, and in various stages of undress. We shifted so easily from sharing clandestine and wonderfully sneaky moments—even in their house while she was there—to him sneaking out of their home to be in my arms and in my bed.

I hated to lie alone at night surrounded by nothing but cool cotton sheets and plush down pillows while she had his hard and warm body to hold close.

I knew the time would come when I would want more from him than just his dick. I wanted his love, his time, his all... for me and only me.

She was my friend—true, but he was my lover, my love, and in this game there could only be one winner, as far as I was concerned.

Me.

Chapter 1

Jaime Hall enjoyed the feel of the steam pressed against her shoulders and her legs where she sat in the glass shower of their bedroom suite. The thick swirling vapors felt like a lover's gentle touch against her skin and those intimate parts of a woman's body. Her breasts. Her nipples. Her thighs. Her lips—both sets.

She relished it. She needed it.

Sadness weighed her shoulders down and soon she felt tears fill her oval-shaped eyes and race down her cheeks. Jaime brought her shaking hands up to hug herself close. "God, I can't take much more of my life," she whispered into the steam as her head dropped so low that her chin nearly touched her chest.

She heard a sudden noise in her bathroom. Her head jerked up as she immediately swallowed back any more of her tears and frantically wiped any traces of them from her face. The last thing she wanted was for him to see or hear her crying.

"Eric," Jaime called out to her husband of the last seven years.

No answer. Nothing to acknowledge her. Seconds later the bathroom door opened and then closed. Disappointment nudged the door to her heart shut as well. The body's automatic defense mechanisms were amazing.

Jaime rose from the bench, turned off the shower, and walked out of the stall. The vapors swirled around her nude curvaceous frame like fog as she stepped down onto the plush white carpeting that felt like mink against her pedicured feet. As she wiped a clear spot in the grand oval mirror over the pedestal sink, she came face-to-face with her unhappiness. She forced a smile and put on her usual mask, but even she could see it didn't reach her eyes.

She grabbed a towel and wrapped it around her frame. She raced out of her bathroom suite through their spacious cathedral ceiling master bedroom and out to the hall. As she raced down the curved staircase, her towel slipped and fell behind her on the stairs, but she didn't break stride.

Thank God she was home alone, because she wouldn't want anyone to see her stark naked and racing through the house like she was crazy.

"Eric!" she called out, striding through the circular foyer to the kitchen.

The house was quiet. She covered her exposed breasts with her arms as she looked out the kitchen windows over the driveway. The sun was just starting to rise. She just made out his tall and slender figure headed down the street toward their friends' home with his tackle box and fishing rods in hand.

He left to go deep-sea fishing and didn't even bother to tell her good-bye. *How much more can I take?* She turned and let her body slide down to the polished hardwood floor as tears racked her body and she could do nothing but wrap her arms around her knees and rock to make herself feel a little better.

"Shit!" Renee Clinton swore as the gray acrid smoke rose from the frying pan with fury. She hurried to turn off the lit eye of the Viking stove before shifting the pan to one of the remaining five burners.

"Damn, damn, damn it all to hell."

Renee could only shake her head in shame at the blackness of the bacon she'd been frying. It was *beyond* crispy.

"Is something on fire, Ma?"

Renee looked over her shoulder as her fifteen-year-old daughter, Kieran, walked into the kitchen on dragging feet in her oversized fuzzy pajamas. "Just breakfast."

"*You* were cooking?" she asked in disbelief as she sat leaned her hip against the island in the center of the kitchen.

"I wanted to fix your father breakfast before he left to go fishing." Renee slid the halfway-decent-looking slices of bacon onto a clear glass plate.

"You never cook." Kieran moved across the kitchen to the pantry.

"I know how to cook," Renee protested as she ran a hand through her deeply wavy natural. "It's remembering that I have food on the stove that I have a problem with."

Kieran stepped out of the pantry digging into a box of cereal before throwing a handful of some sugary-sweet cereal she loved into her mouth. She moved over to stand beside her mother and looked down at the bacon with a frown. "Good thing Daddy loves you," she joked before turning to walk out of the kitchen.

"Yeah, good thing," Renee said hesitantly as she cracked

eggs into a large red Le Creuset ceramic bowl and whisked them with a little extra ferocity.

She poured the eggs into a stainless steel pan and left them so that they would set before she scrambled them. She moved back to the end of the island where her briefcase was opened and instantly became absorbed into the facts and figures of the report she'd brought home to review.

At forty-three, Renee was the vice president of marketing for the CancerCure Foundation, one of the largest nonprofits serving cancer research and awareness in the country. It was her job and her passion to develop partnerships with major corporations for invaluable donations and increasing the national visibility of the foundation. She took her work very seriously—not just for the six-figure income she received, but because it intrigued and challenged her every day. It was very easy for her to get deeply absorbed in her work.

Renee picked up an oversized cup of gourmet coffee with one hand and the open report with the other. Her lips moved as she read. Her face showed her shifting feelings: interest, surprise, discontent. She leaned her hip against the island as she took a deep and satisfying sip of her drink.

"What the hell is burning?"

The words on the report disappeared as Renee closed her eyes and frowned as she thought, "Damn," at the sound of her husband, Jackson's, voice from behind her.

She dropped the report and snatched the burning pan from the stove in one continuous motion. "This just isn't my morning, Jackson," she told him, looking over her shoulder at her tall, solid husband of the last eighteen years.

His handsome square face shaped into a frown as he took in the papers and files on the island. There was no mistaking the immediate look of disapproval.

Renee hated the guilt she felt at that one look that spoke volumes about their marriage. "I thought I would cook—"

"*And* work?" he asked, moving past her to fill the thermos he held with coffee.

Renee swallowed her irritation. She looked down at the burnt bacon on the plate and the brown eggs in the pan and scraped them both into the garbage disposal. "I'm trying, Jackson," she stressed, her eyes angry and hurt.

He just snorted in derision.

Renee felt tension across her shoulders. She jumped a little as he moved close to her to press a cool kiss to her cheek. She closed her eyes, absorbing his scent as she raised a hand to stroke his bearded cheek. He felt familiar and strange all at once. It had been so long since they showed each other simple affection.

She tilted her head back to look up into those eyes that had intrigued her from the first time she saw him on the campus of Rutgers University. "I love you, Jackson," Renee whispered, hating the urgency in her voice as her eyes searched his.

For what seemed forever, his eyes searched hers as well. "We need to talk. We *have* to talk," he said, his voice husky and barely above a whisper.

A soft press of his lips down upon hers silenced any of her words or questions.

Moments later, he was gone and Renee felt chilled to the bone.

"You didn't have to get up so early with me, baby."

Aria Livewell shrugged as she followed her broad-shouldered husband, Kingston, down the stairs of their three-thousand-square-foot home in the family-oriented subdivision of Richmond Hills. A home meant to be filled with children. "It's no problem. You know me and the girls are hanging out today and I wanted to get some housework done before they picked me up."

Kingston sat his fishing equipment by the wooden double doors. "Think you four will be back on time? You know we're supposed to meet at the Clintons' tonight to fry up all the fish we'll catch today."

"Just three, actually. Jessa said she had *something else* to do today." Aria made a playful face and waved her hand dismissively.

Kingston put his broad hands beneath her short cotton robe and pulled his beautiful mocha-skinned wife close to him. "If we whup our friends in bid whist tonight, I have one helluva surprise for you."

Kingston was *so* competitive.

She tilted her head up to lightly lick his dimpled chin as she pushed her hand into the back pocket of his vintage jeans to warmly grasp his firm, fleshy buttocks. "Can I get a hint?" she asked huskily with a teasing smile, the beat of her heart already quickening with anticipation.

"Damn, I love you," he said roughly, his eyes smoldering as he slid one hand up to her nape.

Aria moaned softly in pleasure at the first heated feel of her husband's lips. As she gasped slightly, he slid his tongue inside her mouth with well-practiced ease. She shivered. Her clit swelled to life. Her nipples hardened in a rush.

"Do we have time?" she asked in a heated whisper, barely hearing herself over her own furious heartbeat as Kingston undid her robe and planted moist and tantalizing kisses along her collarbone.

"We'll make time" breezed across her flesh.

As her robe slipped open and his familiar hands caressed her silky skin, Aria enjoyed their passion and wondered if the time would come when she didn't cherish and yearn for her husband's touch. His dick. His kisses. His love.

With his mouth, Kingston made a path to the deep valley of her breasts, bending his knees to take one swollen and taut dark nipple into his mouth. He sucked it deeply and then circled it with the tip of his clever tongue.

"Yes," Aria whimpered, flinging her head back.

Kingston turned them and pressed Aria's back to the towering front doors as he quickly undid his belt and zipper. His hands shook as he placed them on her plush hips and lifted her with ease until her pulsing and moist pussy lips lightly kissed the thick tip of his dick. "Why is your pussy so good?" he whispered against the pounding pulse of her throat.

Aria didn't answer, she just smiled wickedly—and a bit cockily—as she caused the swollen lips of her vagina to lightly kiss the smooth round head of his dick . . . twice.

Kingston dropped Aria down onto his erection, her pussy tightly surrounding and gripping him like a vise. "Damn," he swore, his buttocks tensing as he froze. He didn't want to cum. Not yet.

Aria pressed the small of her back to the door and began to work her hips in small circles, anxious to not just have his dick pressed against her walls but to feel his delicious strokes.

Kingston's jaw clenched. "Don't make me nut, baby." His voice was strained.

Aria raised her hands to tease her nipples with her slender fingers as she enjoyed the tight in-and-out motion of his penis when Kingston began to work his hips. She felt wild and free, uninhibited and sexy. "Umph. I'm gone cum, baby. Please make me cum," she whispered with fevered urgency as each of his deep thrusts caused her pussy juices to smack and echo in the foyer like applause.

Kingston's chest and loins exploded with heat as his primal need to feel as much of Aria's pussy as he could. He pushed deeper up inside her, drawing quick and uneven breaths as his heart thundered. His buttocks clenched and then relaxed as he touched every bit of her ridged walls with his solid inches. “Damn, Aria,” he swore, planting adoring kisses along her collarbone as his dick filled her several times with warm shots of cum.